MERRYWEATHER LODGE: MALEVOLENT SPIRIT

by

Pauline Holyoak

WHISKEY CREEK PRESS
www.whiskeycreekpress.com

Published by
WHISKEY CREEK PRESS

Whiskey Creek Press
PO Box 51052
Casper, WY 82605-1052
www.whiskeycreekpress.com

ISBN 978-1-61160-300-2
Credits
Cover Artist: Gemini Judson
Editor: Marsha Briscoe
Printed in the United States of America

Other Books by Author Available at Whiskey Creek Press:

www.whiskeycreekpress.com

Merryweather Lodge: Ancient Revenge

Emily couldn't wait to visit her Aunt and Uncle in their quaint and mysterious little cottage near Stonehenge. But it doesn't take her long to realize that her fairytale kingdom has a sinister twist. One night in her attic bedroom she is confronted by an evil entity that would taunt her for the rest of her stay and long after that. Who is this hideous creature and what does she want? When Emily meets the gorgeous Jonathan McArthur she is infatuated, consumed with lust and an odd familiarity, as if they had met before. Will he be coaxed by the peculiar old gypsy to enter the dreaded woodlot? Can the bloody ancient curse be removed before it's too late? And will Emily ever get to feel his lips on hers? A chilling tale of love, passion, sorcery and sacrifice; laced with mystery and tied with humor. Inspired by the author's own experiences in a remote little cottage near Stonehenge.

Dedication

This book is dedicated to my parents Reg and Elsie Wellings. They are the diamonds in my collection of treasured memories. And, to the place I will always call home, Aylesham village, and her people.

The Legend of Merthia

Loki, the high Druid priest, was seduced by a beautiful but evil sorceress named Hagmanis. A child was conceived in her sordid womb. When the infant was born, Loki took her and banished Hagmanis to the end of the earth. He called the child Merthia. She was graceful and alluring, with exquisite features and hair like spun gold. But in her heart she carried the evil seed of her mother. As a young girl, for amusement, she would torture the village cats. All the other children feared her. As she grew, she became more alluring and seductive. Her lust for blood also grew. The young men in the village could not refuse her. She conceived two illegitimate babies, who she tried to kill at birth. Loki was desperate to change his daughter's ways. At the age of eighteen she was betrothed to a handsome young priest named Golwin. Merthia was obsessed with her youth and beauty and feared growing old. One day she made a pact with Odina, the Goddess of Immortal Youth. If Merthia were to sacrifice a young virgin every Sabbath, Odina would in turn bestow upon her

1

immortal youth. Merthia kept her promise. Just before her wedding day, Golwin discovered her evil deeds. He called off the wedding and gave his attention to her cousin, Colrea. Merthia was furious and vowed revenge. On the day of the Autumn Equinox, Merthia took her cousin into the forest and tied her to the altar of sacrifice. She was just about to cut off her head when Golwin arrived. He grabbed the axe out of Merthia's hand and buried the blade deep into her skull. As the evil life force drained from her body, she screamed, "I will be back and revenge will be mine." Her spirit is said to roam the earth in search of revenge. On her death bed she was given a gift by Odina: the power to possess the bodies of her female descendents. But only the ones with evil hearts could kill for her.

Chapter 1

"Chicken or beef?" the tall, thin, well-groomed flight attendant inquired, as she bobbed around the cabin like a puppet on a string. I sighed. Why is it always chicken or beef? Why can't they be more creative, and where's my vegetarian meal?

The flight from Edmonton to London was nine hours and I was famished. I hadn't eaten a thing at the airport or thought to bring a snack. The constant dull hum of the motor buzzed in my ears, like the drone of bees. My mouth was as dry as sand paper and the stale air hung around me like a contaminated fog. The plump, red-faced old lady that was sitting next to me had fallen asleep. Thank God. She smelled of cheap perfume and kept going on about her grandchildren, how she loved to visit the little darlings once a year, and about her dog Henry, "poor thing." She had to leave him with her finicky friend in London. Oh how she missed her "dear Henry so." I sat there, politely murmuring the odd "oh dear, how nice," and nodding my head. It was such a relief when she fell asleep. She really was a sweet old lady but her scent was making me nauseous and I just wasn't up to idle chatter with a stranger. I just wanted to be left alone, to wallow in my own self pity and grief.

I was returning to England after a gut-wrenching two weeks at home. My mother had passed away, suddenly. She had taken her cancer medication with sleeping pills and a hefty dose of alcohol. She was at home alone when it happened. My dad blames himself for not being there and is totally devastated. After the funeral he left to visit his cousin in Australia. Everyone agreed it would be the best thing for him, but I had hoped he'd come back to Merryweather Lodge with me. Nonetheless, he wouldn't be moping around home consumed with guilt and grief; he'd be in a whole new environment, meeting new people and, hopefully, healing some of his pain.

It was the last week in November. I told Auntie I would come back for three months, although she wanted me to stay for six, the allotted time given by the UK government to stay in the country without a visa. But I didn't want my dad returning to an empty house and besides, I wasn't sure if I wanted to stay at Merryweather Lodge for any longer than that, not after all those terrifying things that happened there, on my previous visits. What if the hideous creature was still there, determined to get her revenge? The one thing that drew me back like a magnet was the gorgeous Jonathan McArthur, my sensual soul mate, the man of my dreams.

My dad called me just one week after that horrifying

event in the woodlot. He told me that Mom had passed away but I wasn't to rush back home, that he'd take care of everything. But it would have been impossible to let him face our tragic loss alone.

And not to attend my own mother's funeral was unthinkable.

I laid my head on the back rest and sighed. Oh how I wish I'd have been kinder to my mom, more loving towards her. She always rubbed me the wrong way and I was always belittling her. I wanted her to be more like me and she couldn't understand why I wasn't more like her. Now she's gone and I didn't even have a chance to say goodbye. I closed my eyes but the chatter box inside my head would not be still and sleep would not come.

The plane landed with a clumsy bump. I could feel the conflicting tears of loss, longing, excitement, and utter fatigue welling up inside me as I emerged from the large metal doors, dragging my hefty suitcase behind me. My eyes searched eagerly through the crowds of waiting people. Cries of joy, shouts of "there they are" echoed all around. Then I spotted him, a head above the rest, silky black hair framing his gorgeous smiling face. My stomach fluttered as he moved towards me, weaving his way through the congestion of bodies; his velvet, dark brown eyes scanned my face, revealing their undying devotion. I dropped my suitcase, flung my arms around his neck, and snuggled my face into the warm fleshy scent of his naked skin. I was back in the arms of my soul mate, at last. He pulled away and touched my eager lips with his, tenderly.

"How was your flight?"

"Long and boring."

"Did you get any sleep?"

"Nope. None."

He grabbed the handle of my suitcase. "You'll need a nap when you get home then."

Home? Was I really coming home? I hadn't decided yet if I was going to take up residence here in England. Canada was still my home. I had, however, quit my job at the newspaper but I would have done that anyway. Kyle had been promoted to editor and when I broke it off with him he was rude, condescending, and intent on making my life miserable. I knew he didn't care about not dating me anymore but his ego had been deflated and he wasn't used to being dumped. I told him, after one of his tantrums, to stick his job where the sun don't shine. It wasn't very professional but it did give me a potent dose of satisfaction. (I still struggled with my impulsive temper.) I'd saved enough money to last me for a while and I was hoping to pick up some freelance work for a little extra cash while I was in England.

We fought our way through the crowds and into the parking lot. "How's my aunt?" I asked as I threw my tartan duffel bag into the back seat of Jonathan's shiny black BMW. The pavement was gleaming wet, from a typical rainy day.

"She's good. Back to her old self, I'd say."

"That's great! Thanks for looking out for her while I was gone."

He grinned. "It's more like she was looking out for me. She insisted I come for tea every Saturday and a proper roast dinner on Sunday, and she made me eat everything on my plate. 'Waste not want not' she'd say."

We glanced at each other and chuckled in unison. "That's my Auntie Em."

It was a two hour drive to Salisbury Plains from Gatwick and I dreaded the thought of sitting cooped up again, but once we were off the motorway and into the countryside, fatigue was replaced with contentment and a strange sense of belonging. The trees had lost most of their leaves; just a few colorful survivors held on in desperation. The grass held patches of brown. It wasn't as bleak and barren as back in Canada before the first snow fall but it was drab and showing signs of what was to come. My heart leaped unexpectedly as Merryweather Lodge came into view. Dressed now, not in the gay colors of spring, like when I first saw her but cloaked in withering vines, dry amber leaves, and surrounded by bare shrubs and wilted flower beds. But still the gray stone cottage held an air of enchantment and seemed to beckon me with open arms, like a mother welcoming her daughter home after a long journey. I could almost hear the thump-thump-thump of her heart beat. I glanced at the attic room window; it glared at me from under its crown of thatch. I drew my eyes away quickly, just in case.

The front door opened and Auntie stepped outside, her old face beaming, her chubby red cheeks puffed with a wide grin. She hurried towards me, wiping her hands down her floury apron, and then threw her plump arms around my chest, nearly knocking me over. I was treated to the familiar, eclectic smells of her person and well worn apron; cinnamon, apples, fried onions, bacon, rose water, and lemon polish, all mingled together on her motherly form.

"Welcome home, luv."

There goes that word again: "Home!" I took a deep breath and crossed the threshold, inhaling the room's homey aroma. Jonathan followed, lugging my heavy suitcase behind him. "Where do you want this?" he asked.

"In the parlor please."

I threw my coat over Uncle Reg's frayed, wing back chair and flopped into its cushiony softness. Auntie scurried into the kitchen, to put the kettle on and start preparing a feast fit for a king, I assumed. Jonathan squatted on the little wooden stool by the hearth and rubbed his hands together in front of the blazing fire. He looked so at home, as if he'd lived here all of his life.

"Wow!" A strange back cat leaped on my lap, causing me to flinch. "Well, hello there. Who are you?" I ran my hand down its silky coat, as it purred vigorously. Auntie handed me a cup of hot tea. "I found 'im wandering in the yard; don't belong to any of the locals, he don't. I asked around. Thought I'd keep 'im, till someone claims 'im, that is. Called 'im Winston I did, after Churchill, got that same puckered face and 'aughty look in is eye, 'e does."

Jonathan placed his hefty tea mug on the hearth. "He's taken to you already, Emily."

"Just like 'e did with you, Jonny, don't seem to care for me that much though, not until 'e wants feeding, that is."

That's strange, I thought. Animals were usually drawn to Auntie. They seemed to sense her compassion and kindheartedness. "Why did you keep him then?"

"Figured 'e was just shy at first but now I recon 'e's just picky about who 'e likes and don't like. I couldn't leave 'im outside, not when it's freezing out; besides 'e gets along well with the other two, taken to 'im like bears to honey they 'ave. I'm guessing 'e might come around to taking to me sooner or later." She lowered her head and headed back to the kitchen.

I looked down at the finicky feline who was now curled up in a ball on my lap. He did have a very odd looking face, wrinkly and round, with bulging, almond shaped, yellow-green, glassy eyes that seem to imply that this was his domain. "He looks a little bit like Wooky." I was referring to Auntie's old cat, which had come to a mysterious death in the barn.

"He ain't nothing like my Wooky, 'e ain't. Gotta face like a slapped arse, 'e does," Auntie mumbled, as she slammed the kitchen door.

I covered my mouth to stifle a snicker. Jonathan shook his head and grinned. "I have to get up now, kitty" I said, as I nudged the jet-black ball of velvet off my lap. He turned his head and locked his peculiar eyes on mine. His annoyed glare gave me a strange uneasiness. "I'm going to freshen up," I announced. Jonathan winked and wiggled his fingers in a tiny wave. I wandered to the bathroom, hurrying past the attic room as I usually did, not daring to look up, just in case. But after that terrifying incident in the woodlot the cottage seemed at peace; there was no eerie feeling, no strange noises, unpleasant smells, or friendly shadows following me around. Merthia had gone and Mary Eliss was at peace now, or so it seemed.

After a bountiful, proper English tea, of cucumber and cheese sandwiches, pickled onions, Scotch eggs, sausage rolls, and jam tarts, Auntie poured us a glass of her homemade blackberry wine and ushered us into the sitting room. Jonathan slipped his arm around my shoulder as I snuggled beside him on the sofa. Auntie sat in her favorite well-pillowed, comfy chair, her legs propped up on the tapestry stool, her feet ballooned by her huge fuzzy slippers. I was warmed by the ambiance of this familiar, snug little room, the wine and the sensual body nuzzled into mine. My eyes drooped as Auntie's idle chatter droned on and on. The next thing I knew I was being carried into the parlor by a pair of strong, bare arms. Gently, they lowered me onto my make shift bed and laid a soft woolen blanked over my form. I kept my eyes closed, not wanting to spoil the moment. The feeling of his breath on my face and the caress of his moist lips as they touched my cheek made my insides tremble. I wanted to grab him and pull him on top of my needy body but this wasn't the time or place. Soon, I told myself as I placed my hands between my legs to stop the throbbing, nested into the blankets, and slept.

The metallic chimes of the old grandfather clock stirred

me. It was nine a.m. I had slept through the night, sound and undisturbed. Blinking the sleep out of my eyes, I lifted my head and gazed around the room. Auntie had left a bowl of plump apples and pears on the buffet. The frosty sun that streamed though the diamond paneled windows painted the fruit with a beautiful, glassy sheen. There were some new framed photos beside the bowl, one of Auntie and her mother, one of Auntie's dad tending the sheep, one of me when I was a baby, and one of Jonathan and his sister Belinda when they were small. It was strange, I thought, to have a photo of your hired hand's children beside your family photos. And where was the one that usually sat there: the black and white photo of Auntie and Uncle Reg at the beach, on their honeymoon? My gaze wandered to the white panel door. It was only a few weeks ago that the hideous creature burst through that door. She was ready to pounce, to take her revenge, to summon her ancient blood-stained axe and chop me up into fleshy little pieces. I shuddered. The door flew open. I shot up! A burst of fear caught in my throat. "No! No!"

"Flaming Nora, our Emily. What's wrong?" Auntie's eyes were wide; her mouth was covered by a starched white hanky and her head was topped with prickly curlers.

I took a deep breath to regain my senses. "I thought it was....sorry you scared me." She lowered her cushy bottom into the corner of my bed, gave my hand a motherly rub, and lowered her voice. "Sure it weren't one of them there bad dreams, luv, yer still 'avin um, are ya.? Gotta get a 'old of yer self. Yer too old for this now." She stood up, took my hand, and peered into my eyes. "It's that nutty imagination of yers; it'll send ya bonkers it will."

I gave her a false smile. "Okay, Auntie Em. Whatever you say." Too old for this? Nutty imagination sending me bonkers? Was she kidding? If I hadn't gone bonkers after all I'd experienced the last time I was here, there wasn't much chance of it happening now.

"Come on, luv, rise and shine. I'll make ya a full English breakfast."

"Thanks but no meat, remember."

"I remember but I think it's a load of malarkey m' self."

I patted her hand as she rose from the side of my bed. "I see that you have some new photos on the buffet."

"Lovely one of you when you were a baby, ain't it?"

"Yes, and a nice one of Jonathan and Belinda too."

"I took that with m' own camera when they were little, thought Jonny might like to see it up there, being as though 'e's never seen it in 'is mum's 'ouse. Got rid of all the photos when she were expecting Belinda, turned 'er all funny it did. It were hormones they say."

"Where's the one of you and uncle Reg.?"

"Dunno, one minute it were there, next minute it were gone. I must 'ave put it somewhere, 'avent got my 'ead screwed on right half the time." She walked towards the door. "I'll go make us a cupper now, luv."

My nerves were still on edge as I gathered and folded the bedding. I had to stop thinking about what had happened here and focus on the present, enjoy my time with Auntie, convalesce in the arms of Mother Nature, and most of all, spend some quality, romantic time with my luscious soul mate, the gorgeous Jonathan McArthur.

I sat down at the kitchen table, eager to devour the bountiful feast that lay in front of me. Auntie smiled widely, revealing her perfectly straight, slightly stained dentures, as she poured me a cup of tea from her vintage tea pot. "Did ya' know that little Lindy's coming home tomorrow?" Oh yes, Belinda, the bitch goddess herself, Merthia's host and servant, and maybe, my real cousin. After all the frightening events that had occurred here, Auntie wouldn't talk about her husband's death, Merthia, or the fact that she could be Belinda's real mother. If I mentioned it, she'd just shake her head and mumbled, "Lies, lies, lies, all of um." It wasn't that Auntie had forgotten, I concluded, but she was sweeping all those pesky little memories under the rug, as usual. Belinda had been admitted to a psychiatric hospital for treatment. The incident in the woodlot had rendered her mentally ill. Jonathan had informed me yesterday that she was coming home in a couple of days. The very thought of seeing her again gave me goose bumps.

But what would she be like, now that she wasn't possessed? Would she be the sweet young thing they said she was as a child or had she always been evil, as Merthia had contended? Jonathan had told his parents that we found her in the wood lot, agitated and disoriented. What was the point in telling them the truth, he'd said. It was all so crazy, so utterly unbelievable. "Yes, Jonathan had mentioned that she was coming home."

"'Er mums been worried sick about 'er, and it ain't like Maud to fret; it ain't. We'll go and visit 'er once she's settled in." She must have noticed the scowl on my face. "I'll go by m' self if ya want."

"No, I'll go with you. It will be nice to see her again." *You liar.*

"Did you remember that my girl friend is coming next week?" I asked.

"Of course, how long is 'er staying?"

"Just for fourteen days; she wants to be back before the Christmas rush." Skye Jenkins had been my best friend since fourth grade. We hadn't had any quality time together while I was home. My time had been consumed by funeral arrangements, visiting relatives, helping dad get the finances in order before I was to come back to England, and he was to go to Australia. When Skye told me she was coming here for a visit, I was thrilled and I couldn't wait to introduce her to Auntie and Jonathan. Although I wasn't quite sure what they'd think of her. Skye works part-time in her mom's "Enlighten Me" store in the West Edmonton Mall. The rest of her time is spent teaching yoga, meditation, and hypnosis. She is devoted to her spiritual quest and can seem a little strange to people who don't understand her. I had asked Jonathan to try and find an eligible guy friend to introduce her to, preferably someone like-minded. In spite of her being drop-dead gorgeous, Skye has never had a boyfriend. She'd been on a few dates and had crushes on boys in junior high but as far as I knew she'd never had a steady guy in her life. When I asked her about this she just shrugged it off and said, "I'm too busy; besides boys are overrated."

"She's coming all this way just for a fortnight?"

"She couldn't take anymore time off work and like I said she wanted to be back in Canada in plenty of time for Christmas. You don't have to go to any trouble. She can sleep on the pull-out couch with me."

Her brows arched. "Are you daft girl? There's hardly enough room on there for you. She'll 'ave the bedroom upstairs."

"The attic room!" Was she kidding? I shivered as the memories poured over me like a bucket of icy cold water.

"Of course, it's a perfectly good room. Put a lot of work into doing it up, we did." Her sad eyes looked up to the ceiling. A tremor touched the corner of her mouth. "Me and our Reg. God rest 'is soul."

This was the first time I'd heard her mention his name since his untimely death. It was a big step in the healing process. I walked towards her, put my arm around her motherly form, and gave it a gentle squeeze. She was right about the pull-out bed; it wasn't much bigger than a single. I remembered how Mom and Dad had to cuddle real close to stop them from falling off. I didn't think Skye would be impressed at having to get that cozy with me or me with her, for that matter. "I'll ask her if she'd mind sleeping up there."

"Bloody hell, our Emily, why would she mind?" Auntie

blustered. "We'll do it up tomorrow and you can help."

I winced. Had she really forgotten what happened up there? Had she no recollection of the hideous creature, the possession of Belinda, or Merthia's revelation that Belinda was Auntie's daughter? What about the resident ghost, Mary Eliss? Surly Auntie hadn't forgotten her. I wanted desperately to shake her and tell her to stop pretending that none of this happened. But I was too afraid of what it might do to her. She glanced at me out of the corner of her eye, as if she knew what I was thinking. I stood up and announced, "I'm going for a walk, won't be long."

"Don't ya go straying too far. Ya know it ain't safe out there."

Now why would she say that, if she had no memory of what happened?

I grabbed my shoes and wrapped myself in the warm saffron shawl that I bought at the handcraft shop, and wandered into the back yard. The sky was the color of cold stone. A nip of frost laced the air, threatening sleet or snow. The gnarly old cherry tree hung on, hopelessly, to a few dry leaves. The vegetable garden had been tilled and covered with mulch. Sam crawled out of his dog house, came towards me, and shoved his cold nose into my hand. "Hi, Sammy, what have you been up to while I've been gone?" He stared up at me with his dull brown eyes, as if to say, "not much". Then he turned and went back to his house. My thoughts wandered to the funeral home where my mom had been laid out. I didn't want her to be displayed like that but Dad and her sister insisted. She would have wanted people to see her made up and to pay their respects, Auntie Pam said. And made up she was. She looked so radiant, so elegant and poised, lying there in her best evening dress. Everyone commented on how beautiful she looked and I know she would have liked that. I sniffed back the tears and quickly changed my train of thoughts.

I wondered if Jonathan would call. I had fallen asleep before I had a chance to ask if he was staying the night. Auntie said he left after I fell asleep. I couldn't wait to see him. Before I left for Canada we promised each other that we'd never be apart, permanently. Our love was eternal; it had endured many incarnations and would continue its everlasting journey. Our feelings for each other were innate and intense but we had not yet slept together. There never seemed to be an opportune moment or enough privacy, but it was something I fantasized about, often. Even the death of my own mother couldn't keep the sensual visions out of my mind. My body ached for him. We'd experienced so much together, in such a short time; finding out we were literal soul mates, learning that his sister was being possessed by his jilted lover from a past life, grasping the concept that his sister could be my aunt's daughter swapped at birth with his mother's dead baby, the horrifying event in the dreaded woodlot, and getting help from his friendly childhood ghost. I asked myself often, was it real or was I trapped in some sort of nightmare, unable to awake from its hellish trance?

I lowered myself into the white wicker chair beside the back door, huddled into my shawl, and gazed at my gloomy, fairytale kingdom. In the distance I could hear the faint bleating of the few remaining sheep. Suddenly uneasiness fell upon me, like a thin cloak of dread. Something leaped into my lap. I gasped! "Winston? You naughty boy, you scared me!" The sleek black cat had come from no where. I ran my hand down his smooth, shinny coat. His glassy eyes stared into mine; their piercing glare made me nervous and drowsy. He kneaded his sharp claws into my legs, as he purred, a loud, deep throated purr, more like that of a lion than a domestic cat. My heart started to race. His talons dug deeper and deeper, into my jeans, though my jeans, into my flesh. I tried desperately to push him off and to free myself from the invisible glue that bound me to the chair. But my whole body was numb. An intense, stabbing pain pricked my flesh, like someone was plunging a pair of scissors into my legs. Blood oozed from my pants. "Help! Help!" I screamed, in hopeless desperation.

Chapter 2

"Stop! Stop!" My whole body shook uncontrollably.

"Wake up! For heaven's sake, girl, snap out of it." Auntie was leaning over me, her hands on my shoulders, shaking me vigorously.

My eyes sprang open. Auntie stepped back. I lowered my head tentatively and gazed at my lap. There was no blood, no cat, no pain. "Where the hell is he?"

"Where's who?"

"That demon cat, Winston!"

Auntie's forehead wrinkled. "Now 'e might be an ornery old thing but 'e ain't no demon. You were 'avin one of them there bad dreams again. Going frantic you were." She smiled lovingly, then pushed the sweaty hair away from my face with her plump little fingers. "But yer all right now, luv. Come on, I'll make us a nice cupper."

I rose. Feeling a little light headed, I grabbed the back of my chair and took a few gaping breaths. Then I saw him, sitting beside a group of wilted marigolds. His beady eyes were fixed on me, like a stalker watching his victim. He looked like a misplaced lawn ornament. My pulse was still racing. *But it was only a dream.* I gave him a suspicious glare and went inside.

Auntie was sitting at the kitchen table, with a bottle of her homemade blackberry wine and two tiny crystal glasses in front of her. I glanced at the wall clock, then at the wine. "Auntie Em, it's not even noon."

She squinted at the clock. "Who cares? Thought ya'd be needin' something stronger than tea after that episode. You've been through a lot lately, luv, losing yer mum and all."

Not to mention what I experienced here. But that was taboo, for now anyway.

She lifted the bottom of her apron, placed it over the top of the bottle, and tried to unscrew the cap. Her teeth clenched and her face crinkled as she strained to loosen its grip. I knew better than to ask if she needed help. After a few moments of her wrestling with the bottle the lid lost its hold. She poured the thick burgundy liquid into the crystal glass and grinned triumphantly. I couldn't help but smile; she was as stubborn as a mule, my auntie Em. "I almost forgot to tell ya. Jonny phoned."

"He did?"

"He's stopping by after work. Be 'ere around half past six. He's going to his mum's for tea first."

Hmmm, I thought he'd be anxious to see me. But I guess not.

"We'll start on the room upstairs this afternoon. Take off that striped wall paper, make it more grown up for your mate, we will."

I gave her a sour grin and knocked back my wine. The phone rang. Auntie shook her head and sighed, saying, "Ain't no rest for the wicked, there ain't," as she made her way to the curio stand in the hallway. Maybe it was Jonathan. Perhaps he'd changed his mind, taken the day off and was on his way over, because he couldn't stand to spend another moment without me. It was obviously not for me, as she didn't return.

This afternoon I'd be venturing into the foreboding attic room. The muscles in my stomach tightened at just the thought. But at least I wouldn't be alone this time. *I should take some sea salt, just in case. That's if Auntie still has some.* I opened the kitchen cupboard, reached for the old toffee tin at the back of the top self, and pried open the lid. Yes, there was still some in there. I scooped a handful, dropped it into a small plastic bag, and pushed it deep into the back pocket of my jeans. I didn't have time to put the tin away before Auntie entered the room. She wore an elated expression as she waved her white hanky around like a flag. "Well, if that ain't a turn for the books, I don't know what is."

"What?" I was expecting some steamy local gossip.

"It were my old mate Martha Davis. She's 'ere visiting 'er Brother Fred. Thought she'd look me up, see if I were still around. I were gob smacked when she said who she were. Never expected to 'ere from 'er, not in a month of Sundays."

"Is this the Martha you picked chestnuts with? The one that saw Mary Eliss in the woodlot?"

Her eyes grew. "Don't ya go bringing that up. It were a long time ago. She's likely forgotten about it by now.

How can someone forget about something like that? "Okay, whatever. When is she coming?"

"Tomorrow at five o'clock. Better get this place cleaned up."

"Auntie, the cottage is spotless."

"Cleanliness is next to godliness. That's what m' mum would always say. Real 'ouse proud she were." Her gaze wandered up to the ceiling. "God rest 'er soul."

"I'll give you a hand."

"No, you get started on that there attic room. It's gonna take a long time and a lot of elbow grease to get that paper off."

I swallowed and mumbled, "I'd rather not go up there by myself."

She raised her hand in a gesture of hopelessness. "All right. Bobs yer' uncle. That imagination of yours flits about like a blue arsed fly."

Auntie's lingo was getting harder to understand but I was glad she hadn't insisted I go up there alone.

"Come on then, let's get cracking; we can get started on it, at least." As she turned, her eyes caught the toffee tin on the counter. "Suppose I could give this a quick going over in the morning," she said, while fumbling with the corner of her apron and pretending not to have noticed the tin. "Can't stay up there for too long. You'll be needin' a bath before Jonny comes."

Was she trying to tell me something? I lifted up my arm and sniffed my pits. Auntie liked giving me orders. I think it was her way of mothering me.

We gathered rags, soap, a couple of wall paper scrapers, and filled a tin bucket with hot water. Auntie tied a red scarf around her wiry gray hair, pushed her hands into a pair of pink rubber gloves, and headed for the stairs. I followed behind leisurely, hoping she'd go first. When we got to the foot of the stairs she stepped aside. "Go on, luv, beauty before age."

"It's supposed to be the other way around," I muttered as I heaved the heavy bucket up the stairs. There were traces of what looked like salt in the corners of the stairs. *That's interesting.* I rested the bucket on the top step and raised my hand towards the knob. The tips of my fingers trembled, a little. *Don't be silly, Emily. Mary Eliss is at peace now and Merthia's gone.* But why was my gut in a tangle and my inner voice screaming "stay out"? The brass knob was steely cold, at the touch of my hand. The heavy door opened with its familiar eerie creak.

The room was cool, damp, and held a slight musky odor. Everything was the same as the first time I saw it, through the eyes of an unsuspecting fourteen-year-old girl. Annabella was slouched in her child-size rocking chair in the corner. The Eliss family portrait was hanging in its usual spot. The brass bed was dressed in its delicate lace and the dressing table with its huge ornate mirror was neat and tidy. Except for the residue of lingering, frightful memories, all was well, or so it seemed. Auntie was right about the wallpaper; the candy stripes were enough to make you cross eyed. We set to work, soaking the walls in hot soapy water, scraping, peeling long strands of gooey paper off the walls. It had been pasted on with heavy glue. Auntie hummed an unfamiliar tune. Every once in a while I'd glance over my shoulder, just in case. "Didn't they have any strippable wallpaper when you did this room? The stuff with an adhesive on the back?"

"Can't be bothered with that there 'new fangled' stuff. This is proper paper. Sticks like a bad dream it does."

It's a nightmare for sure. "What color are you going to paint the walls?"

"Purple."

"Purple?"

"That's what I said. It were m' mum's favorite color, said it 'ad magical powers she did. Fancied 'erself as a bit of a seer, m' mum. Bless 'er, poor thing."

Before I could open my mouth the smell of something rancid invaded my nostrils. I dropped the scraper and covered my nose. *Oh my God, is it her?* "Can't you smell that?"

She wrinkled her nose. "Got wind 'ave ya, luv?"

"No! I don't have wind!" I gnawed down on my bottom lip as I sniffed the air. It was gone.

Auntie was twirling her hanky in her liver-spotted hands. "Can't smell anything."

"No, because it's gone now. It smelt like cat pee." I

stared at her, pitifully, like a frightened child, hoping my for-lorn expression would encourage her to confess. "Didn't it, Auntie Em?"

She sniffed and faced the challenge. "I don't know," she answered, in a harsh voice. Then in a kinder voice, "The cats won't come up 'ere, except for Winston, that is. I often find 'im sitting on the top stair waiting for me to let 'im in. Funny, that is."

Very funny and suspicious. I raised my voice. I couldn't help myself. "What I think is really funny, Auntie, is the fact that you won't acknowledge what's happened here, Mary Eliss, the creature that you fought with in the woodlot." I drew my eyebrows together. "The one that scared your hus-band to death. Remember?"

She swallowed hard. Her face turned grim. Compassion and regret stirred inside me. I walked over to her, bent down, and gave her a gentle hug. "Sorry, I didn't mean to up-set you."

"M' memory ain't what it used to be, luv." I knew that she wasn't being honest. Her mind was, for the most part, in-tact and there's no way she could have forgotten all those ter-rifying events. For some reason she was pretending to have forgotten, but why?

I carried on scraping and peeling, listening to Auntie's off tune serenade, my senses alert for any sudden changes in the atmosphere, unpleasant smells, or ghostly apparitions.

"Time for a cuppa," Auntie announced.

"Good idea, I'm parched." I placed my tools on the floor.

"No, luv, no need to stop. I'll bring it up here. We may as well finish it up. We'll 'ave it finished in an 'our if we keep on goin'." She wiped the scum from the scraper and tossed the dirty rag into the bucket. "Plunk."

She was right, and what could possibly happen in such a short time? I'd been to hell and back. Surely I was brave enough to spend a few minutes in here, alone? *Then why is there a huge wad of dread in your throat?* "Okay, but leave the door open, please." She shrugged her shoulders and strolled out of the room. Immediately my muscles tensed. *Stop it this instant. Emily Fletcher!* "There's nothing to fear but fear itself," I mumbled as my gaze darted around the room.

I took the little bag of sea salt out of my back pocket and sprinkled it around the room. "Wow! Where did you come from?" Winston was on the bed, his front paws tucked neatly under his chest, his head tilted slightly back, in a regal manner. *He didn't come in after Auntie left. He must have been under the bed and if so, how long had he been there?* The horrid dream of his sharp claws piercing into my flesh was still with me. I tossed the soggy rag into the bucket and walked towards him. His odd shaped eyes watched me intently. His poised demeanor seemed to imply that he was king and this was his castle. I knelt down beside the bed and ran my hands over his silky coat, cautiously, trying to rid myself of my fear; after all, he was just a cat and that was just a dream. He purred, a deep throated purr. Then, suddenly, he sprang up. His back arched, his hair stood erect. I moved back

as he hissed wildly. The room filled with the acrid stench of
cat pee. I turned and flew out of the door.

* * * *

It was twenty past six and I was sitting snug in the arms
of Uncle Reg's deep-cushioned wing back chair, draped in his
old blanket, the one that his mother had stitched for him, the
one that had covered his coffin. I was pondering the promis-
ing events of the evening, with a glass of chardonnay in my
hand, dressed and groomed, waiting for my prince charming
to arrive. The ringing of the phone broke my thoughts.

"I'll get it," Auntie called from the kitchen. "Ain't no rest
for the wicked, there ain't." Her mumbling trailed down the
hall way. Her voice sounded concerned. I moved closer to the
door to hear what she was saying but she hung up abruptly.
She entered the room, head hung, hanky in hand. "Jonny ain't
coming, luv." My heart sank. "It's Lindy, she's poorly, got a
'igh fever she 'as. Their taking 'er to the 'ospital to 'av 'er
looked at. He said 'e'd call you tomorrow but I told 'im to
call us when she's seen a doctor and let us know 'ow she is."

Anger and disappointment whirled around inside me like
a hurricane. "He didn't ask to talk to me?" She shook her
head. "Why couldn't her mother take her? Or why didn't he
just drop them off there?" Oh dear, that sounded selfish and
whiny.

"Flippin' 'eck our Emily, 'av some compassion." She
shook her head. "His sister's very poorly; could be something
serious for all they know. And they could be there all evening. To see a doctor in that there 'ospital's like waiting for

cement to dry, unless ya already got one foot in the grave. You'll be seeing lots of Jonny, don't you fret about that."

I smiled. "I guess you're right. I hope she's okay."

A thin grin spread across her lips. "Me too, luv."

"Maybe I'll give him a call on his cell."

"Yer what?"

I must remember to use the English lingo. "On his mobile phone."

"All right, but give it awhile."

I could feel twinges of utter disappointment stabbing at my heart. I was dying to hold him, to feel the warmth of his manly body next to mine. Had that bitchy sister of his done it again, kept us apart, just like she had in the past? *But she's ill and Merthia isn't controlling her anymore. Is she? What if Belinda really is Aunties daughter? That would make her my cousin. Oh, whatever...* I grabbed my fleecy hoodie from the coat stand and headed for the door "I'm going for a walk. I won't be long."

"Don't ya go wandering off." She hesitated. "It's getting dark out there."

"I won't," I said, as I swung open the door and stepped outside. The air was cold and damp. A gray mist hung over the farm. I breathed in the thick air as I stood in the dense silence. Sam came bounding up to meet me, his tail whipping back and forth, his cold nose nuzzling into my hand. When Auntie had fully recovered, the McArthur's brought Sam back to the farm. She allowed him to sleep in the kitchen at night, as his enthusiasm for chasing the cats had diminished. "Come on, Sam, let's go for a walk." He trotted beside me like a faithful shadow. I pulled the hood of my jacket over my head, as the cool evening air nipped at my ears.

Down the rough country lane, past the foreboding red barn, we strolled, side by side. I stood at the edge of the meadow and stared ahead. In the distance, shrouded slightly by the mist, I could see it, the dreaded wood lot, looming like a great monster waiting to devour its prey. I could feel its strange magnetic pull—a longing, a stirring in my soul—as if I were a pirate being tempted to plunge into the depths of the dark formidable sea, in search of a priceless treasure chest. Through its net of mist it beckoned. I shivered. *Not a chance. Never again!* A sound from behind me caught my attention. "Wow…what the…" A swarm of tiny flickering lights came towards me. I moved back. Sam's ears perked, a low growl vibrated from the back of his throat. "It's okay, boy, they're just fireflies." I thought for a moment. *No they couldn't be fireflies, not at this time of year, not when it's this cold. And anyway it wasn't dark enough.* They came closer. I started to feel uneasy. They were making quick screeching sounds, like chattering little children or fairies. "Fairies! No, surely not!" Suddenly the swarm of colored orbs turned and shot off towards the pasture. Sam took off after them, ears and tail erect. "No, Sam! Come back!" I puckered my lips and gave a sharp whistle, like Uncle Reg used to do when instructing Sam to come. He kept going. I ran after him. I couldn't let him get away; I had no idea where the lights would lead him. It was dusky now. I could hear the bleating of the sheep and feel the squashing of their waste on the soles of my shoes but I could only see vague outlines of white fluff. The tiny lights were luminous as they flew across the meadow, with Sam's dark silhouette trailing close behind. I ran hard to catch up to him. My legs were starting to ache and my heart was racing like a freight train. "Sam, come back! Right now!" The lights stopped for a moment, as if to ponder, then soared up the banks of Beacon Hill right to the top.

Like colored candles on a birthday cake, they flickered and glowed over their delectable mound. Sam was sitting at the bottom of the hill, whining, like some poor wounded animal. I ran up to him and knelt down beside him, wrapping my arms around his neck, as my gaze wandered to the top of Beacon Hill. The little orbs chattered excitedly. "What are you?" I cried. One of them left the swarm and swooped down right in front of my nose. I waved my hand in front of my face and swatted at it. "Shoo. Go away." It weaved back and forth in front of my face. Its aura was that of something sinister. This was no fairy, more like a naughty little pixie, or worse. Sam snarled, and then lunged at it, baring his teeth. Instantly it soared to the top of the hill and joined the others. I bent down and grabbed Sam's collar. "Come on, old boy, we're out of here!" I started to run in the direction of what I thought was the cottage. "Come on, Sam. You know the way." He ran a few strides in front of me, panting, with his nose to the ground. It was getting dark and the cold mist was nipping at my skin.

I stared ahead, looking for some sign of the cottage, but it was getting difficult to see anything. I froze. "Sam, where are you? Sammy!" The thought of what happened to me last time I was here came rushing into my mind. *Now stop it, don't you go panicking Emily Fletcher. Don't you dare… Just use your head and think.* If I kept going in this direction I was bound to see something I recognized. "Sammy…" Why would he leave me? That wasn't like him. Where could he have gone? If he showed up at the cottage without me, Auntie would be frantic.

I wrapped my arms around my shivering form and trekked through the curtain of dusky mist, stumbling over rocks, walking into bushes, my eyes narrow, trying desperately to focus on something, anything familiar, while my chest ached with tension.

A light came in view. I sighed, a deep sigh of relief. It was a dim yellow light coming from a small window. As I got closer I could see that it was a cottage. I hastened my stride but something didn't feel right. This wasn't the beaten path from the pasture that led to Merryweather Lodge and surely I would have noticed the red barn if I had passed it. No, this didn't feel right at all. As I got closer, the knots in my gut tightened. I knew where I was now. This was the peculiar Mrs. Tilly's cottage, the cottage that my dad grew up in. But after the incident in the woodlot she disappeared. "No ones seen 'ide nor 'air of 'er," Auntie had said. After everything Merthia said about Mrs Tilly the thought of possibly seeing her again terrified me.

I pushed my way through the wall of dried vegetation,

tall brittle grasses, dead nettles, and old man's beard. I moved cautiously up the old porch steps and to the back door. Everything was the same as I remembered it, but it had become unkempt, dusty, and dirty. The multitude of chimes hanging from the gable roof were tarnished and jumbled. The rocking chair was covered in dead leaves. Dirt stained the terracotta pots and rust spots patched the watering cans. I shuffled towards the lit kitchen window, cupped my hands around my face, and gazed inside. Through the dirty little window and shabby net curtains, I could only see glimpses of the purple kitchen. If Mrs. Tilly had left, why was the light on? Perhaps there was a squatter here or perhaps Mrs. Tilly hadn't left after all. Taking a deep breath, I put my fist to the door and knocked. The sound broke through the eerie silence like a gong at a funeral march. At first there was no response. Then I heard the squeak of the rocking chair on the porch. I turned to look at it. Ever so slowly it rocked, back and forth—an animated empty seat, beckoning me. My hands shot to my throat. The chimes started to tinkle. I flew off the porch, tripped on the stairs, and landed face first on the ground. Then I heard the creak of the door opening, slowly.

Chapter 3

"Hello, my dear. I've been expecting you." She stepped just outside of the doorway, held out her stubby hand, and motioned me to come inside. I lifted my bedraggled body off the ground and wiped the blood from my nose with the back of my hand. I thought about running, dashing away as fast as I could into the murky void, but where would I go and what if there was something even more threatening than her out there? Maybe she'd have a flashlight I could borrow, or maybe she'd had a phone installed, although the chances of that were pretty slim. "Come in, child. Looks like you need tending to." I pulled a tissue from my pocket, wiped the blood from my nose and the back of my hand, and proceeded to climb the rickety old steps, cautiously, not knowing what to expect. She looked almost the same as she did the last time I saw her. She wore the same cheery expression, and the long purple, cabbage-print dress, and bright colored jewelry, but something was different. "That's it. Come on in." She smiled sweetly. I felt the vibes of my inner voice objecting, as she took hold of my arm and led me through the door.

Woodsy warmth and the smell of fresh herbs, ginger, and pine filled the air. The kettle whistled on the cast iron stove, as though it had been prepared ahead, for my arrival. She guided me to the kitchen table, pulled out a ladder-back chair, and ushered me onto it. One lone beeswax candle sat in the center of the table on a chipped saucer, its glow shadowed by the dull electric light. "Sit there. I'll be right back." I gazed around the room, fiddling nervously with my tissue. Everything looked the same, except it was more distinct. The colors were more vivid, the smells more intoxicating. Mrs. Tilly's white hair shimmered with silver highlights and her face beamed with a radiant, healthy glow. It was captivating and surreal, like a storybook cottage where everything was perfect and enchanting, complete with a charming fairy godmother. "Here, put this on your scrapes; it'll stop them from going septic." She handed me a piece of white gauze that smelled delicious. Then she placed a blue Wedgwood cup and a tiny fancy plate in front of me, sliced a big slab of gingerbread, and poured me a cup of herbal tea.

"You said you were expecting me?" I asked, timidly. She nodded. "How did you know I'd be here?"

"That's for me to know and you to find out, child."

I didn't like the sound of that. "Do you have a phone here and perhaps a flashlight I can borrow? I need to call my aunt as she'll be worried sick about me. I was going for a walk and I got lost." I bit into the chunk of gingerbread. It tasted heavenly.

"My dear, you never got lost. You reached your destination." She glanced at the clock on the kitchen shelf. "Right on time. And no, I have no use for a telephone."

She was scaring me. "How about a flashlight? You must have a flashlight."

"I might have, but why would you need one?"

"To see where I'm going; its pitch black out there." I stood, but I felt little woozy, so I sat back down.

"Contact your aunt through your thoughts."

"You mean telepathically?" She grinned, and I protested, saying, "But I can't do that."

"Nonsense, child, you can do anything you want. You have the gift." I remembered her telling me that once before. "What gift?" I asked.

"The gift of a seer; you inherited it from your great-great-grandmother. She was a white witch and a darn good one, secretly, of course. You wouldn't dare let anyone find out you were a witch, not in them days."

"You knew my great-great -grandmother? That would make you..."

"Very old and very wise."

I started to feel drowsy. "It's been nice visiting with you but I have to go, with or without a flashlight."

"Oh no, you're not going anywhere, my dear." She glared at me with her glassy, turquoise eyes. "Not until you've told me what happened in the woodlot. Were you able to expel the entity Merthia?"

I told her everything that had happened, that the potion

that was supposed to expel Merthia didn't work, that Merthia said that Mrs. Tilly was her real mother, and that she claimed that Mrs. Tilly killed Maud's baby at birth and gave Auntie's baby to her in replacement.

Her eyes were fixed on me with a gleaming curiosity. When I finished she put her hand over her mouth and snickered. "What a load of rubbish."

I got up and looked straight into her strange eyes. "Don't laugh. It was horrifying." I squeezed my eyes into tiny slits. "Perhaps you are her. Merthia's evil mother, Hagmanis."

"Don't be so ridiculous, child," she snapped.

"Then why did you give me the recipe for a potion that would bring her soul back to life?"

Her head cocked and there was a suspicious look on her face. "You must not have added the right ingredients."

"No! I followed your instructions. I did what you told me, and watched her drink it."

"Ahh. That was a mistake. You were supposed to pour it down her throat."

I felt drowsy and a little shaky but I kept my composure. "We couldn't restrain her, and besides, what difference would it have made? You gave us the wrong recipe." Things were starting to get blurry.

"What did you do with the amulet, girl?"

I grabbed the back of the chair as the room stated to spin. "What have you done?" I mumbled. Then, darkness!

I awoke in a haze on the kitchen floor. Rubbing my eyes, I reached for the chair and pulled myself up. Except for the eerie, flickering glow of the candle, the room was pitch dark and bitterly cold. My head was throbbing and my nerves were on edge. Was it all a dream? I asked myself. I took the candle, held it out in front of me, and dragged my feet around the room. It was dusty, dirty, and smelled of mildew. Dirty dishes laced with green mould lay in the sink. Bits of dry herbs were scattered on the draining board. I shivered. A sense of dread balled in my stomach. *I must try to find her flashlight. This candle will not last if there's the least bit of wind out there.* Pulling open the drawers and rummaging through the cupboards, I searched frantically for the flash light that I would need to guide me back to Auntie's cottage. Just as I was about to give up and settle for the candle, I saw it, sitting on the back shelf of the meager pantry: a heavy, gray plastic flashlight. I held my breath and said a silent prayer as I flicked the little switch on the side. "Yes." It worked. I dashed to the front door, turned the handle, and pulled. It was locked—from the outside, but how? I twisted the knob, pushed, and gave the door a swift kick. It wouldn't budge. I went to the back door. It was locked, too. The windows seemed too tiny to crawl through, but were they? The window in the sitting room was a little bigger than the others. I pulled back the grubby net curtains and placed my hand on the latch and tugged, but it was stuck. They were all stuck. "Help! Help!" I cried in utter desperation. The floor boards squeaked. I stood still and stiff, my back rigid against the kitchen sink, my eyes following the beam from the flashlight around the room. Squeak. Squeak. "Mrs. Tilly, is that you?" *She's playing games with me.* "Show yourself. I know it's you." My voice was shaky. My heart hammered under my ribcage. My flashlight caught sight of an axe leaning against the wood stove. I grabbed it and dashed to the door. Heart racing, adrenaline pumping, I lifted the axe and swung at the lock. With all the strength I could muster I chopped away at the piece of metal that stood between me and freedom. And then I heard someone cry, "Corea! Colrea!" "*Oh my God. It's her. The creature!*" Utter fear consumed me. I hacked at the door wildly, as if possessed. The lock fell to the ground and the door swung open. I dropped the axe, grabbed the flashlight, and flew out of the door.

Down the rickety steps, into a pitch black maze of tangled grasses and brittle debris, not knowing what direction I was going or what I was running from. My heart was beating like a hammer inside my chest. Suddenly I tripped; the flashlight fell out of my hand. My precious beam of light had been extinguished. Darkness enveloped me. I fell to my knees and groped around in the dirt. *Please let me find it and please don't let it be the batteries. Why didn't you look for batteries? You're so stupid, Emily Fletcher. Stupid and cursed!* My hand fell on a vertical slab of cold stone. My fingers slid across its rock-hard, smooth surface. It felt like…no, it couldn't be! I shuffled back, my legs throbbing, my hands sore, from the prickly brambles and my mind numb with dread. There was no moon or stars to aid my vision. Then I felt it, the plastic handle of the flashlight. I held the glimmer of hope in my hand and squeezed my eyes shut. "Oh please make this work."

I flicked the switch and the light came on. "Thank you," I mumbled. I lifted myself up from the ground and shone my beam of light on the vertical stone. It was a gray tombstone. The big bold letters etched into its cold, hard surface read BELINDA! "Oh my God!" I gasped, blinked my eyes rapidly, and looked again; now it read MAUD! *What is this? A trick!* I winced and took off.

Out into the dark night I went, weighed down by fatigue, the cold air gnawing at my bones, the beam of weak light stretched out in front of me. The pitch-black cloak of nightfall surrounded me. I was terrified. "Help! Is anyone out there?" I screamed. *Where the hell is my lavender-scented guardian angel when I need her?* "Help!" I heard a sound in the distance. I stopped, held my breath, stood perfectly still and listened intently. The grass rustled. The distant sound of a lone dog's bark hung in the air. "Sammy! Sammy is that you?"

"Emily Anne." That sounded like Auntie.

"Auntie Em!" I waved my flashlight around, sending the beacon of light in all directions. "Over here! I'm over here!" I flung my arms around her, almost knocking her off her feet.

"What the bloody 'ell are ya doing out here? I've been worried sick about ya." She pulled out a large white hanky, licked the corner, and proceeded to wipe my face with it. I cringed but let her carry on. To let her mother me was the least I could do. "And your hands are like a block of ice," she said.

I put my fists up to my mouth and blew into them. "I went for a walk and got lost." I looked into Sam's sad brown eyes. "And he took off and left me." He looked away, as if to acknowledge his naughty behavior. "How did you know where to find me?"

"I didn't." She looked down at Sam. "But 'e did."

I patted him on the head. "Okay, I forgive you. But I still don't understand why you left me like that. Come on, you lead the way, take us home." He turned and headed for home, as if he'd understood every word that I said. I hooked my arm through Auntie's and we followed his lead. I wasn't sure how much to tell her or if I should tell her anything at all. Would she believe me or admit to believing me? "Have you heard from Jonathan? Is Belinda okay?"

"I 'aven't 'eard anything, not before I left, but I've been out 'ere looking for you for God knows how long."

I gave her arm a gentle squeeze. "I'm so sorry, Auntie."

The clock on the mantel read nine forty-five. I threw off my jacket and hurried to the phone, to see if Jonathan had left me a message. "Oh, shit," I mumbled, as I suddenly remembered that there was no answering machine on this phone. *God, it's so primitive here.* I picked up the receiver and dialed his cell phone number.

"Hello."

"Jonathan, it's Emily. How's your sister?"

"Emily, where have you been? I've been trying to get hold of you all evening."

"It's a long story. Where are you?"

"I'm at my mum's. Belinda just has a bad case of the flu and a throat infection. The doctor told her to stay in bed and take lots of fluids. And he gave her some antibiotics. She's feeling a lot better already."

Antibiotics don't work that fast. Are you sure she wasn't faking? I scoffed under my breath. "I'm glad to hear that. When are you coming over?"

"I'll be there in the morning, after breakfast, around eleven if that's all right?"

"You're not going home then?"

"No, I may as well stay here over night. I don't have to work tomorrow."

Then why don't you come here now? "Okay, I'll see you in the morning."

"See you then."

I waited. No "I miss you" or "I love you". No warm words of any kind. He hung up the receiver. Was he going off me? Had these few weeks apart made him reconsider our relationship? Surely not; we were soul mates. Our souls were bound together, for eternity. I'd only been back here for two days and already I'd had a nightmare, encountered some weird flying orbs, been scared half to death by some spooky old woman, got lost, and discovered the grave of someone still living. My emotions had already stared to wrap around me like clinging vines. *Why can't things just be normal here?* I went to the kitchen and poured myself a large grass of wine. Auntie was scouring a dirty pot in the sink. "What did he say? How is she?"

"Oh, she's fine, it was just the flu. She's a lot better now, now that she's stopped me from seeing her brother." *Oh no, I shouldn't have said that. It just slipped out.* She glared at me and drew in her brows. "Sorry, I shouldn't have said that. It was childish and spiteful."

"I'll say." She shook her head. "Don't know what ya were thinking to say such a thing."

I lowered my head. "I just really wanted to see him tonight."

She patted my arm in a motherly fashion. "I know ya' did, luv, but you'll be seeing lots of 'im now, mark my words."

"He's coming over tomorrow morning, around eleven." She gave me a nod and a sweet smile. Then she rubbed her upper thigh with the heel of her right hand. Arthritis, I assumed. I kissed her lightly on the soft skin of her cheek and grabbed my hefty wine glass. "Good night, Auntie Em."

"Good night, luv. Sleep tight, don't let the bed bugs bite."

It's not bed bugs I'm worried about.

I strolled into the parlor, placed my wine on the antique side table, and flopped on my make-shift bed. All the things that had happened swirled around in my head, and I knew that sleep wouldn't't come easy. I lifted my weary form from the bed and lit one of the scented candles that Skye had given me. It promised to soothe, relax, and induce sleep. My eyes were heavy, my body drained, but the voices inside my head wouldn't stop babbling. I kept asking myself, " *Were there any messages encrypted in these experiences?*" and, wondering if it was ever going to stop. After what seemed like hours of internal debate, sleep finally came, a sound, undisturbed slumber, wrapped in the warm arms of Merryweather Lodge.

I awoke early to the sensation of something crawling across my bed. I pried my eyes open and slowly lifted my head from the pillow. "Aaah...it's you." Winny was glaring at me with her baby blue eyes. She had grown pleasantly plump and looked like a snowball with whiskers. I gathered her up in my arms and nuzzled my face into her furry white coat. She purred contentedly, but suddenly, without warning, she flew off the bed and raced out the door, as if being chased by a vicious dog. I sat up and scoured the room suspiciously. That's when I saw him, sitting by the door, back straight, ears perked, exhibiting a commanding air, like a sentry guarding his fortress. "Winston, did you scare her?"

"Meow."

I shoved my arms into my heavy flannel house coat and peered at the strange cat. "You're too weird. I'm out of here." I moved past him cautiously, half expecting him to jump out and pounce on me. The wood floors were like cold stone under my bare feet. Even though Auntie had had central heating installed, the cottage was freezing cold in the mornings. She turned the heat off when she went to bed, then back on again when she got up. She said it wasn't proper wasting good heat at night.

Anxious to greet the day with a positive outlook, I put the cat incident and all the other events out of my mind and proceeded to prepare myself for the gorgeous Jonathan McArthur's arrival. Auntie was in the kitchen, humming a happy tune while frying a pan full of bacon. Her little feet were inflated by her big fluffy slippers. Even though I didn't eat meat, the smell of fried bacon in the morning always made my mouth water. "Hope that's not for me, Auntie Em."

"Morning, our Emily. No it ain't for you but a bit of meat in yer belly would do ya the world of good."

I just grinned. "Is that so?"

"I'm makin' bacon and egg pie for tea. It were Martha's favorite. M' mum used to make extra and give 'er a couple of pies to take 'ome for 'er family, they never 'ad much poor souls, but we always 'ad plenty. M' mum were a charitable woman, always gave to them that were less fortunate, she did. From Yorkshire she were, m' dad were a Londoner. We came 'ere when I was a youngun. She came from a well-to-do family ya know, m' mum. Right posh they were, never met them though. They disowned my poor mum." Her gaze wandered up to the ceiling. "God rest 'er soul."

"Why did they disown her?"

She lowered her head. "Oh it were nothing."

I knew there was no point in pursuing this topic. As usual she was offering me a tidbit and then putting it back on the plate.

After breakfast I took a hot scented bath in the claw-foot tub, put on my low necked, cashmere sweater and fitted jeans, and curled my long red hair. I wanted to look groomed and enticing without looking like I'd made an effort.

Auntie and I were mulling over some old cook books, looking for recipes for Christmas baking, when I heard a knock on the door.

"Hello, anyone home?" My heart leaped.

"Come on in, Jonny. Take a load off." His lanky legs and gorgeous muscular form strolled through the narrow kitchen doorway. "Good morning, ladies."

Auntie beamed, as she motioned him to the chair next to me. "Sit down 'ere. I'll make you a cupper. How's Lindy this morning?"

"She seems fine now, no fever or pain. It must have been the twenty-four hour flu."

I wrinkled my nose, dying to say something sardonic but I knew I couldn't, so I settled for, "Yes, there's a lot of that going about." Auntie must have sensed the sarcasm in my voice. She gave me a reprimanding glare, out of the corner of her eye. Jonathan slipped out of his black woolen coat and draped it over the back of his chair. I felt a lusty, throbbing heat between my legs as his sensual body towered above me. A black knitted sweater hugged his manly chest. A pair of dark blue jeans clung to his thighs. I fought the overwhelming desire to gaze, to feast my eyes on this delicacy that I promised myself I was going to devour, soon. As he sat down I caught a whiff of his cologne.

Auntie placed two cups with saucers in front of us and poured the brew from her hefty brown teapot.

"So what 'ave the two of you got planned for today?"

He shrugged and his dark brown eyes met mine. "Where would you like to go? I'll take you anywhere your little heart desires."

To your bed. "I'd like to go for a long walk and just talk."

I had decided last night, while I was going over the day's events that I would ask him to come to Mrs. Tilly's cottage with me. I had to go back to see if my nightmarish evening was real or just an illusion.

"Didn't you do enough gallivanting last night?" Auntie glanced at Jonathan and shook her head. "Got lost she did, 'ad me worried sick." His brows rose.

"Don't ask. I'll tell you later," I mumbled.

Auntie went to the pantry, pulled out some cookies and cakes, placed them on a fancy platter, and shoved them in front of us. Jonathan put his hand to his stomach. "Oh I couldn't, I'm still full. My mum cooked a full English breakfast."

"Go on, a little bit won't 'urt ya. And ya both could do with a little meat on yer bones." Like a school boy who'd been told to finish his vegetables, Jonathan slid a cookie off the platter and nibbled on the end. "I'll leave you two youngun's by yourselves. I 'ave to get ready for m' visitor."

I smiled. "She's going to be reunited with an old friend."

"Oh, how nice."

"Make sure you're back 'ere by five, I want ya to meet 'er. That goes for you too, Jonny."

"Don't worry, Mrs. Fletcher, I'll make sure we're back for tea." He gave her a reassuring grin as he grabbed his coat from the back of the chair.

She shoved a can of lemon polish and duster into her large apron pocket, headed for the kitchen door, but then turned. "Five o'clock sharp!"

"We hear you, Auntie." She was getting so set in her ways. Tea was always at five, dinner at twelve and she always ate her breakfast at precisely seven a.m.

Jonathan lifted my warm winter jacket off the coat rack and held it out in front of me. I swooned. *What a gentleman.*

A rush of cool morning air greeted us as we stepped out the door. He reached out and grabbed my hand. "Alone at last."

I gave his strong warm hand a gentle squeeze. "I missed you."

He brought my hand up to his mouth and caressed it with his soft lips. "I missed you too." All the doubts I had about him evaporated. He loved me and no one was going to come between us. Not 'her'. Not anyone. He stopped suddenly. "Emily, where are we going?"

"Keep going and I'll tell you." We strolled side by side, hand in hand, as I told him everything that had happened since the time I arrived. He never said a word. He just listened in silence, contemplating, I was sure, the credibility of it all. I stopped and faced him. "Jonathan, after all we've seen, all we've been through, you must believe me. Why would I make this up? And no, I wasn't dreaming or hallucinating. She's back, Jonathan." My lips quivered. "I can feel it."

He pulled me tight to his broad chest and wrapped his strong arms around me. "She's gone, Emily, and all that stuff you just told me could have a simple explanation. It's because of all that you've been through, that you're assuming it's supernatural."

I pushed him away and shook my head. "No! I'm not assuming it was supernatural, I know it was. And I'm going to prove it to you." I grabbed his hand. "Come on."

He pulled me back into his warm embrace. "You're so sexy when you're mad." His breath brushed my face. His long cool fingers cupped my trembling chin. I was captivated. I couldn't move. "Before we go, we have some unfinished business to take care of." I closed my eyes as I felt the soft touch of his lips on my cheek, slowly working their way to my lips. Hungrily his lips devoured mine, as the tip of his tongue probed the inside of my mouth. A hot wave of utter passion and need consumed me, as he whispered, "I want you Emily."

Chapter 4

The realization of where we were and what had happened here suddenly kicked in. *What if she came?* "We can't. Not here."

"Why not? I don't mind roughing it." His long finger pushed a loose strand of hair away from my face. "It might be fun."

I stepped back. "Soon, Jonathan. Soon."

He rolled his eyes. "It better be soon or I'm going to combust."

I put my hand over my mouth and snickered. "Is it that bad?"

"Yes, every time I'm near you I get this longing in my heart and this throbbing in my…" I put my fingers over his mouth, as my brows rose. "Come on, let's go before you burst into flames."

We walked, making idle conversation, through the sea of rolling pasture. Waves of green smeared with brown and dabbed with dots of heavy coated sheep. "I'm sorry for getting so annoyed at you," I said. "I have a tendency to open my mouth before my brain kicks in. I had always blamed my parents for my defensive nature. My mother's subtle way for making me feel judged—and inadequate and my dad's sarcasm and disapproval of my unorthodox views."

"We all have our crosses to bear and certain personality traits that we're not proud of," he said. "That's what makes us human. I'm sure your parents did their best."

"I know they loved me but it was their approval and acceptance I needed. How about you? It couldn't have been easy knowing you were adopted and having a ghost for a playmate." *Not to mention a deranged sister.*

"I didn't find out that I was adopted until I was about twelve and having a ghostly friend felt normal to me."

"Really?" I was amazed.

"She was like a visible imaginary friend. Like a secret companion, I suppose."

"I have a feeling she still is."

We stopped by the earthy mound of Beacon Hill. "This is where I last saw those weird lights. They hovered at the top, then one flew down and almost hit me on the nose. They were pretty, like little Christmas lights but there was something sinister about them. They gave me the creeps and I'm sure they were trying to tell me something. And the hill, I saw it move, pulsating as though it were alive." He cleared his throat. I looked into his face. *Did I detect an expression of doubt and amusement, perhaps?* I felt a twinge of annoyance but I just grinned and kept my mouth shut. "I think Mrs.

Tilly's cottage is this way," I said, as I linked my arm through his and led him on.

We walked, this time in silence. My mind and body were a hive of emotions; a swarm of thoughts buzzed around in my head; the sticky nectar of lust still clung to my skin. I cringed when we passed the spot where Merthia possessed me. I could still feel the sensation of her rancid flesh devouring me, like maggots burrowing into my skin. My gut clenched when the cottage came into view.

We plowed our way through the untamed, withering garden, brambles, and pieces of broken fence. The porch was in the same bedraggled condition as I'd seen it the day before but the door was unscathed and closed. I climbed the rough steps to the porch; slowly, my legs unsteady, my throat as dry as sand paper, clutching on to Jonathan's hand with a tight grip, eyes and ears alert for any sudden movement or sound.

He cupped his hands and glared through the tiny kitchen window. "Looks deserted."

"The light was on when I was here last night." He gave me an "are you sure about that?" glance out of the corner of his eye. "Knock on the door," I commanded authoritatively, still slightly wounded from the questioning glance. He clenched his fist and rapped on the thick wooden door. I stood back and took a couple of deep breaths. Nothing. "Open it."

"I don't think we should go inside; that would be trespassing."

"It's deserted. You said so yourself." He placed his hand

on the iron doorknob, turned it, and then pushed the door open. "Hello, anyone home?"

I crept behind him tentatively and took a quick glance back at the door. There wasn't a mark on it. We moved timidly, from room to room. It was desolate, grubby, and smelled of wet wood and mildew.

Jonathan ran his slender finger over the dusty mantel. "It looks like no one has lived here for sometime, Emily."

I grabbed his sleeve and turned him around to face me. "You weren't listening; she was here last night and the cottage was warm, clean, and very much lived in. I took an axe to the door when she locked me in and hid from me." *Or was it all just an illusion?* I pointed to the vintage axe, leaning against the wood stove. "That axe."

He looked at the axe, then at the door, shrugged, and managed a patronizing comment. "It's all right now."

He thinks I've lost it. I plunked myself down on the threadbare sofa. I wasn't going to succumb to my volatile nature. What good would it do me to get angry at him? I had to convince him that I was not going crazy. I covered my face with my hands and sighed. Jonathan lowered his muscular body on the cushion beside me and slid his arm over my shoulder. "You've been through a lot of stress. Your mind and your emotions have been pushed to their limits. It's no wonder you're…"

That did it. "Hallucinating?" I pushed his arm off my shoulder and stood up. "Don't you remember what Merthia said? That Mrs. Tilly was really her mother, Hagmanis? And if that's true, she'd be able to appear and disappear whenever she wished. Right? She's probably playing some sort of malicious game with me, trying to make me believe I'm insane." I glared at him. "Or to convince other people that I am." I dashed from room to room. "Come out and show yourself. You evil witch! Come on. Come on!"

He grabbed my arm and pulled me in. "Emily, get a grip! She's not here. No one's here."

I turned and buried my face into his chest, frustration burning inside me, dread simmering in my soul. "You don't think I'm losing it, do you?" He buried his hands in my hair and planted a gentle kiss on my forehead and said, "No, I don't think your losing it; I just can't stand to think that it's starting up again. I thought that it was all over, that all this stuff had been put to rest. I'm sorry, Emily, it's me, not you." A picture of the ominous tombstone came to mind. "Let's go," I demanded. "I have something to show you." I hurried down the rickety steps and through the tangled garden. *Now where was it? The grass was shorter and there were no bushes.* I tried to recall how far I'd gone before stumbling on it.

"What are you looking for?" he asked.

"It was dark but it can't be too far."

"What can't?"

"The grave stone I tripped over."

"A grave stone? Well, maybe it's disappeared."

I ignored the sarcasm and continued to search. "I was running—fast, in a straight line from the porch. It must have been only a minute or two before I stumbled on it." *Oh no, was that an illusion?* "Wait a minute. Here it is. I've found it!" I knelt in front of the gray slab of stone and rubbed my hand over its cold, soiled surface. "Where's the inscription?"

Jonathan bent down and peered over my shoulder. "There's no inscription."

"I can see that! But there was an inscription there yester-day. It had Belinda carved into it in big bold letters but then it changed to…"

"Belinda!" he interrupted, before I could finish.

"That's what I said."

He stiffened and moved back, as if I had stuck him. "You imagined it."

I held my ground, my voice firm and final. "No, I did not!"

"Maybe that's what you want to believe," he said, and then his tone softened. "Unconsciously, perhaps."

"What?" I gasped, incredulously.

"To see my sister dead and buried."

Now I was livid. "Are you crazy? Why would I want to see her dead?"

"Because you think that hideous creature still has a hold on her, I'm guessing."

"Well, guess again! And even if I thought that I wouldn't want her dead. I wouldn't wish that on anyone, Jonathan. What kind of a person do you think I am?" I could feel myself starting to well up.

He walked towards me, gathered me in his arms, and

held me tight. "I know you're not that kind of person, Emily. I'm so sorry. I just find it so hard to get my head around all of this stuff, even after all that I've seen and a grave with my sister's name on it? Come on, let's just go."

I inhaled the mouth-watering aroma of almonds, nutmeg, and fresh baked pastry as I stepped inside the door of the cottage. Everything was spic and span, and the wood furniture gleamed. Auntie's eyes lit up when she saw us. "How was ya walk?"

"Uneventful," I said. She glanced at me out of the corner of her eye, as her mouth widened in a phony grin. It was as if she knew exactly where I'd been and what I was up to. "Something smells good."

Auntie picked up the bottom of her apron, wrapped it around her hand, opened the oven door, and pulled out the tart pan. "Bakewell tarts," she said, in a boastful tone.

"Another one of Martha's favorites?" I asked.

She nodded her head. "Where are you two off to now?"

"We're going into Salisbury for lunch."

"Better make that dinner. I'm only making a light tea."

I looked at the old kitchen table, loaded with pies, cakes, eggs, flour, and such. "A light tea, is it, Auntie?" I kissed her on her soft, flour-spotted cheek. She flashed me a coy, thankful smile. "Enjoy your visit with Martha. Bye the way, is she staying over night?"

"I 'aven't the foggiest idea, luv."

"If she does she can have my bed. I don't mind sleeping on the sofa."

"Don't be silly, she can have the bed upstairs. I'll tidy it up at bit and I'm sure she won't mind the unfinished walls, not for one night."

Not the attic room. I put my hand over hers and said, in an authoritative tone, "No, I don't want you going up there. She can have my bed."

She scoffed and shook her head. "All right, bossy britches."

"You could stay at my place," Jonathan said to me, in a confident tone.

Auntie's brows arched. "That wouldn't be proper and what would the neighbors think?"

I rolled my eyes but couldn't help laughing under my breath. *Was she that naïve and archaic? Was she under the impression that I was still a virgin?* Probably. Then in a not-so-confident voice, "I meant on the couch, of course." Then he gave me a quick wink and one of his sexy lip-twitching, half smiles, where the corner of his mouth raised slightly and his cleft chin tightened. My body and heart responded with a resounding, *Yes!* "Auntie Em, I'm twenty years old. Don't you trust me to look after myself?"

"I do, m' luv." She gave Jonathan a crafty grin. "But I'm not so sure about 'im."

"You can trust me to act like a perfect gentleman with your niece, Mrs. Fletcher."

"All right, Jonny. I believe you, thousands wouldn't"

"'Bye, Auntie. We'll be back by five o'clock."

"And no 'anky panky. Do ya 'ear me, little Jonny?"

"I hear you, Mrs. Fletcher." His hand was over his mouth, stifling a snicker when we stepped outside.

I was still shaking my head. "The stuff she comes out with."

"What would the neighbors say?' And to think that I would take advantage of her poor, innocent niece."

"Well, wouldn't you?"

"Of course," he said with a smile.

We climbed into Jonathans pride and joy, a black BMW with all the bells and whistles, still caught up in the light-hearted amusement of Auntie's lingo. "I have to stop at my parents' place," he said. "I left my mobile phone there." That put a damper on my mood. "If it's okay with you?"

"No problem." I'll stay in the car and wait, I told myself. The last person I wanted to see right now was the strange, unpredictable Belinda McArthur and I'd rather not see her miserable old mother either.

We took the back route, a rough dirt road that rolled like a long brown ribbon before us, with groves of half naked trees on either side, flanked by ploughed farm land as hard as cement, hilly pastures with faded grass, cows, and lots of bulky coated sheep. Autumn's cheerful melody was slowly giving way to the deeper serenade of winter but it still held a sense of enchantment for me.

Like a lot of the homes around here, the McArthurs cottage had a fairytale façade. It might have belonged to a rich toymaker or a wicked fairy godmother. It was built with stone and red brick and topped with a shingled gable roof.

The windows were modest in size, etched with tiny squares and flanked by gray wooden shutters. A porch wrapped around the front, like a frilly skirt. The garden was tidy with a large lawn, empty flower beds and neatly trimmed privet hedges. Auntie owned this cottage and I wondered why she chose to live at Merryweather Lodge and not here. This seemed much more fitting for a farmer than his hired hand. But Uncle Reg's grandfather built Merryweather Lodge and keeping it in the family seemed to be extremely significant and the honorable thing to do. Uncle Reg was a stubborn man, with principles that were etched in stone.

We drove around to the back of the cottage and parked beside a weathered old pickup truck. "Are you coming in?" he asked.

"No, I'll just wait for you here."

"I'm sure my parents would like to see you again."

It's not your parents I'm worried about. "I'll visit them some other time. Tell them I said hi."

"Suit yourself. I won't be a minute."

I gazed around the back yard; it wasn't as neatly kept as the front. Parts of rusty farm machines and tools littered the lawn, a ramshackle potting shed sat at the bottom of the garden, and next to it two sturdy oak trees anchored a huge truck tire, attached to heavy rope. I wondered if Jonathan and Mary Eliss had played on that swing when he was a child. I pictured him pushing her back and forth, her long green dress fluttering around her dainty legs, her childish giggles echoing though time and space. I saw them... "Jeez!" I gulped, my mental picture suddenly broken. "Where did you come from?"

She was staring at me through the window, wide eyed, with a strange grin on her face. I hadn't seen her in the yard or coming out of the house; she just seemed to appear from nowhere. I grinned back at her. "Belinda?" She was dressed in a simple blue dress and a hand knitted white cardigan. Her hair was loose, with one side pulled back with a comb shaped barrette. She wore no make up and looked more like a little child than an eighteen-year-old. This was not the evil, provocative, manipulating Belinda I knew.

She cupped her hands around her eyes and peered at me through the glass with a pitiful expression on her face, like a poor muted child. I waved my fingers and mouthed hi. She frowned, as though her feelings were hurt. *What is wrong with you, Emily? Go out and speak to her. She's obviously harmless. And she seems to have regressed back to the lovely young thing they all said she was.* I was just about to open the door, when her expression and demeanor started to change.

I moved closer to the window and watched dumbfounded, as her face began to twist and pale and her eyes sank slowly, deep within their dark pockets. Big black pupils peered up at me through the matted hair that now hung over her face. Her clothes became tattered rags. Teeth clenched, shoulders hunched, arms hanging limp by her side, like a vampire stalking its prey, her dirty bare feet paced, back and forth, in front of the window. I could sense the anger and hate emanating from her savage form. Anxiously I pushed the lock on the side of the door. Then I felt it, in the bottom of my gut, moving up to my throat, that familiar, gut-wrenching feeling, of utter dread.

Chapter 5

Jonathan. Where the hell are you! Belinda stopped pacing and came to the car window. Glaring through the glass with her gaunt eyes, she snarled and hissed. I could smell the foul stench of her breath through the pane of glass. She raised her fists and started pounding on the window. *There was no way that this evil creature could have come from the loins of my dear Auntie Em.* I cringed. "Stop it! You silly bitch, you're going to break the window!" The car vibrated from the force of her blows. I was scared that her hand was going to come crashing through the window, all mangled and dripping with blood. I lowered my head onto the back rest and squeezed my eyes shut, took at few deep breaths, and tried desperately to go within and block her out of my mind.

From far away I could hear the sweet sound of Celtic music, a harp, a flute, and soft guitar, all mingling together in joyful harmony, getting closer and closer. The aromatic scent of roses, lavender, fine herbs, and sweet red wine filled my nostrils as the music and a group of white-robed young men moved in my direction.

"Knock! Knock!" I bolted upright and my gaze flew to the window. "Jonathan! Thank God."

"Open the door," he shouted.

I took a quick look around before lifting the latch. "Where have you been? You said you'd only be a few minutes." I shoved him out of the way. "Where is she?"

"Who?"

"Belinda!"

He pointed to the gnarled oak trees. "Over there." Rocking to and fro on the makeshift swing was the childish little teenager I first saw. Her pretty dress and soft wavy hair fluttered in the breeze as she swung to and fro. She looked up at me, gave me a mischievous smile and held up her hand, wiggling her fingers in a waving motion. *I don't know how you did that, you malicious little bitch, but now I know what I'm up against.*

"She said you told her to go away. She only wanted you to play with her."

"What's wrong with her? She looks like and acts like a little child."

"They're not sure; she'll be fine for a few days, and then suddenly she starts to regress again. Her doctor thinks it might be schizophrenia but they're still running tests on her. They say it could also be post-traumatic stress. By regressing to her childhood, she can forget all the terrible things that have happened to her since then. She goes back to being eight years old, before she discovered Lizzy Lunn's body, before any of the other…crazy stuff started happening"

Crazy stuff? "She goes back to being a lovely young thing?" I asked, with a hint of sarcasm.

"Yes."

Yeah right! Merthia said, "She fools you all with her false innocence."

"Why does she dress like that?"

"My mum dresses her. I think, secretly, she wants to keep her that way. She feels like she has her little girl back, at long last. I know she looks ridiculous but even when she's her normal self she still dresses modestly and wears outdated clothes. Not the Belinda you remember, eh?"

I smiled. *Not even close.* It did make sense. The trauma of finding a mutilated body and being possessed by an evil spirit was enough to make anyone loopy. Maybe she didn't mutate. Perhaps it was me. Did I drop off to sleep? Was I dreaming? My dreams had become so vivid; the distinction between my night visions and daydreams were faint and blurry. Or, was I going loopy? Had the schizoid gene finally kicked in like my dad said it would? Why was Belinda McArthur a sick, deranged young woman withdrawing back into her childhood, unable to face the terrifying things that had happened to her? Or was she still Merthia's faithful servant and a master of disguise?

"I'm sorry Jonathan, I just can't forget what she was."

"She was possessed, under some sort of spell. But I'm sure that creature's gone now, Emily; you banished, remember?" His vice chocked. "She left my sister mentally ill."

My heart ached for him. "I'm sure she'll recover. It's just a matter of time."

He nodded his head, then dug into his pocket and pulled out his keys. "Let's go."

I climbed into the passenger's seat and laid my head on the cushiony, black leather head rest, my emotions and mind still reeling from what I had just witnessed. Merthia hadn't been banished, I was sure of that. The potion hadn't worked. And all those killings and disappearances, Merthia had to have been the slaughterer? But surely Belinda was too small and frail at the age of twelve to have butchered Lizzy Lunn. Maybe Merthia was using another family host to kill for her, or did she even need a host to carry out her bloody, evil deeds? So many questions, yet to be answered.

"Emily."

I raised my head, startled at the sound of his voice. "What?"

"I was asking you where you wanted to eat."

"We can pick something up and go to your place if you like."

The curves of his mouth turned up ever-so-slightly, revealing what he had in mind. "That's fine with me."

I yawned drowsily, as I gazed out of the tinted window. Jet lag and fatigue were finally catching up with me. On one side of the road, in the middle of a flat open field, surrounded by a tall fence and photo-taking tourists, the great monoliths of Stonehenge oozed out of the ground like the petrified trunks of ancient trees; huge monstrosities concealing hidden secrets of worship, astronomy, or horrific sacrifice. On the other side of the road, gentle rolling hills stretched for miles, pimpled and blemished by their somber Bronze Age burial mounds. My eyes felt heavy. Then darkness.

The air was warm with a soft breeze that carried the fragrance of primroses, new leaves, and fresh green moss. My long red hair fell about my thinly clad form like a veil of pure woven silk, as I danced around the bright crackling flames in the middle of the circle. Round and round the blazing fire we flew, hand in hand, six beautiful maidens, with creamy white skin and flowing hair laced with fresh flowers and berries, twirling, giggling, chanting, "Anam Cara. Anam Cara." Their transparent gowns of delicate skin-like fabric clung to their bodies, revealing their most private parts. I felt my body tingle with an erotic sensation as I glimpsed their hard breasts and perfect naked forms lost in a euphoric haze of pure ecstasy. "Hush…" They stopped, suddenly. Two of the maidens grabbed handfuls of dirt to smother the fire. They scattered swiftly, like frightened sheep with a wolf at their heels, crouching behind tree trunks and thick tangled bushes. I stood, glued to the ground, feeling the air of panic and fear but unable to move my limbs, pinned down—a succulent piece of flesh, waiting for the wolf to rip it to shreds and devour it. A young girl's screams echoed in the distance. Utter fear consumed me. A soft hand clasped onto mine and pulled forcefully.

My feet thawed and I followed her lead. She dragged me behind the thick trunk of a large birch tree; pieces of its bark were peeling away like bits of skin from raw bone. She put her delicate finger over my lips and whispered, "Anam Cara." The cries grew louder. Then I heard it, the dreaded sound of rustling grass and breaking twigs. I tucked my body behind the trunk and peered around its pale, woody knolls. A woman in a long purple cloak led the procession. She held her head high in a regal fashion. Her wavy hair flowed over her shoulders and back like a long veil of gold and red satin, with fresh leaves and berries woven into its fibers. Behind her walked men, young and old, with long beards and dirty white robes. Belts of rope encircled their loins. Two of the older men were carrying a bed made of sticks. On the structure lay a young naked girl, her limp yellow hair dangling through the twigs like bits of straw. She was tied with heavy rope. Her cries and pitiful sobs hung in the air as they passed us.

My companion took my hand and we crept from behind the tree. Quietly, cautiously, trying not to disturb a blade of grass, we followed the procession. They stopped in a clearing beside a huge oak tree. We crouched behind a bush. The men lowered the naked girl to the ground, untied her, and led her, bawling and struggling, to a large slab of gray rock.

The scene resonated inside me and I trembled with dread. The woman pushed back her purple cloak, raised her hands to the heavens, and chanted something I didn't understand. The sky became a kaleidoscope of swirling color; crimson, orange, sapphire and magenta whirled above my head in a frenzy of vivid hues. One of the men drew an axe from his robe and handed it to the woman. "No!" A hand shot to my mouth. The maiden shook her head as she pushed her hand tight over my mouth. "We can't let them do this," I mumbled between a mouthful of fingers.

The executioner turned and looked in our direction. My heart sprang to my throat. *She knows I'm here.* She grinned, then turned away and lifted the axe. A blood curdling scream echoed through the woods as the blade fell and severed the young girl's head. Bright red blood squirted into the air. The woman dropped the axe, turned her head, and gazed again in my direction. I held my breath. Her face dripping with warm blood, emerald eyes gaping with furry, she looked towards me and called, "Colceathrar."

"Emily. Wake up!" My eyes sprang open but part of me was still in the woods. I could feel her eyes on me, piercing into my soul like daggers, and feel my gut churning. I shook my head and grabbed Jonathan's arm as I tried to bring myself out of the hellish nightmare. "It was her," I mumbled.

He had stopped on the side of the road. "You dropped off and had a bad dream. All the stress and excitement is getting to you."

"Excitement? I was in the woodlot and I saw her. She was performing one of her sacrifices, on a young girl. It was barbaric. She called me cousin." I glared into his dark eyes. "She was warning me, telling me that she's still after me. Still out for revenge!"

"I'm sure it was just a bad dream." He put his long fingers over my cheeks and turned my face to meet his. "Look at me. We have to believe that she's gone, Emily, for good, forever." Then he planted a soft kiss on the tip of my nose, smiled, and started the engine.

I slumped back into the seat. "How can you be so sure?"

We stopped at a small bakery on a narrow cobblestone street in Salisbury and picked up two vegetable pasties and two butter cream cakes. I was sure that they contained no less than eight hundred calories apiece. The remnants of the dream had left me and I felt a sense of calm as I stepped inside Jonathan's colorful flat. He took my coat and motioned me to the knobby red sofa. "Sit, my lady."

"Thank you, sir." I snuggled into its soft, lumpy fibers.

"Can I get you a drink?"

"Wine, if you have it." He scurried into the tiny kitchen, carrying the brown bags containing our lunch. "Can I help you?"

"No thanks. I can handle this. As long as it doesn't have to be cooked, mixed, or prepared, I'm okay." Five minutes later he came out of the kitchen with a wide smile and a tin tray covered with a blue-striped tea towel. On the tray were two paper napkins, a clay plate containing our pastries, cream cakes, a bottle of red wine, and two glasses. "Bon appétit, my lady." His voice was low and raspy.

I flashed him a thankful smile, as my eyes raked over his tantalizing form. "It felt so real."

"What did?"

"My dream, even when I woke up I could feel it, as though I had really been there, physically I mean. Perhaps my soul had been there and witnessed that horrid scene eons ago." I took a deep breath. "It wasn't all bad. I was dancing with a group of girls that I felt a real kinship to. They were chanting 'anam cara'. Do you know what that means?"

"It's Gaelic for soul mate."

He placed the tin tray on the wooden chest in front of us and sat down beside me. "Let's not talk about that; not now, all right?" I gave him a quick nod and a half smile and watched him fill my glass to the brim. "You're not trying to get me drunk so you can take advantage of me, are you?"

"And what if I am, would you hold it against me?"

I brushed the pastry crumbs from his cleft chin with the tips of my fingers; the feel of skin on skin sent a pleasurable sensation up my arm.

Ooooh, how I'd love to hold it against me. We broke out in laughter. For the first time since my return, I felt relaxed. My mind was calm and my guard was down.

After we'd finished our pastries and I'd almost downed my second glass of wine, Jonathan took the glass out of my hand, placed it on the tray, and with an air of urgency he lead me to his bedroom. As soon as I started to move I felt a familiar pressure in my lower abdomen. *Oh shit, I have to pee, damn you, wine.* "I have to go to the bathroom. Sorry, I'll be right back." I hoped that this wouldn't spoil the moment but I'd be no use to him in there with my kidneys about to bust.

"Okay, but hurry or I'll need a fire extinguisher to put out the flames."

I giggled. "I won't be long, I promise."

I scurried to the shared bathroom at the end of the hall

and prayed that no one was in there. I was finally going to bed the man of my dreams, to run my hands over his sensuous body, and feel him inside me. I could feel the sexual energy building inside me as I closed the bathroom door.

As I stepped into the hallway, an unpleasant smell greeted me, and as I got closer to his room the smell became rancid and the air bitterly cold. I could hear the sound of someone groaning and panting. The door was open, but I was sure I'd shut it behind me. A chill raced along my spine. I moved timidly, though the sitting room, shivering, my fingers holding my nose. I reached the door of the bedroom and gasped! Dumbfounded, I watched as Jonathan's hips pumped up and down. His eyes were closed, his face rippled with pleasure, cries of arousal escaping from his moist lips. "Yes. Ooooh yes!" The bed squeaked. The sheet below his waist was levitating and moving as though something was underneath it. His hands seemed to be caressing an invisible form. He was panting like a horny dog, his head pushed back into the pillow, his naked chest wet with sweat. Rage and jealousy gripped like a vise at my rib cage. *Oh my God. It's her. She's on top of him!*

Chapter 6

I lunged towards my invisible adversary, my eyes wide, fury raging within me. "Get off him, you bitch!" A force, like a powerful gust of wind, hurled me back. I crashed into the wall in a heap. *You have the gift, Emily.*

I closed my eyes tightly and concentrated. "Wake up, Jonathan. Wake up now!" His eyes opened. He shrieked and shuffled back in the bed, brushing at his skin with his long fingers frantically, as if his body were crawling with red ants. The sheet collapsed. I pulled myself up from the floor. My right arm throbbed from the impact. Jonathan's mouth was agape; his face wore a look of shock and confusion. He lifted the sheet, and then lowered it. He gave me a sour grin; his eyes searched mine. "What just happened here?"

"It wasn't a wet dream, I can tell you that. She was here, on top of you." I swallowed the wad in my throat. "She was fucking you, Jonathan."

"Don't be ridiculous." He sat up, holding his hand to his head, dazed and unsteady. "My head's throbbing; I feel like I have an enormous hangover."

"What do you remember?"

"After you left I took my clothes off and got into bed." He hesitated. "But I left my underwear on. The room got really cold and the smell of…"

"Cat pee?"

He raked his fingers through his hair, took a whiff of his hand, and screwed up his nose. The blood drained from his face. "How?"

"I don't know how." I lifted his clothes from the foot of the bed and threw them at him. "You'll need a shower." My voice was edged with hostility.

"Hey, whatever happened here was not my fault." Then he grinned mischievously. "We have some unfinished business."

"Are you insane? After what I've just seen!"

He stood, his muscular naked body still damp with sweat, his private parts still partially erect and wet. He was a luscious picture of pure sensuality; surely even a nun would be aroused by such a perfect physique. But all that I could think of was her on top of him and the look of pleasure on his face. He grabbed his clothes and a towel and left the room.

I sat on the corner of the bed, my eyes still watery from the foul stench, my arm sore and bruised. The anger that burned inside my guts flared. She had got to him before me. She threw her disgusting body on his and raped him. I could almost hear her scornful laughter, mocking me. The satisfaction she must feel knowing she laid him before I did. I felt like it was me that had been violated, shamed, and degraded in the worst way. *"I'll get you, Merthia, and this time I won't fail."* A faint, lifeless voice whispered in the ether, "He's mine now, Colrea. Mine."

I covered my ears. "No!"

Jonathan strolled back into the bedroom; his hair was wet, his chest damp; a large white towel of soft terrycloth was wrapped around his waist. The towel bulged at his crotch and he smelt tantalizing. I looked away; all I could feel was disgust and betrayal. He dressed and sat down beside me on the bed, bringing with him the smell of fresh soap and sandalwood. I gazed into his dark eyes. "Now do you believe me? She raped you, Jonathan. That foul-smelling, hideous creature raped you."

He took my hand and held my gaze. "I don't know what just happened. All I know is how much I love you." His lips crept closer to mine. *Where have those lips been?* I turned my head. "Tell me what you remember."

"Not much, just getting into bed and the smell. Then I woke up and heard you screaming, felt something creepy on top of me and the sensation of…" He hesitated.

"Being fucked!"

He scratched his head and shrugged. "For a moment I thought it was you."

"Oh right! I'm creepy, smell rancid, and can make myself invisible. Tell me, did you enjoy it?"

"Calm down and don't be so absurd. If what you're saying is true, then I'm the victim here." He lowered his head

73

and put his hands over his face. *It wasn't his fault.* I dropped my arm over his shoulder. "I'm so sorry, Jonathan. I know it wasn't your fault. I'm just so angry, hurt, and scared. She's back, with a vengeance more powerful than before."

He sighed. "Then we'll have to get rid of her, and this time we'll do it right."

It was ten to five that afternoon when we arrived at the cottage. Auntie was in a flurry of preparation. She was wearing her best pleated skirt and white blouse, covered by a starched, blue apron. Her prickly curlers had been removed and tight gray curls sat on top of her head like a scouring pad. Her feet were still covered by her huge fuzzy slippers. They made her legs look like short, thick sticks, wrapped in brown pantyhose below her skirt.

The kitchen table was set with her best china and lace tablecloth. She whipped off her apron and glanced at her watch, when she heard the sound of crunching tires on the gravel driveway. "Right on time, like she always were." She scurried to the door, primping her hair along the way. "Well, I'll be bowled, ain't ya a sight for sore eyes."

"Emily Fletcher, you haven't changed a bit."

"Fiddlesticks. Come on in, take a load off." Auntie ushered her in, took her full length mink coat, carried it over her arms and lowered it ever-so-carefully on to the chair as if it were a fragile piece of glass.

Martha gazed around the room, with a suspicious look on her face. She was tall and thin, with a long nose and deeply set brown eyes and she reminded me of a Doberman pinscher.

She wore a tweed suit with a striking gold brooch on the lapel, a felt hat with mink trim, and her fingers were decorated with manicured nails and diamond-studded rings. Her dress and demeanor indicated a woman of some sophistication and she looked at least ten years younger than my aunt. Auntie looked much older than herself; her weathered, makeup-free face, gray hair, false teeth, and arthritis aged her considerably. "This must be your niece, the one you told me about on the phone." She had a slight Australian accent.

"That it is, named after me she is, Emily Anne Fletcher." I stood and held out my hand. "Pleased to meet you. I've heard so much about you." She smiled and shook my hand feebly and her lips twisted in a woeful smile.

"And this is 'er boyfriend and a good friend of mine, Jonny McArthur." Her voice rang with affection and pride.

"Nice to meet you Mrs...."

"Call me Martha."

Tea was a smorgasbord of English delicacies, traditional homemade pies, sweets, and preserves. Martha and Auntie chatted on and on, about school, their teachers, children from surrounding farms, and local gossip. Their obvious differences seemed inconsequential, as they reminisced. Jonathan and I sat in relative silence, giving them the odd nod, "that's nice" and laughing when they laughed. Auntie had asked me not to mention the incident in the woodlot but I was itching to ask her about it. Jonathan yawned. I waited for a lull, then I asked, "Martha, do you remember that time when you and Emy went to the woodlot and saw the ghost of a young girl?"

Auntie's eyes grew big as she moved her head back and forth, in a scolding manner. "Oh that was such a long time ago, she won't remember that now."

Martha straightened her back. "How could I ever forget such a thing?" She glanced over her right shoulder, suspiciously, as if someone might be listening to her and then relayed the whole story, exactly as Auntie had. She turned to me and said, "This area is cursed, you know. That wasn't the only thing that happened to us." She leaned over the table and whispered, "I could tell you some stories that would make your hair curl."

Auntie coughed, stood up, and pushed back the chair. "Well, maybe some other time. Right now we're going to sit by the fire and 'ave us a nice glass of wine. Made it m'self I did."

Bossy old mare. What was she so afraid of? I was up for the wine though. I never had understood why it wasn't proper to have wine with tea. Even though it was a light meal, like our midday lunch, it was still an evening meal.

Auntie took Martha's arm and led her into the sitting room. "You sit down in 'ere while I get the wine." She came back with two bottles of blackcurrant wine and four small glasses on a deep oval tray. Her hands were a little shaky but I knew better than to ask if she needed help. " Now, I want to 'ear all about yer life, down under. I've always fancied a visit there one day, I 'ave."

"Will you be staying over night?" I asked.

Martha's fingers twitched and her eyes grew, as if I'd

asked her to sleep in a den of vipers. "Oh no, dear, I promised my brother and his wife I'd be back by ten."

Auntie frowned. "Well, that's a blinking shame. Are ya sure ya want to be driving on that there motorway when it's dark? And we get a lot of fog this time of year. It's like pea soup sometimes."

"I'll be fine, Emy. I've been driving since I was seventeen and there's a lot less traffic on the road this time of night. Besides I'll come back. I'm not going back home until after Christmas. Hey, maybe we can go out for fish and chips and a movie, just like we did when we were kids. But this time it'll be my treat."

"We 'ad some fun when we were young'uns," Auntie said. "Do you remember that brazen hussy…"

We left them to their gossip and reminiscing, and went into the kitchen and started to clear the table. A few minutes later Martha came in and slipped me a piece of paper folded in half. In a low voice she said, "My brother's phone number and address. Come visit me; I have something to tell you." She glanced over her shoulder. "About this place and what goes on here." I nodded and shoved the piece of paper into my pocket.

Jonathan left shortly after Martha. I didn't' long for him to stay, as I usually did. The memory of Merthia's spirit having its way with him and the look on his face was still with me, along with the feeling of disgust. I felt like I had been betrayed and violated. But it was him that was raped, not me. I shook my head, trying to dislodge the vision and depressing thoughts. I had to find a way to banish this evil entity once and for all.

Auntie was sitting in her cushy chair, nibbling on a thin tea biscuit, her gaze fixed on the T.V screen. She was watching the ten o'clock news with her favorite television personality, meteorologist Trevor Spenser or "Trevor the weather" as she called him. He was a handsome middle-aged man, dressed in a sharp blue suit and tie, with a posh British accent, babbling on with his usual nonspecific forecast: "Cold, mostly dry, sunny spells, with the odd wet patch." Auntie was infatuated, by the weather man?

I filled my glass with the last of the wine and went to the parlor to change into my housecoat. My new fitted jeans were starting to itch and rub my thighs. When I returned, Auntie had a brush in her hand and her feet were dangling on either side of the foot stool. "Come 'ere, luv; ya hair looks like rats' tails." I'd grown accustomed to her brutal honesty and parked my buns on the stool between her ankles. She must have sensed that I needed the soothing touch of a motherly hand. She ran the brush down my fine, red hair and began her maternal, grooming procedure. "I liked your friend; she seemed like a very nice lady."

"She's changed. All hat and no knickers she is now, luv. It would do 'er good to get off 'er 'igh 'orse and remember where she came from. 'Er dad were a drunk and 'er poor mum suffered. Raised those kids on 'er own she did, took in other people's washing and ironing to make ends meet." She looked up. "God rest 'er soul."

"Well, she didn't't seem like a snob to me and she seems to have done very well for herself."

"She married a 'igh faluting business man. But I'm willing to give 'er a chance, being as though we were such good mates and all. Judge not and ya shall not be judged."

"That's generous of you, Auntie," I said, with a silent snicker.

She ran her hands through my hair as she brushed. Every stroke told me she that she understood how painful these past few months had been for me, and that she felt my sorrow, loved me, and accepted me just the way I was.

I remembered my mom brushing my hair when I was a child, in front of her dressing table mirror. I would sit on her silk-covered stool, admiring her cosmetics and jewelry. Every tug of the comb, every glance from her reflection seemed to utter disappointment; a recollection perhaps, of what she'd always imagined her daughter might look like. Not this ginger-headed, freckled-faced child that stared back at her, but a pretty, rosy cheeked, blonde-haired little girl—a clone of herself. Nevertheless, she borne me and I believed that her sense of love for me surpassed the disappointment of my image. If only she knew how transparent she was.

Auntie finished her grooming and patted me on the head. "That's better, luv."

After the brushing and my third glass of wine, I felt lightheaded, stress-free, and happy. I wasn't about to let this joyful feeling evaporate. I hadn't felt this good in a long time. "Auntie, do you have anymore wine?"

"That I do, luv; it's in the root cellar."

I knew where it was. Just off the kitchen, there was a hobbit-sized door, with rough grimy surfaces. I had seen Auntie go up and down there with her vegetables and preserves. It reminded me too much of the attic room door and I knew what lay behind that door. "You wouldn't mind going down there to get some, would you?"

"Not on yer nelly. I've been on m' legs all day and m' blinking feet are giving me jip."

"Ok, I'm sorry. I'll go." I felt a sense of confidence that came with the alcohol buzz. And, what could possibly be down there that I haven't seen before? I should have been immune to it all, so why was my gut starting to churn over?

I opened the drab little door and gazed down into the pitch black pit. A dank earthy smell invaded my nostrils. I fumbled for the light switch on the wall inside the door. A lone bulb hung from the low ceiling, its dull yellow light illuminating the rough plank stairs. Tentatively, one shaky foot after another, my hand gripping the narrow wooden rail, I ventured into the creepy, dark, dingy root cellar.

Chapter 7

It was a crude dugout. The atmosphere was stuffy, dismal, cold, and eerie. Rough planks had been set into the dirt walls. Along one of the walls a row of wooden shelves held jars of pickles, beets, jams, and jellies; beside it sat a crate containing potatoes, carrots, and onions, and on the other side of the room was a variety of bottled wine and brandy, with fancy white labels.

I felt something under the sole of my shoe and grabbed the side of the shelf to steady myself. I stooped down to take a look. It was a tiny mound of fresh dirt and all around it were small animal prints, like the paws of a cat. I dug into the dirt with my fingernails. It was Auntie's pendant. *Now how did that get here?* Something moved. I froze. My gaze moved around the room. Two beady yellow eyes peered at me from behind the vegetable crate; it took me a heart-racing moment to realize what it was. "Winston? What are you doing down here?" He must have followed me but surely I would have noticed him. "Come on, kitty, you can't stay down here." I went to grab him, but he hissed and scurried back. "Ok, I'll send Auntie down after you. She won't put up with your non-sense."

I picked up the dirty pendant and shoved two bottles of wine under my arm. Just as I was about to put my foot on the bottom step the light went out. "Oh, shit!" I scampered up the stairs, guided by the light from the half-opened kitchen door; before I reached the door, it closed suddenly—as if someone had shoved it. My breath caught in my throat. My fear exploded into panic. "Help! Auntie Em!" I shoved the pendant into my pocket and twisted the brass handle. It wouldn't budge. I pounded on the door. "Auntie Em! Auntie Em!" The blackness was closing in on me, choking me with its foreboding grip. I couldn't breathe. I stood, perfectly still, too afraid to turn around, my hand throbbing from beating on the rough wood. *Just breathe and relax, Emily. She'll come looking for you soon. Unless... No! That's unthinkable.* "Meow! Meow!"

"What is it, Winston? What's wrong?" The cat growled and then let out a harrowing shrill. Something touched my arm. I dropped the bottles, grabbed the pendant out of my pocket, put it up to my lips and prayed.

The door creaked open. "Flippin' heck our Emily. What's all the hullabaloo about? All ya had to do was turn the handle and push."

I dashed though the door, my heart still in my mouth, my senses drenched in fear. "I tried to open it. Didn't you hear me knocking? Someone or something locked me in."

"For heaven sake, girl, what ya' talking about? There's no lock on that door. It must 'ave got stuck, somehow, and no, I never 'eard you knocking. I came looking for ya. Thought ya'd got lost down there." She ran her gaze up and down my trembling form. "Looks like ya seen a ghost." She dug up her sleeve and pulled out her hanky. "And where's that wine you went down there for?"

I took a deep breath and tried to regain my composure. "I dropped it. The light went out and something touched me."

She nudged me aside. "Well, it's on now."

I turned my head to take a look. The light was on but I wasn't surprised. The cottage was playing tricks on me again or was it 'her'? "Well it went off while I was down there and scared me half to death. By the way, Winston's down there." I handed her the silver pendant. "I think he was trying to bury this."

"Well, I'll be blowed. M' mum's star. I've been looking all over for that."

"The last time 'we' saw it Merthia was tossing it into the woods. But how did it get back here and why was Winston trying to bury it?"

She lowered her head and started rubbing the pendant with her hanky. "Ya still want that there wine?" she asked, changing the subject.

"Yes, but I'm not going back down there."

"Don't be barmy. What do ya thinks down there? The devil himself?" *No, the devil 'herself.'* "I'll go," she said.

"Put the pendant on first." She shook her head and rolled

her eyes as she hung the silver chain around her neck. I moved aside and pulled the door as wide as I could. With both hands I held tight to the door knob, to make sure it stayed open. I called through the doorway, "Watch for broken glass."

"Bring me a plastic bag, a cloth, and a bucket of water," she hollered.

Oh no, I'd have to let go of the door. I looked around for something to secure the hinge. A wooden box sat in the corner by the back entrance, full of Auntie's gardening tools. It looked strong enough to hold the door open but it was too far for me to reach.

"Emily Anne, what's keeping ya?"

"I'll be right there." I let go of the door and dashed towards the box, dragging it frantically across the floor, and shoved it against the door before it was able to close. Then I made another frantic dash to the kitchen cupboard where her bucket and rags were kept. All the time thinking to myself, *What if it locks her in? How will I get her out?* I remembered what Merthia said to her in the woodlot: "I should have killed you years ago but I needed you then. Now I have no use for you."

The door was still open. Thank God. "Here you go, Auntie." I met her halfway up the stairs.

"About blinking time." I handed her the bucket and scurried back. I could hear her calling for the cat, "'Ere, kitty, kitty." A few minutes later she appeared, lugging the bucket and two bottles of wine. "He ain't down there."

"Who?"

"Winston. Didn't you say he were down there?"

My mind was in disarray. "Yes, he was down there. I saw him. And I haven't seen him come back up."

"There must be something funny goin' on around 'ere then."

No. You don't say. "Not funny, Auntie Em. Sinister!"

She gave me one of her half grins and reprimanding glances, which said, "I don't want to hear about it."

"Well, I'm off to bed. Been a long day, it 'as."

"You're not kidding," I mumbled.

"What's that, luv?"

"Oh nothing. Good night, Auntie."

It had been a long day—an eventful, stressful, unnerving day. I wasn't sure how much more of this I could take. I popped the wine cork and poured myself a glass. The buzz that I'd had from the wine I'd drunk earlier had evaporated, shortly after I entered the root cellar. Fear has a way of sobering you up. I had to get the events of the day out of my head, so I could rest and get some sleep. Getting drunk was the only way I could think of to put my mind at rest. I would talk to Jonathan, I concluded, and tell him that we have to get to the bottom of this; we have to get rid of this evil Druid priestess, once and for all. I wasn't going to allow him to sweep it under the rug anymore, and I wouldn't take no for an answer. But there were so many unanswered questions, so many pieces that didn't fit the puzzle. Somehow I had to complete that puzzle and find a way to banish her, if I was to get any rest here at Merryweather Lodge. Skye would be here next week and I could hardly wait. She would know exactly what to do in this place of horrors.

I reached for my duffel bag, opened the zipper, and fumbled inside for my journal, but I pulled out my mom's instead. I was surprised when my dad handed it to me. I had no idea my mom kept a journal. As far as I knew she hated writing and only read gossip and beauty magazines. The cover was rose pink with embossed gold edging. I felt a twinge of guilt as though I were peeking into someone's most private and intimate thoughts. Would she want me to read it? I had no way of knowing. I had to concentrate. The print was a little blurry and the words seemed to run together in a train of squirmy lines. Was it the booze or my mother's writing?

On the first page in fancy handwriting: *To my big little sister, with love.* It must have been a gift from my Auntie Pam, Mom's older sister. She always called my mom her "big little sister," and my mom called her, "her little big sister." Mom was two years younger than Auntie Pam but a good five inches taller. Their mom, my grandmother, had been five feet and their dad six foot three. I remember them laughing about their height difference and how they wished they could have met somewhere in the middle.

The more I read the more legible it became. She wrote about the weather, the neighbors, the "would-be divas" at the salon. There were a lot of entries about her feelings and dreams; how she felt trapped in a life that was going nowhere, how she hated spending her days trying to make homely women beautiful, how she felt inadequate and self conscious about her height, her bouts of depression, and her lifelong dream of becoming a model. In the middle of the journal she wrote something that tore at my emotions. She wrote about how beautiful I was, how the deep, maternal love she had felt for me was too profound for words, and how very much she had wanted to give me a brother or sister but after my difficult birth she was never able to conceive again. I had always assumed that she didn't want to have anymore children, that she was afraid of pregnancy spoiling her perfect figure. My mom was a lonely and unhappy woman. But she loved me and had a depth that I never saw.

I grabbed my glass and gulped my comforting elixir, and then I poured another one. Hugging the journal to my breast, I laid my head back and sobbed. "Oh, Mom, I'm so sorry. Sorry for the way I treated you, sorry for the way I always put you down. I miss you so much. Why couldn't you have told me how you felt? I would have listened. If only I had one more chance to talk to you, to tell you how much I loved you. But you're gone forever. I'll never see you again." I turned over and wept into the pillow, my face drenched in the tears of grief and regret, the loss burning a hole in my heart. Sleep came quickly.

I was in a dark, dank pit that stank of manure. A single candle burnt on a ledge in the corner. A swarm of flying imps with pointed wings, tiny red horns, and grotesque faces circled my head. They were giggling and pulling at my hair. One of them nipped at my cheek with its sharp teeth; then another and another. I swatted at them frantically and tried to move my feet, but they wouldn't budge. I was paralyzed from the waist down, unable to free myself from this hellish dungeon. They started to peck at my ears and my eyes, piercing my skin with their razor-like teeth; blood trickled down my face; every jab sent a shock wave of excruciating pain though my body. I opened my mouth to scream but nothing came out. Something grabbed my ankle. I looked down. Pushing their way through the dirt floor were hands; pale hands, hands with long rough fingernails, hundreds of them, grabbing and clawing at my feet. One of them gripped my ankle and started to pull me in. I squeezed my eyes shut. Slowly I sank through the black sludge into a thick dark, lair.

The atmosphere changed. Carefully I pried my eyes open. I was standing barefoot in the dreaded woodlot, by the ancient oak tree, but I felt no fear. A warm breeze carried with it the fragrant sent of blossom, wild flowers, and fresh pine. I felt carefree and giddy, like a schoolgirl on her first day of summer vacation. I looked down at my form. My hands and feet were child size. I was wearing a plain cream colored dress, with a thin sash of rope around my waist. The image of a woman appeared from behind the oak tree; a radiant aura of white emanated from her delicate frame. Raven-black hair, crowned with a halo of daisies, tumbled in graceful curves down her back. She was dressed in a pure white, silk gown, with a band of silver thread resting on her hips. She smiled and opened her arms. "Come to me, Colrea."

I felt a sudden sense of recognition. It was my friend Helgara, one of the goddesses of light. I ran to her and buried my face into her silky, soft gown and sniffed its sweet perfume. "I missed you."

She pulled away, took my small hands, bent down and looked into my eyes. "You have to go back, Colrea. The battle is not yet over. Call on your spirit friends to help. The secret lies beneath the…"

Something moved. She looked up. A gust of icy air caught my back. I turned, ever so slowly. Two female figures stood before me, their heads slightly bowed. One was an older woman in a drab brown dress; it hung like a burlap sack from her bedraggled frame. Next to her, holding her hand, stood a little girl clothed in green rags. Methodically, in unison, like animated dolls they lifted their heads. Through their strands of dirty, limp hair I saw the face of Maud McArthur. The little girl looked a lot like Belinda. With their distorted mouths gaping, their devilish, unblinking eyes fixed on me, they moved forward. I spun around to seek protection from my beautiful friend but she was gone.

The atmosphere in the woods had changed. It was damp, cold, and stank of trepidation. Closer and closer they came. I moved back, then turned and ran, into the shadows of the giant trees. They kept coming. I picked up the pace. I could hear their morbid moans and the ground vibrating under their swift, clumsy feet. They moved with rapid speed, like hungry vampires after their first taste of blood. My heart thumped like a drum inside my ribcage; sharp stones and twigs cut into my bare feet. I could smell their rank breath on the back of my neck, then something grabbed my hair and jerked my head back. "No! No!" I screamed.

I jerked bolt upright in my bed. My head was spinning. Food and wine began to rise in my belly. I hurled myself out of bed and dashed to the bathroom. Crouching in front of the toilet, my hands on each side of the cold, porcelain bowl, I heaved and spewed the foul contents of my guts. My head throbbed and spun, my body ached, my mind was disoriented, still stunned by the vividness of my nightmare. I leaned my back against the wall and drew my knees to my chest. My dreams were becoming more lucid. I could remember every detail, every emotion, every smell, as if I had just lived it.

There was a tap, tap on the door. "Can I come in, luv?"

I didn't want Auntie to see me like this but I knew that there was no point in trying to send her away. "Yes, come in," I muttered.

"I could 'ear ya being sick from m' bed. What's ailing ya? Was it something you ate?"

"The wine."

She sighed. "'Ave told ya' before, ya' can 'ave too much of a good thing and it ain't proper for a young girl of yer' age, getting drunk, it ain't." I buried my face into my knees as another bout of nausea stirred in my stomach. Auntie went to the sink and ran a facecloth under the cold water tap. "There, there luv, you'll be as right as rain in a few minutes. I'll make ya' a strong cup of tea. That'll cure ya," she said as she knelt down beside me, pushed the sweaty strands of red hair away from my face, and dabbed my cheeks and forehead with the cool compress. This was a bad hangover and I knew from experience that it would take more than a wet cloth, a cup of tea, and a few minutes to cure it. Later that day I wrote this metaphor in my journal.

> *December 3rd*
>
> *Dear friend. I have done it again; I have consumed the blood of the serpent. Its pleasant aroma and exquisite taste enticed me and flooded my mind with giddy thoughts and bold confidence. "Indulge," it whispered softly. I drank its sweet, ruby red, sensual elixir and allowed it to have its way with me. But now I see it for what it is; cold, venomous, deceitful, destructive, false and fleeting. I want to expel its poison from my form but it runs though my veins like a raging disease. My mind cannot function; its mental capacity is inhibited, fuzzy and vague. My form is sluggish and achy. My soul weeps with regret. For a few hours of pleasure, I suffer. The snake has revealed itself and I will never partake of its blood again.*

My inside voice whispered, *How many times have you made that morning after promise to yourself, Emily Fletcher?*

It was the day of Skye's arrival. I couldn't wait to see her, to hug her, to tell her about my experiences and share my innermost thoughts and feelings with her, as I was used to doing over the years of our friendship. Jonathan and I had talked, and he had confessed that he had been trying to suppress what he feared in his soul to be real, but I could tell that part of him did not want to believe that his sister was involved. He had agreed that something needed to be done and that we would wait for Skye before trying to expel Merthia. We thought Skye might have some ideas on how to get rid of this evil entity and her metaphysical expertise would be an asset.

The cottage had been quiet for the past week, no paranormal activity, dreadful nightmares, or sinister encounters. It seemed to have regained its peaceful, warm, homey character. Perhaps it was all over finally, and all would be well at Merryweather Lodge from now on? Perhaps.

Chapter 8

We had been waiting at the airport for two hours; the plane had been delayed because of fog. I trudged back and forth from the message board to my spot by the gate, until I saw the word 'landed' appear on the screen. "Jenks!" I shouted, as soon as I spotted her coming through the metal doors.

"Fletch!" She waved enthusiastically. Her suitcase was painted with huge brightly colored flowers. The backpack draped over her left shoulder was mauve with pink stripes; she wore a long denim skirt and an orange t-shirt complemented by heavy silver chains. A barrette, in the shape of a white flower, was holding one side of her dark hair away from her face. Everything clashed. She looked like a hippie from the sixties, but her face and tiny, perfect form were to die for. I envied her beauty, her self confidence, and her 'I couldn't care less what people think about me' attitude.

We flung our arms around each other and squeezed. I felt my eyes welling up. Skye was like a sister to me. We had been best friends since we were nine years old. Jonathan stepped forward to take her suitcase. I grabbed his arm. "Jenks, I'd like you to meet the gorgeous Jonathan McArthur." He paused, momentarily abashed, cleared his throat, and then stuck out his hand. Skye ignored his hand, reached up, pulled him down to her level, and gave him a warm hug. "Your prince charming," she declared, with a half smile.

"It's so nice to finally get to meet you," he said, looking a little bashful and shocked by her exuberance and assertiveness. "I've heard so much about you."

"All good, I hope." She linked her arm through mine. "I've been looking forward to this forever. What's happening at the cottage? Has the Druid priestess come back, any paranormal activity, sightings, ghosts, vampires?" she asked all in one breath.

"No vampires."

She sniffed. "That's a shame."

I laughed, drew her closer, and whispered, "But there has been lots of activity. Wait until I tell you what happened to Jonathan."

"Tell me. Tell me."

"Not now, later."

On the way back to the cottage I sat in the back seat with Skye, so we could talk. We giggled and chatted like a couple of school girls, sharing our naughty secrets. It felt so good, so comforting, to have my best friend with me. She was the only one who really understood me, the only one I could trust with my innermost thoughts and feelings. I had often wondered, since I first found out about my reincarnation, if Skye and I had been friends, sisters, or even lovers in another life. We had a connection, not unlike the one I had with Jonathan, but on a more intuitive level—a magical feminine link bound by a deep sense of understanding and sensitivity.

Skye's eyes lit up, and her smile grew, as her face filled with awe. "Aha, so this is Merryweather Lodge. It's just how you described it." She climbed out of the car and gazed at the cottage dressed in its late autumn attire. Her gaze fell on the attic window; she grimaced and looked away.

Auntie stepped out of the door, rubbing her hands down her clean apron and grinning like a Cheshire cat. Skye ran up to her and threw her arms around Auntie's chubby waist. "I've really looked forward to seeing you again and getting to know you." Auntie looked over Skye's shoulder, smiled, and gave me a wink of approval. She stepped away from Skye's embrace and scanned her with her discerning old eyes. "Well, ain't you a lovely little thing but a sight for sore eyes, I must say."

Skye's brows arched with surprise when she spotted the chain around Auntie's neck. She touched it carefully. "So this is the pentagram." Auntie pulled away, and then she took hold of Skye's hand and led her into the cottage. "Its m' mum's star," she mumbled. I had warned Skye about my aunt's lingo and told her that I would translate—if I could!

Jonathan lifted her luggage from the trunk of the car, carried it inside, and sat it down in the narrow hallway, just inside the front door. "I'm going to leave you ladies to it. I have to work tomorrow."

"But don't you want to stay for dinner? Auntie will be expecting you to stay."

He smiled and kissed my pale cheek. "You need some time to get re-acquainted with your friend. I'd only be in the way. Besides, I have so much paper work to catch up on for work. I'll stop by tomorrow evening. Have a nice visit," he called from the front door.

Skye was the only one that answered. "'Bye for now. Thanks for picking me up." Auntie mustn't have heard him; otherwise she would have protested and insisted he stay.

Skye and Auntie hit it off immediately. They had met once before but only briefly: when Auntie Em and Uncle Reg came to Canada for my eighteenth birthday. I had pre-warned Skye not to mention any of my past encounters or talk about ghosts, possessions, or anything related to the paranormal.

We sat around the scrubbed kitchen table, Auntie with her steak and kidney pie, me with my veggie burger, and Skye with her bean and rice casserole. I had lied to Auntie and told her that Skye had food allergies but really she was a strict vegan. I thought it was easier than explaining why Skye wouldn't eat anything derived from animals. Auntie would not have approved.

"Leave the dishes, Mrs. Fletcher, Emily and I will wash them. We have so much to catch up on." Skye gave me a wink and a nod.

"Oh don't call me that, luv, makes me feel old. You can

call me Auntie, just like my niece does. I'll leave you girls to it then might catch forty winks in m' chair." She had got up very early to finish and prepare the attic room for Skye. I had no idea what it looked like. I couldn't bring myself to go back up there. We had hired one of the neighbors who did part-time home renovations to finish stripping the paper and painting the walls. I told Auntie that I'd never speak to her again if she insisted on doing it herself and I even offered to pay the man we hired but she wouldn't take my money.

We started to stack the dishes and clear away the food. "So, what do you think of him?" I asked Skye anxiously.

"Who?"

"Jonathan of course."

"He's okay."

"Okay? He's gorgeous!"

"If you like that sort of thing."

"And you don't? When I showed you his photo back home you said he was really hot."

She yawned. "I'm sorry, Fletch, I'm just tired. I couldn't sleep on the plane and now it's catching up with me."

"I know what that feels like; I can never sleep on that night flight either. Maybe you should have an early night and we can have a long talk in the morning. I can finish these."

She squeezed the dish rag and pulled the plug out of the soapy sink. Leaning towards me, she said, "No way. I want to hear all about what's been going on here, now." She was all of a sudden emotionally charged.

And I was anxious to fill her in. I lifted a couple of

Auntie's generous wine glasses off the top shelf and filled them with her home-made brew. Then I placed a half-eaten box of chocolates in front of her. "Milk Tray. They're to die for."

"No animal products, remember?"

"In these?"

She lifted the box and read the list of ingredients on the side. "They contain dairy products." She put the box on the table and met my gaze. "Did you know that Aztec women were forbidden to drink chocolate because Montezuma feared it would unleash feminine magical powers?"

I grabbed the box and opened the lid. "In that case I'll eat the lot." We laughed.

"This looks yummy." She lifted the heavy glass of wine and arched her brows. "Wow, where did she get these glasses from?"

"A boot sale, I think she said. You should see her 'proper' wine glasses; they're like tiny glass thimbles."

She grinned. "What's a boot sale?"

"It's the same as a garage sale."

"Your aunt's adorable."

"I think the feeling is mutual. She doesn't seem to mind Jonathan or his friends calling her Mrs. Fletcher."

"You don't mind me calling her Auntie, do you?"

"Of course not, we are like family."

I told Skye everything that had happened since my return. I tried to remember every little detail, every emotion, and even the smells. I wanted to give her as much information as I could, in hopes that she would come up with a solution, a suggestion as to how we could get rid of this powerful entity and all the hellish activity in the cottage. She listened intently, a furrow of deep thought across her forehead, sipping her wine and nodding. Every once in a while she'd raise a brow or gnaw on her lip. When I got through it all, I leaned back into the chair, sighed, and folded my arms. "So what do you make of all this? Are you going to be able to help us get rid of her?"

She scratched the side of her head with her neatly trimmed fingernails, while rearranging herself on the seat. "Oh my God, Fletch, this is not good. Merthia's back for sure and from the sound of it, more manipulative and vengeful than before." I swallowed hard.

"If this Mrs. Tilly is really Hagmanis, then she will protect and assist Merthia no matter what it takes. I don't think your eyes are playing tricks on you or that you're schizophrenic. You have a profound connection to the spiritual realm." She leaned over the table, moved the chocolates aside, and took hold of my hand. Her fingers were warm and silky soft. "It's a gift, Emily."

"That's what I've been told but I'm not sure I want it. It feels more like a curse than a gift." She smiled, sympathetically. "You're caught between two worlds and until you can deal with this karma from your ancient incarnation you won't get any rest. You might be able to use this gift. Hopefully I can help you and show you how. As for Belinda, if she is mentally ill then she's more vulnerable than ever. Merthia is probably using her as a host again. That is, if she needs a host. That's something we have to find out. Those little lights you saw in the pasture were probably will o' the wisps."

"Will o' the what?"

"Will o' the wisps. Some people call them corpse candles. They're mischievous little spirits that watch over the dead. They can be vicious. There must be bodies buried in Beacon Hill and if the mound is as big as you say, there could be hundreds."

I shivered and took a mouthful of wine. "What about the rape? Tell me she didn't need a host to do that, because if she did…" I took a deep, gasping breath.

"We don't know. If she is gaining strength she might not need a host."

"Except to kill for her."

"Right. I've brought some of my books and my laptop. I'm going to do some research and hopefully come up with some sort of exorcism or spell to banish her."

"Shhh…what's that?" I could hear footsteps shuffling across the wooden floor boards, getting closer and closer. I held my breath as the door slowly opened. Then I exhaled with a long sigh of relief. "Auntie, I thought you'd gone to bed."

Skye's lips were clenched, to smother a giggle. Auntie was wearing a huge fleecy housecoat of red tartan that was at least three sizes too big for her and it looked like a lumberjack's bedspread. It was long and met with a pair of green woolen slippers. There were prickly curlers stuck all over her head like porcupine quills. Her lips had caved in and the bulge in her pocket revealed where her false teeth were. A hot water bottle was tucked under her arm. "I couldn't go to bed without saying good night to my favorite girls, now could I. Ya've bin 'avin a good old chin wag by the sounds of it." Her words were slurred and it was all I could do to restrain myself from bursting out in laughter. Skye's lips were tight. Auntie kissed us both on the head and gave us a toothless, lopsided smile. "Night, night, luvs." She turned before closing the door. "Don't you go leading your friend up the garden path; our Emily and ya best sleep up there with 'er tonight, just so as she don't get lonely, that is." *Now what did she mean by that?*

"Good night, Auntie Em."

"Good night, Auntie," Skye said. As soon as the door closed she burst out laughing. "How does she sleep with those spikes on her head, and you never told me that she had false teeth."

"Are you making fun of my aunt, Skye Jenkins?"

"You know I'm not; she's really sweet."

"She is and she has a heart of gold but you don't ever want to get on the wrong side of her. She can be your worst enemy. I know she's hiding something from me, and I wish I knew what it was."

Skye's eyelids were closing, her head was drooping.

"Jenks'!" She jumped. "Go to bed. You must be exhausted."

She rubbed her eyes, stretched out her legs, and yawned.

"You're right—I am."

"Do you need help with your suitcase? Those stairs are steep." I had asked her before she came if she minded sleeping in the attic room. She said it would be a thrill to sleep in a haunted bedroom but I wasn't sure if she really meant it or if she was just being accommodating and brave. I knew that she was fascinated by the paranormal and didn't fear it, but sleeping in a haunted attic, by yourself, seemed ludicrous.

"Aren't you coming with me?" she asked.

"I thought you said you didn't mind sleeping up there by yourself."

"I don't, but wouldn't it be fun? It would be just like when we were kids sleeping in that old shed on your acreage, the one we called spookula castle."

"Not really, Skye. This is not make-believe; it's very real and dangerous."

"Are you scared; are you chicken?"

"You betcha. I'm terrified of that room."

"Oh come on, Fletch. I won't let anything happen to you, I promise. If we hear any weird noises, smell anything funny, or even sense any activity at all, we can come back down here. It'll be a hoot." She put her hands together. "Please."

Perhaps she really was scared to be by herself, and she had come all of this way to spend time with me and to help me. "Are you sure you wouldn't rather sleep down here in the parlor?"

"Yep, I'm sure."

"Okay. But I'm out of there at the first sign of anything spooky and don't you try and stop me."

"I won't, honest."

I gathered my night clothes, housecoat, and little bag of sea salt, all the time asking myself, *Are you out of your mind Emily Fletcher?* and disregarding the subtle objections of my inner voice.

It was pouring rain outside. I could hear it gushing down the drainpipes and lashing against the window panes, propelled by heavy gusts of wind. I prayed that the lights would not go out.

As I helped Skye lug her suitcase up the old attic stairs I thought about the first time I went up here, as an unsuspecting fourteen-year-old about to meet her unearthly adversary, a hideous creature bound for revenge. A soft voice whispered from behind the door, "Come, Emily, come."

Chapter 9

"Did you hear that, Skye?"

"What?"

"Oh, nothing."

Auntie had certainly done a good job of decorating. The walls were a soft lilac with cream trim. The frilly lace bed linen had been replaced with a plain chenille bedspread of dark mauve, with a pillow sham to match. Simple white sheers hung from the strange little window. The Eliss family portrait was accompanied by a pair of charcoal drawings of sheep in a meadow. The kidney-shaped dresser had a new coat of paint and was accompanied by a ladder back chair instead of the cushioned stool. A couple of shelves had been installed on the wall next to the dresser. The child size rocker that had cradled Annabella was gone; her china body was slouched to one side, on top of a storage ottoman covered in brown velvet. The room smelled of paint and freshly ironed linen. Auntie had attempted, I assumed, to make it look more grown up and contemporary but it would take a lot more than that to hide what lay beneath the room's new facade. The atmosphere was still tainted with trepidation.

Skye heaved her suitcase onto the bed and undid the zipper. Then she glanced over her shoulder, suspiciously, as if someone was watching her.

"What is it? Did you feel something? A presence?" I asked eagerly.

"No, I'm just looking for somewhere to hang my clothes."

"Oh, there isn't anywhere. Just put what you can in the dresser drawers and I'll hang your good clothes in Auntie's wardrobe. That's where I hang mine. It's massive and she only has a few dresses in there. Are you sure you can't feel anything?"

"I'll see." She sat on the bed, closed her eyes, joined her thumb with her middle finger, and took a few deep breaths. Then her eyes sprang open, and her head turned to one side, as if someone had struck her hard across the face. She looked stunned.

I rushed to her side. "Are you okay? What was that?"

She turned to me and smiled awkwardly "I don't know. It felt like someone slapped me."

I stood up. "That's it! I'm out of here and you're coming with me."

She grabbed my hand. "No, Emily. We can't go; we must stay. You want to get to the bottom of this, don't you? You want me to find out as much as I can so I know what we're up against?" I nodded. "Come on—let's get ready for bed. I'm totaled."

I grabbed my pajamas and turned my back to Skye for privacy as I disrobed. I could see her out of the corner of my eye, standing by the bed, peeling off her clothes, until she was completely naked, with not a shred of modesty or reserve. Skye had a thing about being nude; she often went skinny-dipping in the lake near her home and when her mother wasn't home she'd walk around their house stark naked. She was so comfortable in her own skin; she said it made her feel liberated and alive. I was exactly the opposite, shy and un-comfortable with nudity, as though it were something un-clean, something to be hidden, revealed only in the privacy of one's mind or behind closed doors.

She walked toward the dresser, still naked, carrying a bundle of neatly folded clothes. "It's a good thing Auntie left the central heating on tonight; you'd freeze your butt off up here normally." My flannel pajamas felt soft and warm against my skin.

"You don't mind, do you?" asked Skye. "I've been sitting in those clothes for hours and I've been dying to get them off and let the air at my skin."

Of course I mind. It's disgusting walking around like that. "Whatever." But I couldn't help looking and feeling a twinge of envy. She was such an enlightened soul. Her energy drew you in and radiated confidence, compassion, and love. Her face was that of an angel, her tanned body sensual and perfectly shaped in all the right places. Skye's father was of African descent and had died when she was a baby; her mother had a pale complexion and blond hair, and the combination of the two parents' skin tones created Skye's flawless, year-round tan. She was the envy of every pasty-skinned, freckled-faced girl in our school, including me.

I tuned my head and tried not to look as she walked back to the bed, exposing the full frontal view of her naked body. She was beautiful. Oh God, she was beautiful. She slipped an oversized t-shirt over her head and removed a square cardboard box from her suit case.

I recognized the graphics and name on the box. "You are kidding. We're not doing that, are we? Not here, not now!"

"No, I'm too tired tonight. We'll do it another day. I need to evoke your spirit friend Mary Eliss. She might be able to help us. This was her bedroom, right?"

I nodded my head. "But an Ouija board? I thought you'd have a more professional way of getting information. This seems so...well, amateurish."

"The talking board is still one of the best and easiest ways to contact the dead. I've been waiting to do this ever since you told me what had happened to you..." She gazed around the room. "In this fascinating bedroom."

Fascinating? "Creepy, is what I'd call it. Put that box away. I don't want to look at it."

She closed her suitcase, lifted it off the bed, and climbed under the covers. "Switch the light off, Fletch."

I lifted the sheet and snuck in beside her: we were squished together like sardines in a can. "I want it left on."

"Suit yourself. Emily, I have something to tell you but I don't want you to be afraid."

"What?"

"I do feel something?" I held my breath. "But we're in no danger," she said quickly, in a reassuring tone. "There's more than one presence here, I'm sure of it. It feels like..." She took a deep breath, in and out. "A paradoxical essence of heaven and hell is the only way I can describe it."

"That's exactly it; sometimes this place feels like heaven and other times like hell. Didn't I tell you that?"

"Yes, but I had to feel it for myself to really understand what you meant." She turned her head towards me and grinned. "Isn't this neat and cozy? You and me, spending the night in a haunted bedroom, in an eerie old cottage, deep within the English countryside?"

"Yeah great." I froze, as my ears caught the sound of scratching. "Did you hear that?"

"Sounds like scratching." She sat up. "Something's scratching at the door." She pulled back the covers and lowered her feet onto the floor.

I could feel my guts stating to contract. "Where are you going?"

"To see what it is." I gripped the end of the sheet and dragged it slowly up to my face and over my eyes, shutting out anything unpleasant that might appear, just as I had done as a little child. My gut tightened. Then I suddenly remembered... *The sea salt! I forgot to scatter the sea salt.* The heavy wooden door opened with its familiar eerie creak.

"Well, hi there. Who are you?"

I breathed a sigh of relief at the sound of Skye's friendly tone. "Who is it?"

"A cat."

I drew the sheet away from my eyes. "Winston." The odd looking feline wove his way through Skye's legs, brushing his whiskers on her bare skin. She giggled and bent down to pick him up but he slipped from her hands and strutted over to the bed. He leaped from the floor to the bed and sat in a pompous fashion, head held high, yellow beady eyes gazing around the room, as if he were surveying his kingdom. Skye jumped on the bed next to him and ran her hand down his soft coat. "Is this the one you told me about? The one that tried to bury the pentagram?"

"That's him. Strange looking thing, isn't he? There's something about him, something that makes me leery."

"He's part Himalayan and there's definitely something about him." Winston purred, a deep resounding contented purr, as she ran her fingers under his chin. "I'm picking up some sort of vibe from him and I'm not sure what it is."

"Is it good or bad?"

"Good I think, but I'm not sure." She climbed back under the covers. The cat strolled to the foot of the bed and curled up in a ball.

"I keep wondering why he was trying to bury Auntie's pendant in the cellar."

"Why do you keep calling it a pendant? It's a pentagram."

"The word pentagram gives me the creeps. I guess I've always associated it with witch craft and Satanism. Merthia called it the symbol of the goddesses of light. She said her father made her wear it to protect her from her mother's influence. She threw it into the woods but somehow it's returned."

"The pentagram has had so many meanings," Skye said.

"The ancient Celts ascribed it to the goddess Morrieval, as her symbol of truth and protection. To the Druids it was the symbol of the Godhead or Goddess. Before the inquisition, Christians used the pentagram to show the five wounds of Christ. After that it became the head of the goat or devil. In white witchcraft it represents the elements, the head being spirit, the hands air and water, and the feet fire and earth. It is the ultimate symbol of the Devine, of power and protection."

"Wow, I didn't know that. So I really shouldn't fear it?" Skye nodded her head. I glared at Winston. "But then why was he trying to bury it?"

"It could have just been instinct. Cats bury things, right?"

I took his odd furry little head in my hand and turned it to face me. Scowling at him, I said, "Or he could have been hiding it from us, so we'd have no protection, so we were vulnerable." He gave me a soft throaty meow. Was that an acknowledgment or a denial?

The rain had stopped, giving way to an unnerving silence. I took my little bag of sea salt and scattered it about the room, rubbing a little on my pajamas, just incase. "Sea salt?" Skye mumbled.

"Yep," I mumbled back. Then I slid in the bed, trying not to get too close to her without falling off the edge. She was already asleep; I could tell by the short snorting sounds coming out of her nose. I had forgotten that Skye snored. How was I going to get any sleep with that noise, no room to move, a sinister cat at the foot of the bed, and spooky thoughts flying around like ghosts, inside my head? Ever so carefully I turned my body to my right side; it was my most comfortable position. Skye turned and drew her delicate form close to my back, and then she slid her arm around my waist and nestled tight against my spine. So tight. Too tight. I could feel her firm breasts on my back and her moist private parts pressed against the cheeks of my bottom. Part of me wanted to leap out of bed and brush myself off, but another other part wanted to… *No that wasn't me. I wasn't like that.* I could hear the shrill sound of my mother's disapproval as I closed my eyes, wrapped in the warm arms and sensual body of my very best friend.

I woke up to a strange sound and darkness, total darkness. I listened intently, my gaze scouring the inky void, my heart picking up pace. It was a ghostly child's voice, a repetitive menacing echo from far away. The voice came closer, its ominous words penetrating the darkness, ringing in my ears, pounding in my head; "Emily, Emily two by four. I saw you at the cellar door. I pushed you on the dirty floor and cut you with a chainsaw." I recognized the voice. "Skye, wake up! Wake up!"

She lifted her head. The singing stopped. "What is it? What's wrong?"

"The lights have gone out, and I heard someone singing,

and it was Belinda's voice," I babbled all in one breath. I was trembling.

She put her arm around me and drew me close. "Calm down, Fletch. It's okay. There's nothing here. It was probably a bad dream."

I moved away from her embrace. "Don't you go patronizing me too. I heard what I heard and it was no dream!"

"Sorry." She coved her mouth and yawned. "Can we talk about it in the morning?"

"But what about the light?"

She sighed. "Well, we can either fumble around in the dark and try to find some candles or we can go back to sleep and wait for the light to come back on or wake up when it's daylight. Just go back to sleep, Fletch."

"I'm cursed, Skye."

"No you're not. You just have one shitload of karma to sort out."

I turned to my right side and closed my eyes. She was right about that. I had one shitload of karma to sort out. When I woke up, the lights were back on and daylight streamed through the net curtains.

Auntie had a big pot of porridge simmering on the stove. The oaty smell permeated the kitchen and made my mouth salivate. She had also prepared a platter of fruit and nuts, keeping with the list of 'good foods and bad foods' I had given her. I still felt bad about lying to her about Skye having allergies but it was better than explaining Skye's philosophy which would have caused all kinds of aggravation. She complained continually about me being a vegetarian and not eating "prop-erly". After breakfast we were going to Salisbury. I wanted to visit Martha and planned to phone her as soon as we got to town. I'd been dying to hear what she had to say about "this place and all that goes on here".

Auntie had given me the keys to Uncle Reg's old car but she demanded to see my international driver's license before she handed them over. I was a little nervous about driving the weathered old vehicle but our only other option was a local bus that stopped by the roadside at one p.m. and returned at six p.m. I wanted to take Skye shopping and to see some of the tourist attractions in the town, as well as going to visit Martha, and I wasn't sure how long it would take us. Besides I had to get used to driving over here. I couldn't always depend on Jonathan.

It was a bright, chilly morning; yesterday's rain had left everything soaking wet and the stones on the driveway shone like fish scales in the sun. Puddles of water glistened in the ditches and potholes along the road. The subtle aroma of Un-cle Reg's pipe smoke still lingered on the black leather seats. Skye gazed out of the passenger window, seemingly en-thralled by what she saw. When we passed the giant mono-liths of Stonehenge she asked me to slow down and said, "I have to go to Stonehenge while I'm here. I can almost feel its ancient, mystical energy."

"Yeah, I know what you mean. It's not just Stonehenge; it's this whole area." She tuned her head to face me and beamed, as if suddenly elated. "Hey, I just thought of something. Why don't we go there and celebrate winter solstice with the Druids? Wouldn't that be amazing?"

"Isn't solstice after you go back to Canada?"

"No, the winter solstice is on December twenty first, the day before I go back."

"Oh, right. Don't you have to be a member or something?"

"No you just show up. I've read all about it on the web and seen pictures. There's dancing and chanting, offerings, modern-day Druids, and white witches casting spells. Hundreds of people go. It's a spiritual festival, one big pagan party."

"Sounds like fun." But I wasn't sure if I wanted to be around witches casting spells, pagans chanting, and Druids. There was enough of that sort of thing in my life already and it was no party. It was the least I could do, though; she seemed thrilled at the prospect and she had spent all that money to come here, and it was a chance in a lifetime for her. "Okay, we'll go." After I'd said the words, a tiny voice inside me whispered, *you'll regret it.*

Chapter 10

We visited Salisbury Cathedral, the local museum, stopped in the curio and clothing shops along the high street, and had lunch at a quaint vegetarian restaurant on a cobbled side street. I had stopped at the public telephone box and called the number that Martha gave me but there was no answer. So I had decided that we'd go to the house just in case.

It took me a while to navigate the old car through the narrow streets teeming with pedestrians, carrying brown parcels, black umbrellas, and plastic shopping bags, towing little children and well mannered-dogs. The narrow roundabouts were a challenge, and nerve-wracking—numerous vehicles going round and round at full speed, branching off here and there. It took me four full circles to get to the outside lane and even then I wasn't sure I'd taken the right turn, but we arrived at the street where Martha's brother lived without too much trouble, thanks to the precise directions given to me by a kind man in the whimsical antique shop we had visited.

Rows and rows of dull gray terraced houses stretched before us, each with its own square privet hedge and little wooden fence bordering a small front garden; some were neatly kept while others were littered with garbage. A tattered Union Jack served as a curtain in one of the upstairs windows. Identical brick chimneys with clouds of dirty gray smoke coiled up into the heavens. The acrid smell of coal fire smoke lingered in the air. A couple of stray dogs wrestled with a stick in the middle of the street, and a postman politely tipped his starched blue hat as he mounted his bike to continue his late afternoon rounds. It was a common, dated, working class area where life was simple, predictable, and unchanged by the hands of time. It didn't seem fitting for a sophisticated woman like Martha. I pulled the piece of paper out of my pocket and then inspected the numbers on the front doors. "73 Kings Road. This must be it."

Skye followed close behind me. "Doesn't look like there's anyone home."

I opened the latch on the little picket gate and climbed the three concrete steps up to the dreary front door and knocked. The net curtains on the front window moved slightly. I knocked harder. Skye was flicking the latch on the gate. "No one's home, Fletch."

"Yes there is, someone was at the window." Just then door the opened, slowly. A short plump lady with large rimmed glasses and a head full of curlers stood behind the half opened door. "Hello, can I help you?" Her voice was courteous but leery.

"Hi, my name is Emily Fletcher. We're looking for Martha Davis. I'm the niece of a friend of hers, Emy Fletcher, and this is Skye Jenkins." I glanced over my shoulder and motioned her up the steps. Skye stuck out her hand and smiled but the gesture was shunned.

"From Merryweather Lodge?" the woman asked, with a stern-faced expression.

"Yes. Do you know my aunt?"

"No, but I've heard about her." She started to close the door. "Martha's out. She won't be back until later."

"How much later? We can wait." Skye pinched my arm. I ignored her impatient gesture. "There was something she wanted to tell me and I might not be able to come back again."

Her eyes narrowed behind the lenses of her frumpy glasses. "Likely she was going to tell you to get out of that place. She's told us all about what goes on there. I'll tell her you called," she said as she started to close the door.

I put my hand to the door. "What goes on there? What did she say?" She shut it in my face and locked it behind her. I left disappointed but vowed to return.

I was pleasantly surprised to see Jonathan's car parked on the gravel driveway in front of the cottage. It was only six o'clock and I wasn't expecting him until at least seven. I wanted to give him the royal-blue woolen sweater I'd bought for him at the handcrafter's shop on Main Street. I had meant to save it for Christmas but I couldn't wait that long. Blue was his favorite color and he always wore sweaters like this one over his shirt on cold days. I was sure it would look gorgeous on him.

A feeling of uneasiness came over me as I stepped inside the cottage door. There were voices, women's voices, voices I recognized, voices of people I didn't want to see. Sitting in Uncle Reg's wing-back chair, chin raised, lips puckered, holding a cup of tea, was the stocky, self-righteous, grim faced Maud McArthur. Next to Auntie on the chintz sofa sat the mysterious Belinda. She was wearing blue jeans and a simple green t-shirt. Her hair was pulled back into a ponytail and she wore no make-up or jewelry. Her legs were crossed and her hands sat demurely in her lap. She looked fresh-faced and pretty, with a respectable young lady appearance, but seeing her still made me cringe. Jonathan was sitting in Auntie's chair. I took a deep breath and entered the sitting room. "Well, Mrs. McArthur, Belinda, what a nice surprise." I gave Jonathan a quick disapproving glance. "I had no idea you were coming to visit."

Before I could introduce her, Skye stepped from behind me and stuck out her hand. "Mrs. McArthur, how lovely to meet you. I'm Emily's best friend, Skye Jenkins." Maud put down her cup and saucer and shook Skye's hand, enthusiastically and with a warm smile. Skye flinched, slightly. "Emy's been telling us all about you. How do you like our country so far?"

"I love it—the ancient buildings and monuments, the quaint countryside, the slower, simpler lifestyle. It's all so enchanting!"

Maud laughed. "You were right, Emy, she is a lively one."

Auntie heaved herself up off the sofa and took Skye's hand. "Like a cat on hot bricks, she is and a brazen madam at times, but she's a lovely little thing and we've all taken to 'er." *And I had worried about people not liking her. She's draw them all in with her charisma and magnetic personality, even the disagreeable Maud McArthur.* Auntie ushered Skye to the sofa. "And this is Maud's daughter, Belinda or Lindy, as I call 'er."

Belinda rose fluidly from her seat and took hold of Skye's hand as if it were a precious jewel. Her lips quivered with a small smile as her eyes roamed Skye's delicate form, with an expression of sheer delight. "It's a pleasure to meet you, Skye." Her voice was low and soft.

Skye's reply was an uncharacteristic shaky whisper. "The pleasure's all mine." They held onto each other's hand for a few uncomfortable moments.

Auntie disrupted the awkward silence. "You girls must be starving. Bet ya' never 'ad any tea." She didn't give me any time to reply. "Thought not, we left ya some grub on the kitchen table. Covered it in cellophane, we did."

Maud stood and smoothed the wrinkles out of her skirt. "We have to be going; John will be wondering where we've got to." She crooked her finger at Belinda, who was quick to respond. They gathered their belongings and headed for the door. Jonathan followed behind them.

"It's a pity ya' can't stay a little bit longer and visit with our guest," Auntie said, as she reached for the door knob. The two women engaged in idle chatter at the door.

Belinda turned her head, caught Skye's attention, and flashed her a wide friendly smile. Skye moved towards her intently. "I hope that we meet again before I go back."

Belinda gave her a cheeky grin. "Oh, we most definitely will." I didn't like the sound of that. Auntie finally opened the door and said goodbye to her neighbors.

Jonathan gave me a quick glance and a wink as he walked out the door. "I'll be back after I've dropped them off."

I wandered into the sitting room and pulled back the heavy net curtain from the window. It was dusky outside but the inside of the car was lit. Belinda was sitting in the back seat, and immediately her eyes caught mine, as if she had sensed me watching her. I lowered the curtain but not all the way, just enough to see the icy scowl on her face and her lips moving: "Emily, Emily two by four. I saw you at the cellar door. I pushed you on the dirty floor and cut you with a chainsaw." I put my hands to my ears and moved back away from the window. Her mouth had been moving but I was sure there was nothing coming out. Somehow her words were being transmitted from her mind into my head. We had a telepathic link! Oh, my God. I shivered all the way to the kitchen.

Skye was sitting at the kitchen table, picking at a bowl of purple grapes, while twirling her wavy black hair around her fingers. She nudged the leg of the chair with her foot, inviting me to sit. I grabbed a china plate from the cupboard shelf and filled it with scones, jam tarts, egg sandwich's, and fruit; my hands were shaking and my gut was grumbling. I was famished and frightened. I intended to gorge myself to try and take away some of the edge and erase the words that were echoing in my head. I lowered myself onto the hard wooden seat beside her and asked, "What was all that about, Skye?"

She sniffed and carried on picking at the grapes. "All what?"

"That with Belinda. The way you looked at her all googly-eyed and wouldn't let go of her hand." Her head was bowed, her eyes focused on the great big cluster of grapes. I plopped my elbow on the table, rested my chin on my hand, turned my head towards her, and stared, trying to force her gaze to meet mine.

She swept the long strands of velvety hair away from her face with the tips of her fingers and looked up at me. "She's...charming."

I sprang from the chair, knocking it back on to the floor. "Oh she's charming all right; she could charm the crucifix off a priest!" I could feel the familiar surge and uncontrollable steam rising in my gut, like a boiler about to explode. "She's a surrogate for an evil, vindictive entity, Skye, a changeling, a manipulative, foul bitch! I swear, Skye, if I didn't know better I'd think you were..."

She lifted up her chin to meet my icy glare, calm but with a despondent look on her face. "Go on, say it."

I couldn't. I sat back down and bit into a jam tart. "I'm sorry, Jenks, but you're supposed to be helping me get rid of Merthia, not fraternizing with her host."

"Calm down, Fletch, and take a breath."

I covered my face with my hands. "I just want things to be normal here. And I'm scared, so scared."

As she removed my hands from my face, her index finger brushed against my cheek ever-so-slowly, ever-so-gently. It was like being touched by an angel. The pleasurable sensation made me uncomfortable. Her soft, compassionate eyes met mine. "I know you're scared, Fletch, and I'm going to help you get rid of her but I have to do it right. So it's going to take some time and planning. First I want to summon the spirit of Mary Eliss. I have a feeling she can help us. Then I have to consider all the other elements to this mystery before I can come up with some sort of exorcism." Her fingers wrapped around my hand and squeezed lightly. "We might have to go into the woodlot."

I sighed. "Whatever it takes. But what about Belinda? What vibes did you pick up from her, besides the charming, pretty, innocent facade?"

It took her a moment to answer. "Deep down inside her there is a kind heart and a gentle spirit."

I almost choked. "Hello! Are you crazy? Are we talking about the same girl? You do remember the things I told you about her, don't you? And the things that Merthia had said? Belinda had an evil heart from the day she was born; that's why Merthia picked her for a host. And if, by some slim chance, deep, deep down, there is some good in her, how come I can't sense it and how come—"

Skye interrupted. "Probably because the emotion of hate is so strong and powerful, it won't allow you to see beyond its control." She thought for a moment. "Didn't Merthia say that Belinda was given to Maud after being taken from your aunt, who had given birth to her, right?"

"Yes, but I don't know that I believe that."

"If you believe one thing she said, then you have to believe it all. How old was your aunt and Maud when they were pregnant?"

"I don't know their exact age but they were old, both of them. Auntie had had a miscarriage some years before that, I think."

"And Jonathan was adopted?" I nodded my head. "What are the chances of that, Fletch? Doesn't it seem odd and unlikely to you that two middle-aged women, both with fertility problems, conceived at the same time and then delivered their babies three days apart? And if your aunt's baby was three days old when it was given to Maud, wouldn't she have known that it wasn't hers? Three-day-old babies look a lot different than fresh-out-of-the-womb babies."

"You're right. I'd never thought of that. Are you saying that Maud knew Belinda wasn't her baby?"

"Either that or Merthia lied about the whole thing, and your aunt's baby did die and Belinda is Maud's own child, but I think there's a lot more to it than that. What do you know of Maud McArthur?"

"Well, she was my Uncle Reg's cousin and Auntie told me that she wasn't always a 'miserable old bat'. Before she had Belinda she was a quiet, soft-spoken, kindly woman but Auntie said 'avin a baby at such a late age threw a spanner in 'er works and sent 'er body skew-whiff, 'ormones is what it was, been a grouchy old git ever since, she 'as." Skye giggled. "Maud got really irate with me once and told me that this farm should go to her when Auntie dies, something about her granny selling it to foreigners. Jonathan thinks he was adopted as a newborn baby because they've got photos of him when he was only a few days old."

"Got it sussed out yet 'ave ya'?"

I was startled to hear Auntie's voice and wondered how long she'd been standing outside the door. "Sussed what out, Auntie?"

"Whatever ya've been gabbing on about. And I 'erd ya' giving each other jip, like two old fish wives, ya' were. Be nice to each other. Yer' supposed to be best mates."

I was getting familiar with her convoluted lingo but I wondered if Skye was able to understand any of it. I was glad that she hadn't heard what we were discussing, or so it seemed. "Even best friends have disagreements, Auntie Em."

She pulled out the chair across from us, sat down, leaned forward, and laid her arms on the table. She was clutching a large white hankie in her hand. "Would you girls like to 'elp me get ready for Christmas?" Her brown eyes danced with enthusiasm. "We've gotta get us a Christmas tree and I've got loads of decorations and we 'ave to 'ave holly and mistletoe, lots of mistletoe. I'm going to be doing some of m' Christmas baking tomorrow, plum pudding and fruit cake." She gave me a nod and a wink. "Ya' ain't tasted nothin' like yer' Auntie Em's plum pudding, ya ain't."

I didn't have the heart to tell her that Skye wouldn't eat it if it contained anything dairy. But the Christmas preparations were something positive to think about, to take my mind off the gloomy shadows that lurked in the cottage. It would be fun to be decorating this place for Christmas; a real tree in the corner, holly and mistletoe over the fireplace, bulky red candles and stockings hanging over the mantel. And Christmas baking with Auntie would be a real treat.

Skye could hardly contain herself. "That would be so awesome! Can we make apple cider? I love apple cider and rice crispy cookies with sprinkles, and we can decorate the tree with strings of popcorn." She put her hands to her chest and flashed a silly grin. "An authentic country Christmas, in a remote little cottage, amidst the English countryside; how quaint, how splendid."

Auntie threw back her head and roared with laughter. I shook my head and chuckled. "Really, Skye Jenkins, you are such a fantasist. Are you ever going to grow up?" I teased.

"Never!" she replied, which made Auntie laugh even more.

I suddenly remembered that Jonathan should have been here by now. I pushed back my sleeve and glanced at my watch. He'd been gone for an hour. "I wonder where Jonathan's got to." I turned to Auntie. "He didn't ring, did he?"

"No luv, 'is mum's probably kept 'im talking, can talk the 'ind leg off a donkey, that woman can, when she gets goin'."

Or maybe it was his strange sister…or worse. "I wonder

if I should call him. Just to make sure he's okay, that is." Just then the front door opened.

"That'll be 'im now, "Auntie said, as she rose from the table and stuffed her hanky into her baggy apron pocket.

"Hello, it's only me."

Auntie beamed, as Jonathan stepped into the kitchen. "We're ya' been, Jonny, yer' girlfriend's been worried about ya.' Gonna send out a search party we were," she said with a big grin on her face.

I was quick to respond. "I wasn't worried about him. I just wondered where he was." I gave him a sharp, disapproving glance. "He told me he was just dropping them off and he'd be right back."

He took off his heavy winter jacket and draped it over the back of the chair. Then he sat and ran his fingers over the tiny bristles on his cleft chin. "Belinda wanted to show me some of her paintings. She's taking art classes. And we've just discovered that she has a unique artistic talent."

"Just like 'er brother," Auntie interrupted.

I knew it would have been Belinda, keeping him from me. "How lovely," I said, not making any effort to hide my sarcastic tone.

Auntie ambled to the door, her feet dragging her big fuzzy slippers across the hardwood floor. "I'll leave you youngun's to it. Gonna 'ave an early night I am." She glanced over her shoulder, then took out her hanky and put it to her mouth as she walked out the door. I knew what she was doing and shuddered at the thought. Auntie always took her false teeth out in the evening, usually right after tea, if we didn't have company.

"Good night, Mrs. Fletcher," Jonathan called.

"Good night, Auntie," Skye and I blurted out in unison. Then we giggled like school girls.

There was a look of disapproval in Jonathan's dark brown eyes, as he lowered them to the table. He fidgeted with his hands.

"Can I get you a drink?" I asked.

"No thanks; I can't stay." His glance was still focused on his hands.

"Is there anything wrong? You seem quiet and aloof."

The pupils of his eyes moved to look at Skye. Was he uncomfortable in her presence or did he want to talk to me alone? I gave Skye a quick 'get out of here' nod but she never moved.

"I'm fine," he said. "Just a little tired, have a bit of a headache and I have work in the morning." He swept his hair back and went to stand up. I grabbed the sleeve of his sweater. "Don't you want to hear what happened today? And you won't believe what we're going to do in the attic room." Skye's head began to shake and her lips folded over, in a 'no don't tell him' fashion. He must have noticed.

"No, really, I have to go." He moved towards the door. I followed close behind. "You can tell me all about it later. 'Bye, Skye, have a nice evening."

"You too," she mumbled, in a dull tone.

"Will I see you tomorrow?" I asked, when we got to the door.

"Why don't we wait until Saturday, then we can spend the day together." He hesitated. "Just you and me." His lips moved to meet mine and once again I felt the heady sensation of his soft embrace. "I love you," he whispered, as he closed the front door.

Skye was opening the half finished bottle of wine, left from last night. "We're going to need this," she said. "Tonight we are going to summon the spirit of the little girl that lives here: your friend Mary Eliss.

Chapter 11

Once again I found myself entering the foreboding attic. Skye had brought with her all the necessary tools for contacting the dead. A round tablecloth of white silk surrounded by a ring of sea salt lay in the middle of the floor. In the center of the cloth three candles flickered, casting ghostly shadows around the room. The spicy aroma of incense floated towards us from the burning sticks on the dresser.

We sat cross-legged, hair loose, no make-up, wearing white, so as to emanate purity. Annabella sat between us to help evoke Mary Eliss's spirit. Skye said that it would be helpful if we had something that belonged to Mary Eliss and I was sure that the porcelain doll had been her closest companion. In front of us sat the ominous Ouija board. The goose bumps under my pure white robe ran all the way up my arms. I sat motionless, glued to the ground, waiting for Skye's command. "Hold Annabella's hand, join together your index finger and thumb on your other hand, and breathe in through your nose and out through your mouth," she whispered.

"Deep breaths, empty your mind, focus only on your breath, and envision a white light around you, an aura of protection and love." As I inhaled the spicy, intoxicating aroma, a warm radiant white light enveloped me, my body relaxed and my mind was still. "Breathe," Skye muttered softly. Suddenly— darkness! A deep void of cold ghastly, pitch-black darkness. The walls started to vibrate. Harrowing voices of long dead occupants emerged from the pulsating plaster. The room vibrated with the haunting sounds of wailing, gut-wrenching sobs, cries for help; they closed in around me, bombarding my ears. The candles were gone, and in their place lay a pile of severed limbs—hands, feet, arms, heads—covered with blood. Ruby-red stains soaked through the pristine white tablecloth. Hovering over the carnage was my dreaded adversary, in her hideous form. I opened my mouth to scream but nothing came out. Vomit rose in my throat as her stench filled my nostrils. Through the matted hair that clung to her ashen face, green eyes peered at me from their dark sockets. Her mouth opened and through her jagged yellow teeth she hissed, "Revenge is mine." Something cold and hard gripped my finger.

The terrifying vision left me. I opened my eyes and looked down. The tiny alabaster fingers of the porcelain doll were wrapped around my thumb, as if to comfort me. *Did she do that?* Skye's head was still bowed in silent meditation and the room seemed peaceful again. I inhaled the silence but was afraid to close my eyes, terrified now of what I had just envisioned and of what might be to come.

"Are you ready?" Skye asked, as she lifted her head. "I think we've rid the room of all its negative energy."

You've got to be kidding. "Ready as I'll ever be."

She drew close to me. "Keep hold of the doll's hand and put your other fingers on the Ouija board slider."

My fingers twitched as I placed them on the plastic slider. "I'm not liking this, Skye."

She closed her eyes, bowed her head, and then spoke in a low raspy voice, "We are looking for the spirit of Mary Eliss. Is anyone here with us?" At first nothing happened. Then slowly the marker began to move. My fingers trembled and I could feel my heart rate elevating, as the marker slid across the board. It stopped at the word yes. Skye turned her head to the side and shot me a quick grin and a nod. "Are we talking to the spirit of Mary Eliss?" The marker slid swiftly to the word no. Skye shrugged. I swallowed the lump that was working its way up to my throat. "What is your name?" The marker moved; A.N.N.I.E. *Annie?* Our eyes met in silent query. "We're glad you have joined us, Annie." *I'm not. I thought we were trying to contact Mary Eliss.* "We need your help. Do you know the evil spirit that haunts this place?" Skye asked eagerly. The marker immediately raced across the board to yes. I gulped. "Could you help us get rid of her?" The black marker went wild, racing and spinning all over the glossy surface. The board started to shake. I let go of the slider and scurried back, away from the animated Ouija board.

There was a strong scent of lavender in the air. I heard

someone giggling, a child-like giggle coming from the corner of the room. "Come, Emily, come."

I sighed, a breath of utter relief when I saw the radiant, angelic form of Mary Eliss. She was sitting on the bed, her legs dangling over the edge, her hands lying poised on top of her lap. Her milky complexion and strawberry pink cheeks were lit with a wide smile. Her emerald, unblinking eyes were glossy and perfectly shaped, as if they'd been painted on her face. I felt like I was being reunited with an old friend. "Mary Eliss," I said softly, still in awe at the presence of my pretty spirit friend. She held out her hands, palms facing me, warning me not to come any closer. I stayed back and took Skye's arm; her mouth was ajar and her eyes were big and bulging with utter amazement. "This is my friend Skye Jenkins. Skye this is…"

"I know who she is. It's great to meet you, Mary. How did you get here? Where do you come from? I have always wanted to meet a real spirit."

Mary Eliss giggled, ignored Skye's questions, and looked at me. "You don't need the talking board to contact me, silly. If I can come to you I will."

"I need your help," I said eagerly. "I have to get rid of the evil spirit that haunts this place. Is there anyway you can help me."

She lowered her head. "The mystery is yours to solve, Emily, but I will help you whenever I can. Watch out for the malevolent spirit and bury…" Her form faded and vanished in an instant.

"Come back!" I pleaded. "Bury who? What? Do you know someone named Annie?" I cried in hopeless desperation.

"She's gone, Fletch," Skye said sympathetically, as she flicked on the light switch.

"Shit! There was so much I wanted to ask her. She mentioned a malevolent spirit once before and she was going to tell me to bury something or someone."

"There could be any number of malevolent spirits in this place. I guess we have to find out which one she's referring to. Maybe she was telling us how to get rid of Merthia, by burying her."

"Oh, that should be easy."

We gathered our paraphernalia, tidied the room, and changed into our night clothes. "I can't sleep here tonight, Jenks." My gaze wandered around the room. "When I'm in here the veil between my other life and this one seems so very sheer." I could feel the raising tide behind my eyelids.

Skye sensed my frustration. She reached up and wrapped her arms around my neck and drew me close, too close. I buried my face in her shoulder as she brushed my hair ever so gently, with her small fingers. I felt comforted by her caress and the warm fragrance of her body. She was like a spiritual salve soothing my soul. "I won't let anything happen to you while I'm here, I promise. We are going to banish her," she said, in a firm reassuring tone.

I pulled away from her embrace and sniffed back the

tears. "We're going to send her vile soul back to hell, whatever it takes!"

"Whatever it takes." She dabbed a teardrop from under my eye with a soft tissue and stared into my face with such tenderness, as if I were something rare and beautiful. "I couldn't stand it if anything happened to you, Fletch."

That night I slept on the pull-out couch in the parlor. Skye wanted to sleep on the couch with me but I told her she should stay in the attic just in case Mary Eliss came back. A small, unfamiliar part of me was afraid of what might happen if we kept sharing the same bed.

The next morning I tried to phone Martha again when Auntie went outside to hang clothes on the washing line, but there was no answer. Today we were decorating the cottage and baking Christmas cake and Skye's favorite, crispy, rice cookies. Tomorrow I would ask Jonathan to help us search for the perfect tree. The Christmas activity was a welcome reprieve from the horrible thoughts that had occupied my mind for the past few weeks. Christmas had always been my favorite time of year. I loved the food, the decorations, school concerts, Santa, the Christ child, the hunkering down in front of a cozy fire, listening to carols, and sipping eggnog. It had always been so magical and enchanting for me and no one was going to spoil my first Christmas at Merryweather Lodge, not even 'her'!

The old kitchen table was crammed with scrumptious ingredients, waiting for Auntie's skilled hands to mould them together into fine edible, works of art. A dog-eared, flour-spotted cookbook lay opened at the end of the table. Bing Crosby's voice crooned from Auntie's C.D. player on the corner shelf; 'I'm dreaming of a white Christmas…' My Christmases had always been white. I couldn't imagine a green Christmas, but I knew that they seldom got snow here at this time of year; it usually came in the later winter months.

The mixed fruit peel, cherries, and raisins had been chopped and soaked in brandy overnight. Auntie peeled back the cheese cloth from her earthenware bowl, and uncovering a rich fruity aroma. She had insisted that we wear aprons to save our clothes from spills or stains. Mine was blue, splattered with white daisies. Skye's came down to her ankles and the tie wrapped around her waist three times. It had a Union Jack motif on the front with the words 'I love Britain' underneath. Auntie had bought it at a novelty shop especially for Skye but it only came in one size, which clearly wasn't Skye's. We sieved, mixed, baked and sampled, while singing carols, sipping home-made apple cider and giggling like little children. After the cake and cookies were out of the oven, we took off our aprons and gathered the decorations and foliage that Auntie had collected early that morning.

We hung wreaths and strung home-made paper chains around the doors and windows, draped holly and pine twigs over the mantel and stuffed mistletoe in heavy glass vases. Skye said that mistletoe was sacred to the ancient Druids. I wasn't sure if that was a good thing or bad. Auntie had a collection of hand-painted glass angels that we arranged on the buffet and an antique nativity scene that looked charming beside the hearth. All that we needed was the Christmas tree. There was only one place close by, that I knew of, that would have the perfect Christmas tree, but the thought of going there filled me with dread. I tried to forget all about Merthia, and the dark mystery that shrouded Merryweather Lodge. Today it was a cozy, enchanting little English cottage, alive with the essence of Christmas. If only it could be like this all the time.

After dinner, which was, as always, at twelve o'clock, I decided to take a bubble bath in Auntie's claw-foot tub. Every time I stepped into that tub the frightful memory of what happened here when I was fourteen years old came flooding back to me. But what choice did I have? It was the only bathroom in the cottage. Sometimes I would put the bath off for days, but tomorrow I was going to be alone with Jonathan, and I was planning to have my way with him. It had been a long time since I made love to a man and it was making me so raunchy that I was getting inappropriate feelings for my girlfriend. But I had had those inappropriate thoughts before, in the secret world of my fantasies. They allowed me to act out unacceptable tendencies in the safety of my own mind. But, I reassured myself, everyone has secret taboo fantasies, especially those of a sexual nature. As soon as I made love to Jonathan these uncomfortable feelings will go away, I told myself, because I wasn't like that.

I lowered myself into the fragrant, silky water, laid my head on the back of the foamy tub and wallowed in the luxury of this simple pleasure. This evening we were going to try to piece together more of the puzzle, to see if we could come up with a means to banish Merthia. I had a feeling that there were still too many missing pieces. Skye was spending the afternoon, meditating and going through her books and papers on paranormal phenomenon and white witchcraft. I wanted to wait for Jonathan before we discussed it but she didn't want to wait. I was just about to close my eyes when there was a knock on the door. I froze. *Oh no, not again.*

"Yer' dad's on the phone, luv." *Thank God.* I sighed. It's only Auntie. "Didn't want to ask 'im to call back. Costs ya' a bob or two to phone long distance, it does."

"Tell him I'll be right down," I called, as I dragged myself, somewhat reluctantly, out of the soothing, warm water and into the cool air.

It felt so good to hear my dad's voice again and it reminded me of how very much I loved him and missed him. He sounded cheerful and was excited to tell me about the new people he'd met and the adventures he'd been having. And I was so relieved to hear that he was enjoying himself and not consumed with grief. "Is everything okay there?" he asked me. "I'll call you again before Christmas. Keep safe and away from trouble, princess."

Keep safe and away from trouble? That was not the sort of thing you'd normally say to someone on vacation. I knew that my dad was aware that this place had an ominous history but, like a lot of the locals here, he was bound for some unfathomable reason to keep it a secret.

Bare footed, and still wrapped in a damp towel, I walked back to the bathroom. My feet left wet prints on the polished hardwood floor. The room was filled with steam. I fought my way through the cloudy vapor and pulled the rubber plug in the tub. When I turned I noticed something on the mirror above the pedestal sink. I moved closer to take a look, and gasped! On the steamy surface of the oval mirror written in bold capital letters was the word RETRIBUTION! My mind and limbs turned leaden. I felt like I was going to pass out. She was here; she had never left; her disgusting, invisible, dark shadow followed me around like a deranged stalker waiting for the opportunity to butcher its victim. I didn't know how much more of this I could take.

Chapter 12

I gathered my clothes and scurried out the door. I knew there was no use in telling Auntie; the word would be erased by some devious invisible hand and all the evidence gone by the time she got here, like all the other times.

I went into the parlor to see how Skye was doing with her research but she was gone. "Jenks, come out come out where ever you are," I called playfully, as I dashed from room to room. Auntie was polishing the curio table by the front door, with beeswax and lemon oil, one of her many home-grown, organic cleaning products. "Have you seen Skye?" I asked her, eagerly.

"'Avent seen 'ide nor 'air of 'er I 'avent." She pointed to the ceiling. "'Be in 'er room, won't she? Ave ya' checked up there?"

I grimaced and shook my head. "She said she was going to catch up with some reading, in the parlor, but I can't find her anywhere."

She shoved the can of polish and duster in her deep apron

pocket and stormed past me, shaking her wiry gray head. "Blinking heck our Emily, I'll go look. That imagination of yours working over time again, is it? It didn't seem to bother you last night when ya' were up there kicking up a hullaba-loo."

How much did she hear? Did she know what we were up to?

I stood at the bottom of the daunting attic stairs. "I ain't no spring chicken," she mumbled, as she ascended the stairs one foot at a time. As usual, the creak of the heavy wooden door filled me with apprehension. "Ain't no one in 'ere but Winston." The strange cat came slinking down the stairs with Auntie close behind. "Shoo, you naughty boy, told ya' not to keep coming up 'ere, get yer' self locked in every time ya' do."

But how does he keep getting in there? And why is he so drawn to that room?

Auntie went right back to her polishing. "'Er must 'ave gone out."

"Yes she's probably gone for a walk. I'll go see if I can find her."

I started to feel anxious when I noticed Skye's jacket next to mine on the coat rack. I shoved my arms into my heavy winter coat and hurried out the door.

Sam came running to meet me, and I bent down and gave him a quick pat on his black and white head. Then I pulled my fur-lined hood over my head to protect my ears from the brisk, icy wind.

Dark gray clouds raced across the sky like shadowy ghosts. Great gusts blew into my back propelling me forward, as I held on to my hood and called, "Skye! Skye Jenkins, answer me!" She'd never go out in this weather without her jacket, I told myself. I looked around the yard back and front. My eyes watered against the strong wind. I pushed a few loose strands of red hair under my hood and started down the beaten path that led to the barn. Sam trotted faithfully, behind me. The trees tossed their few remaining leaves into the air like confetti. The hip-roofed barn stood before me like a huge red monster ready to devour anything that dared to enter its domain. I had never been inside it before. Uncle Reg had told me that there was nothing in there but an old tractor and some rusty farm tools, but I felt the need to check, just in case. As I lifted the latch, I suddenly remembered that this was where they found Auntie's beloved cat Wooky, "dead as a doornail," as Auntie said. I often wondered what really happened to that cat.

The weighty plank door opened with a groan. Sam stuck his nose inside but I pulled him back. I was bombarded with the unpleasant smell of wet wood and rotting hay. I stepped inside the huge gloomy structure but kept my hand on the door, just in case. "Skye." She wasn't there. I stepped outside, closed the door, and hooked the latch. *Oh my God, where could she be*? She would never wander off by herself, like this, without telling anyone, without wearing a coat. What if Merthia's taking her to spite me or in exchange for me? Panic consumed me, as I ran to the side of the building. The thoughts of what could have happened to her clutched at my throat. I stopped. Someone was coming. I could hear distant voices, two voices, female voices.

I moved to the edge of barn, commanded Sam to sit, and peeked around the corner. I blinked, stunned. Strolling towards the barn, hand in hand, swinging their arms like windswept, frolicking little girls, were my best friend and the evil Belinda. I took another quick look. Skye had my heavy knitted shawl wrapped around her and tied in a big knot in the front. Belinda was wearing a long bulky, black cardigan and a pair of high boots. Their long hair was flapping erratically around their giddy faces. Their voices rang with jubilance and affection as if they'd known each other all their lives. What the hell were they up to, I asked myself. Had Belinda put Skye under some sort of spell? Given her a potion or hypnotized her perhaps? I asked myself. That must have been it. They came to the side of the barn. They were only a few feet away from me, I had to be super quiet to keep from being discovered and find to out what was going on. Sam was still sitting dutifully as he'd been instructed to do. "Stay," I whispered to him. They were laughing now but it was hard for me to understand what they were saying with the wind howling around my ears.

Ever so slowly I stretched my neck to peer around the corner. Belinda was standing directly in front of Skye; so close, in fact, that if Skye suddenly came to her senses she wouldn't be able to escape. Then Belinda started to slowly trace patterns on Skye's face with her fingers. Skye just stood there in a trance-like state with a stupid grin on her face. Oh my God! Belinda was kissing her. That did it. I couldn't let my best friend be seduced by a woman, especially not this woman. What if Merthia had taken over her body and planned to rape Skye as she did Jonathan but this time in flesh and blood?

My hands curled into fists by my side. It felt like my blood vessels were going to burst from the fury building up inside me. I took a gasping breath and stepped from behind the wall. "Get away from her, you evil bitch!" I screamed as I stomped towards them. Sam stood, pricked up his ears and then dashed out in front of me, barking and snarling ferociously at the two women, as if he had sensed my fear and anger. When he got to their side his tail started to wag. They moved away from each other, eyes wide, brows arched, stunned at my sudden appearance. Belinda was wearing make-up, jewelry, and piercings; I scowled at her, raised my chin, straightened my back, and said, injecting as much threat into my voice as I could muster, "What have you done to my friend?"

She threw her head back and laughed, mockingly, and then asked, "What are you doing here? Watching us? Spying on us? Sick bitch!" she snarled. She was no longer the confused little girl or genteel teenager but the nasty mini diva I had met the first time I came here.

I grabbed Skye's arm. "You're coming with me."

Belinda's nostrils flared as she lunged towards me and clenched her fingers around my wrist like a vice. Skye pulled away from me. Belinda loosened her grip. "Stop it, both of you!" Skye demanded, as she tried to tuck the wisps of lashing hair behind her ears. She lowered her head, and then lifted it. Her face wore an expression of sadness as she shifted from one foot to another. "I am sorry, Fletch, I should have told you before now. But I was so afraid of losing your friendship. "I am and have always been…" she hesitated, and then finished her sentence, "gay." Part of me wasn't surprised but to hear it from her lips and in this situation, made me feel betrayed and uncomfortable. She took Belinda's hand. "From the moment we set eyes on each other we knew it was meant to be. When Belinda called me to meet with her I knew that she had felt that same connection." They smiled at each other fondly.

I felt like throwing up. My temper pounded at my temples. The words tore from my throat. "No! She's using you, manipulating you. How can you be so naive? After all I've told you about her. She's not gay; she tried to seduce her own brother for God's sake. Merthia controls her; Belinda's her servant, and her host. For all we know," I glared at Belinda, "Merthia could be inside that body right now!"

Belinda's face was flushed and I could see the blood vessels in her long neck protruding as she clenched her teeth. Her wide eyes cut into me like the sharp blade of a knife. I was starting to get nervous. What if she was Merthia? We wouldn't stand a chance against her, not out here in the open, without any protection.

"No, Emily you're wrong," Skye pleaded. "She has

schizophrenia and if she is being possessed by that creature, it's not her fault. Merthia got inside you and made you do awful things and you had no control over it, right?"

She was right, but there was more to Belinda than that, much more. "Don't trust her, Skye. It's a trick to get back at me."

She turned to Belinda. "I'm really sorry about this. I'll call you tomorrow. I promise." Skye's voice dripped with disappointment. "Come on, Fletch, lets go. We'll talk about this later."

"We most certainly will," I mumbled as I glanced over my shoulder. Belinda stood stiff and still, wind-swept, her face twisted, her fists clenched, glaring at us. Then she mouthed something to me. The unspoken words I read rang in my head, "Revenge will be mine."

As soon as we were out of sight I took another shot at Skye. "How can anyone as intuitive and intelligent as you be so naive?"

She started to laugh. "Please, Fletch, give me some credit. I know what she's trying to do and I'm only going along with it to see what makes her tick and how much control Merthia has over her. Perhaps if I can get close to her I can excavate some of that good she has lodged deep down inside her."

I was relieved to hear that. "And you're not gay, either?"
"Sorry, Fletch, that part was true." I sighed, on the inside.

Auntie was wrestling with a large pair of white knickers on the clothes line. Sam dashed up to her, wagging his tail, as if he hadn't seen her for weeks. "Well I'll be blowed. Ya' found 'er then," she mumbled through the two clothes pegs between her teeth.

She was struggling to get the damp clothes off the line, as they flailed about fiercely in the squally wind. Auntie had no dryer, only a small spin washer tucked under the kitchen counter and usually only did a wash when the day was good for drying. She insisted that laundry should be hung out in the open air; it was only "proper". But the drying days were few and far between in the winter. "Can we help you with that, Auntie?" I asked.

She spit the pegs into the wicker basket full of damp clothes and, with a grunt, hitched the heavy basket up to her hips. "No ya' can't. You two get in the 'ouse and warm up," Ya'll catch your death of cold out 'ere, ya' will."

The ambiance inside the cottage, with its Christmas dé-cor, blazing fire and scrumptious smells was cheery and calm-ing. A huge pot of something that smelled like beer and ap-ples was bubbling on the little gas stove. "Wassail," Auntie said, when she saw me sniffing the steam. "It's an old recipe and custom. Folks used to go from door to door at Christmas time with baked goods and bowls of wassail, to wish their neighbor's season's blessings. Used to do it ourselves years ago."

"Smells heavenly. What's in it?"

She took off the lid and stirred the contents of the pot with her well-worn wooden spoon. "Dark ale, apple cider, cinnamon, cloves, and what ever else takes m' fancy."

Auntie scooped a spoonful of the steamy brew out of the pot, blew on it, sipped, then puckered her lips. "Could do with a bit more sugar, it could." After adding a full cup of sugar she proceeded to hang the damp clothes on the vintage clothes-horse to dry beside the fire. I went looking for Skye who had seemed to have disappeared again or was hiding from me, unable to face me after being discovered with my rival, revealing her real identity and years of deceiving me.

I could hear the bath water running so decided to wait for her to finish her bath in my makeshift bedroom. I took some sheets of lined paper from the buffet drawer, ready to make a list of all the strange and horrid things that had happened here since my first visit, and things that could be clues to solving this mystery and getting rid of my unearthly adversary.

My mind was so frazzled from all the weird and terrible things that were happening to me that I couldn't think straight. If everything was documented, Skye might be able to put some of the pieces together. I was getting so tired of all of this. All that I wanted to do was spend time with Auntie and Jonathan, enjoy the simplicity of this slower and simple life style in this beautiful, enchanting land, and be safe. Oh, how I wanted to feel safe.

As I reached inside my bag for my journal I noticed a bungle of dry lavender sprigs tied with a faded piece of red ribbon, on the window ledge. I had seen a similar bunch by the window, on my last visit but it had vanished mysteriously as soon as Auntie came into the room. She hated lavender and said it was bad luck. I ignored it, opened my journal and clicked my pen.

> *December 10th…Dear friend, I am perplexed and weary of this place. Yet sometimes I feel like I belong here, like it was always meant to be my home. I miss my dog Merlin, my mom and dad. I miss the snow that blankets Canada at this time of year. I will miss my best friend; things will not be the same between us now, the trust and closeness we shared is lost. She is not the girl I thought she was. I feel like I'm in a boat stranded in the middle of a vast lake, not knowing which way to turn and deathly afraid of the deep dark waters that lie beneath., The notes of nostalgia are tugging at my heart strings, longing for home and safety, wherever that might be. I know there is a direction that will take me ashore. If only I knew which way to paddle.*

"Fletch. We need to have a talk."

Skye's voice startled me. She was wrapped in a large terry bath towel "You're not kidding." I tucked my pen and journal back into my bag and asked, "Need a drink?" She shook her head. "Well I do." I went into the kitchen and gathered two of Auntie's hefty wine glasses, a corkscrew and a bottle of store bought Chardonnay that we had picked up at a grocery shop in Salisbury. When I got back to the room Skye was wearing a flimsy, saffron-colored, rayon shirt. It hung over her tiny form and clung to her gentle curving breasts and hips like liquid gold. Her damp dark curls trickled over her shoulders and down her back like a waterfall. I turned my back to her and poured the wine. "So how come you didn't tell me?" I asked her in an accusing tone.

She took the wine glass from my hand. "I told you, I didn't want to run the risk of losing my best friend. I knew this time would come, but honestly, Fletch, I thought you would have guessed before now."

"Who else knows?"

She ran her fingers around the rim of the glass. "Everyone."

I took a swig of wine then lowered myself onto the couch. "Everyone but me. You could have come to me. You know I'm not homophobic. I've always been in favor of gay rights, gay marriage, and you know I can't stand intolerance. And what about the boys you had crushes on at school? You were obsessed with Matt Hasselman."

She placed her glass on the buffet and sat beside me. Her shirt rose up her thighs and she smelt like she'd been dipped in almond and honey. A warm shot of heat from my face told me something I didn't want to know. Why was I having these feelings? Was I gay, or was it just that I hadn't been laid for so long?

"I tried to like boys and pretended to have crushes but it was all fabricated, a cover up for my true feelings. I knew you weren't prejudiced, but there was another reason why I didn't tell you," she said as she stroked the back of my hand with her dainty finger. My hand trembled, ever-so-slightly.

Chapter 13

I tore my hand away and bolted off the couch, afraid of where this was going. "I don't want to hear anymore. You're a lesbian, so what, big deal. Now let's get on with it." She turned her cheek as if I'd just slapped her. I shrugged and handed her the lined paper and pen. "And we'll start with," I threw her a mean scowl, "Belinda. I want you to promise me that you won't see her again, not until we've banished Merthia."

"I told you, I want to get close to her, to see what I can find out."

I shook my head. "It's too dangerous. Now write this down."

I told her everything I could think of about Belinda, her hateful attitude towards me, her inappropriate fondness for her brother, her possession, and what Merthia said about her being Auntie's biological child and having an evil seed. I reminded her about my recent incident with Belinda in their back yard and hearing her unspoken words. Her hand moved swiftly over the paper as she chewed on the inside of her mouth. "Now do you see why I don't want you to see her? She could turn on you, especially if she finds out you don't really have feelings for her. Just help me find a way to stop Merthia from using her."

She sighed. "I might be able to do that if she thinks I have the hots for her." I shook my head. "Okay, you win, I won't see her until this is all over."

I smiled sympathetically. "Next page, the peculiar Mrs. Tilly." With glass in hand, I tucked my legs under my bottom on the soft cushions of the pullout couch, and proceeded to recount all of my experiences at Merryweather Lodge. She had heard them all before but I hoped that having a summary of each occurrence would help us to start fitting some of the pieces together.

She turned to the back of the writing pad and scribbled some words down.

"Here is the list of the things I think are significant," she said. "First on the list is the legend. It was the goddess Odina that gave Merthia the gift to possess the bodies of her female descendants. Perhaps it's only Odina that can take it away? Merthia's spirit is said to roam the earth looking for revenge, but now she knows that you're here why hasn't she killed you? Her first victims were cats but she hasn't bothered your aunt's cats. There's the pentagram—a symbol of magic, good fortune, and protection, so why was Winston trying to bury it? Merthia said that this cottage was built on sacred ground but was it sacred to her people or to her? If Mrs. Tilly is who you think she is we'd better stay as far away from her as we can, but if she's just a wise old witch then she could be of great help to us, and we have to find out who this malevolent spirit is. We can call on the friendly goddess you saw in your vision for help and on Mary Eliss of course. But whatever we do, whatever ritual we perform, it's going the have to be done in the woodlot. It was there that it started and it will be there that it will have to end."

I shuddered at the thought of going back into that dark haunted forest. "Whatever it takes. Just figure out a spell or exorcism of some kind and I'll do it. " I sighed. "All that you've come up with so far is more questions."

"I told you it takes time."

"But we're running out of time, Skye. Any day now she could come through that door and..." The door sprang open. My gut clenched.

"'Ellow m' luvs. Sorry to bother ya'; thought ya' might like a little bit of my wassail."

She was carrying a tin tray with two cups and a plate full of gingersnap biscuits on it. I felt badly that we'd left her to sit alone in the other room. I put down my glass of wine and took the tray from her. "Thank you, Auntie. Why don't you get another cup and join us?"

"Can't, not now luv, m' Coronation Street's on the telly." She glanced at Skye. "Best cover up, luv. I'm turning the 'eat down and ya' showing all ya' naughty bits in that flimsy thing."

I could feel the tickle of laughter at the back of my

throat, trying desperately to escape. Skye put the pad of paper over her mouth.

Auntie turned just as she was exiting the door. I squeezed my lips as tight as I could to stop myself from laughing. "There's a spotted dick in the kitchen if you want some," she said as she closed the door. That did it! I couldn't restrain it any more; Skye lowered the paper and together, we rolled up in laughter, holding our sides and wiping the tears from our eyes.

"A spotted dick in the kitchen?" Skye teased, through her chuckles and tears. "That's for you, Fletch, as you now know I don't like dicks, especially not spotted ones."

I held my hand between my legs, while I laughed uncontrollably. "Shut up. I'm going to pee myself if you don't stop. Spotted dick is a cake made with raisins and suet. Now get some clothes on and stop showing your naughty parts." We broke out in another bout of laughter. It was as if things were normal between us. Just two best friends with no secrets, having a laugh at someone else's expense, as we often did. We had the same sense of humor, but we weren't cruel; we'd would never laugh at someone in front of their faces or make fun of a person's disability, and I knew that even if Auntie could hear us she'd never dream that we were laughing at the things she'd said. She was under the assumption that everyone understood her lingo, although for the life of me I never could fathom how she could think that.

The wind outside was howling, rattling the window latches and pushing its way through the cracks in the doors. I snuggled under Auntie's cozy patchwork blanket and yawned. The warm spicy flavor of the wassail, on top of the wine that I'd consumed before, was making me sleepy. "Do you have enough information to get started?" I asked Skye. She smiled, nodded, grabbed her towel and pad of paper, and said, "Good night, Fletch", in a cheery, tone. The bouncy steps of Skye's bare feet prancing up the attic stairs echoed her high spirits. Winston followed behind like a faithful dog. He had been sitting beside her the whole evening, his fluffy head and strange eyes looking at me, then her, then back again, as we spoke. I could have sworn he understood our conversation and was taking in every word. How can she go up there alone? I asked myself. To sleep in that eerie room all by herself, all night long. Does she have no sense of fear? *What sort of person would allow her friend to take such a risk?* I ignored my inner critic, bent down, pulled the metal rod at the bottom of the couch, and unfolded my makeshift bed. I couldn't possibly spend the night with her now, now that I knew what she was. The thread that bound us had been cut.

I climbed into my bed, burrowed beneath the covers, and sank my head into the pile of plump pillows. I couldn't get the picture of her and Belinda out of my head. Was Belinda bisexual and genuinely attracted to Skye or was she manipulating her, trying to win her trust to get to me or prove that I was delusional? A sound broke my thoughts, a loud thud coming from the ceiling, coming from the attic room! Something scurried across the floor, followed by the stomp, stomp of heavy footsteps, a piercing hiss like that of a large cat and then a pitiful yelp. Oh my God! "Skye!"

I threw off the blankets and flew out of the door. I raced through the dark passage and up the foreboding attic stairs, the terrifying sounds of a tortured animal getting louder and louder, ringing in my head, fear running through my veins like a fast stream of icy water. I held my breath and flung open the heavy wooden door. Silence.

The room was bathed in a soft light coming from the moonlit window. I gazed at the dark shadowy shapes of the furniture from the safety of the open door. Skye's petite form was tucked neatly under the bedcovers; her heavy breathing and odd snort were the only audible sounds, but through the hush I could sense the voices of the long dead residents, their agonizing cries seething through the walls.

I couldn't leave her there without checking for anything suspicious. I flipped on the light switch. Winston rose and stretched from his nest at the end of the bed. Skye was still. My gaze wandered around the room. Everything was in its place, except for Annabella. I crept around the room searching for the missing doll. Perhaps Auntie had taken it, but why? It was Mary Eliss's doll and had never left this room, as far as I knew. I crouched on all fours beside the bed and lifted the blanket that draped over the edge, to take a look underneath. Nothing. Just as I drew my head up, the bed squeaked. Skye bolted upright. She screamed! I screamed! Hand over her heart and mouth agape, Skye threw back her head and roared with laughter. I laughed along with her. "You scared me to death, you freak! What are you doing in here?"

I dropped down beside her on the edge of the bed. "I heard a noise coming from up here, footsteps and hissing and yelping, like some sort of animal."

A frown creased the skin between her brows as she peered around the room, then she shrugged. "Whatever it was, it's gone now."

"The doll's missing," I said.

She slid her hand under the blankets and pulled Annabella from beneath the sheets. "You mean this doll."

I grinned. "You took her to bed with you? Aren't you too old for that?"

"No, she was in here when I got into bed. I thought maybe you put her there."

"Why would I do that?" I thought for a moment. "That happened to me the first time I came here. I found her in the bed but no one had put her there."

"Mary Eliss must have, or the doll climbed in by herself. This was Mary Eliss's bed and the doll most likely slept in here with her. Annabella was probably lonely," Skye said, in a matter-of-fact way. I wasn't about to dispute any paranormal activity no matter how ludicrous it seemed, not after everything I had experienced here.

"I don't want you to stay up here. I can't sleep while you're up here alone."

She smiled a warm and gentle smile. It was not an ordinary friend to friend smile. She lifted up the blanket. "Then join me."

I tuned my head. "No, you come downstairs. You can

sleep in the parlor with me on the floor. The cushions from the pull-out couch are quite comfortable I've slept on them before."

"I was just joking, Fletch, and that sounds more like a command than an invitation."

"You'll get no invitations or propositions from me, Skye." *That wasn't nice.* What was I saying? What was I thinking? Was I mad at her for being a lesbian? Had my dad's narrow views or my mom's conservative, Catholic upbringing rubbed off on me and left traces of prejudiced residue in a corner of my mind? Or was I just annoyed that she evoked some feelings in me that I never knew I had.

I turned to her. She was gathering her papers and clothes lethargically, wearing a grim expression on her face.

"I'm sorry, Jenks. I'm just having a hard time getting my head around all of this."

She looked at me sympathetically. "I know, my being gay has just added another stressful item to your lengthy list and you're really mad at me for not telling you."

I wanted to hug her but I couldn't. "Let's just forget about all of that for now and concentrate on getting rid of the curse." She held her hand up to give me a high-five as she passed me with an armload of stuff. "By the way," I said, as I followed her down the stairs, "I found out who Annie is."

"Really."

"She was Auntie's Mom, and I think she was a white witch, although Auntie would never admit to it."

Skye's eyes gleamed. "That's great! We can summon her

spirit and ask for her help."

"At least I think she was a white witch, and not the other kind," I said.

"I guess we'll find out."

Oh whoopee.

* * * *

I woke early the next morning. My throat was dry from the alcohol and I was craving my morning fix of orange juice and coffee. I reached for my terry housecoat and wrapped it around me, pushed my feet into the warm velvet slippers that Auntie had bought me and insisted I wear; then I tiptoed past Skye who was curled up in a ball on the cushioned floor and strolled into the kitchen. Auntie was still in bed and the cottage was hushed—a pleasing hush that I hadn't felt for awhile, as if something pleasant was about to happen.

I was going to see Jonathan today and I couldn't wait to hold him and feel his manly body next to mine. I poured myself a large glass of orange juice, filled the coffee pot, and went to the window. Snow! Through the frosted window pane I could see the still, white yard bathed in silver moonlight, with a black, diamond-studded backdrop. Delicate, intricately-petalled snowflakes drifted in front of the window, like the heads of tiny white daisies. I felt a surge of excitement, like a little child anticipating all the fun things she would do on her first snowy day; build a snowman, make snow angels, go tobogganing. Today we were going to look for a Christmas tree. I couldn't wait to see what Merryweather Lodge would look like in her new winter attire.

Auntie got up just after I did and demanded I sit down while she cooked me a hearty breakfast of eggs, beans, tomatoes, and vegetarian sausage, with a plate full of toast on the side. She wouldn't eat breakfast herself because it wasn't the "proper" time but she drank three cups of tea and polished off a plate full of digestive biscuits. I told her that Jonathan was coming by and we were going to search for a Christmas tree. She asked if we were taking Skye and said it wouldn't be nice to leave her behind. I had to agree but I wasn't sure how I was going to tell Jonathan as he wanted to spend time with me alone. And then Auntie said, "Lindy's going too. Jonny promised he'd take 'er. They're goin' in them there woods, I think."

How could he have decided that, without asking me? And the dreaded woodlot, with Belinda. Was he crazy?

Chapter 14

But Auntie wasn't sure if Jonathan was going to be able to make it. There were no snowplows to dig us out or trucks to salt the narrow icy roads out here, and when it snowed you either took a chance on the slippery, heavy laden roads or you hunkered down and stayed put until it melted. I opened the back door, sucked in the crisp air, and feasted my eyes on the perfect Christmas card scene before me. Sam stuck his nose out of the door and then retreated to his warm mat in the corner of the kitchen.

The morning sun reflected off the pristine landscape. It was as though Mother Nature had taken her spatula, spread pure white icing over the countryside, and sprinkled it with glittering candy. It looked deliciously festive and enchanting. I was just about to close the door when I spotted something in the distance coming along the snow-covered country lane toward the cottage. As it got closer I could see that it was a tractor, an old fashioned tractor with rust patches, wide meaty wheels, and a huge steering wheel; the driver was bundled up in a heavy winter coat with a black balaclava and a thick woolen scarf wrapped around his head. "Jonathan?" I put my hand over my mouth and compressed my lips to quash a chuckle. He was alone. No Belinda. Thank God.

Auntie yelled at me from the kitchen. "Shut that bloody door. Yer' letting all that cold air in 'ere. It's cold enough to freeze the thingamabobs off a brass monkey. 'Ave a little common sense, m' luv."

Auntie never minced her words. "Okay, but come and see this first."

She came to the door with her arms wrapped around her chest, shivering, her false teeth chattering, overstating her discomfort, as she often did.

I pointed to the odd looking spectacle coming towards us. "Just take a look at this."

She squinted and stuck her head out the door. "Who the 'ell's that?"

"It's Jonathan."

She put her hanky to her mouth and started to giggle. "Well, I'll be blowed. It's little Jonny, bless 'im' and 'e's brought old Betsy. Been around for a long time that old tractor 'as. But where's Lindy?" Auntie nudged me inside and closed the door. "Ya'll catch a death of cold standing 'ere, ya' will. Let's go put on the kettle, make 'im a nice cupper."

Something stirred inside me when I heard him walk through the door. I went to greet him and helped him remove his bulky winter clothing. He slipped his arms around my waist and kissed me soundly. His lips were dry and cold but they warmed my heart and tantalized my senses as if they were made of fire. "I've missed you," he whispered, as he snuggled his face into my neck. The twinge and needy sensation between my legs reminded me of how much I wanted him, how much I loved him.

"Come in 'ere Jonny, sit yer' self down, take a load off," Auntie said as she loaded the table with scones, crumpets, jams, butter, and thick Devonshire cream, along with a pot of freshly brewed tea.

"How was the highway this morning?" I asked

"I decided to drive from the city yesterday evening after work, as soon as it started to snow. I knew I might not make it if I waited until today. They were forecasting snow all night."

"You were at your mom's all night and you didn't call?" My tone was steeped in accusation.

"I was working on an art project with Belinda and I thought you'd be busy with Skye."

"Did I hear my name mentioned?" Skye came bursting through the door full of "vim and vinegar" as Auntie would say. She was back to her high-spirited self, smiling and emitting her wonderful lively energy. She brushed Jonathan's shoulder with her hand. "Hi, prince charming, are you here to take your beautiful princess and her lady in waiting into the dark kingdom?"

Jonathan was not impressed by her playful wit and I knew he'd wanted to spend some time alone with me. He smiled awkwardly and gave an impatient shrug, suggesting he didn't know what she was going on about.

"She's talking about the woodlot," I said, "We're supposed to be getting a Christmas tree today, but I think we should get it somewhere else. I really don't want to go back to that place."

Auntie was standing at the sink, up to her elbows in soapy dishwater. She kept taking quick, discreet glances over her shoulder, making sure that she took in every word that was said.

Skye interrupted the silence, saying, "I thought you were bringing your sister along."

Now where did she hear that? I never told her, unless Auntie did.

"She's not well today; besides there's only enough room on that tractor for one."

"What's wrong with her?" Skye asked anxiously, as she plunked herself down in the chair beside him.

He gave her a 'what business is it of yours' look and said, "She's a little depressed, must be the medication."

"Poor thing, she would 'ave loved to 'elp pick out a Christmas tree and I was going to 'ave 'er decorate it too," Auntie said, as she left the room, drying her hands on her checkered apron.

"She's not a child; she's eighteen, for goodness sake." The disdain in my voice was obvious and I wanted to take my words back as soon as I'd said them.

Skye rolled her eyes at me, and then leaned across the table. Her gaze shifted from Jonathan to me and back again and then she whispered, "So, are you guys ready to try to banish Merthia? I've come up with a spell that might work and I thought being as though we're going into the woodlot today anyway we might give it a try." She straightened in her seat, folded her hands on top of the table, and waited for a response.

Jonathan raised a sardonic eyebrow, and then bit into a thick piece of scone; the strawberry jam and cream oozed out from the middle. He lifted his scolding eyes to meet mine, indicating that he had wanted me all to himself today. He might have planned something romantic, a walk in the snow hand in hand, stealing the odd kiss, making out by the barn on a blanket perhaps. Whatever it was it did not include Skye, spells, or Merthia, that was for sure.

I dabbed the cream from the side of his mouth with a paper napkin. "Today is as good a time as any. It's worth a try."

"I thought we were going to get a Christmas tree."

"We can do that as well," Skye said, hastily. "I'm going home in a few days and I'd like to know that Emily is safe before I go."

"And I'm never going to be safe here as long as the unearthly woman's around looking for revenge."

Jonathan raised his hands. "Okay, you guys win. I guess we're going ghost hunting."

Skye grinned, stood, and pushed back her chair. "I'll go gather my things." She scuttled out of the door wearing an expression of cheerful expectancy, as if she were getting ready for a party. But this would be no party.

Jonathan took another huge bite into his messy scone and said, through the crumbs between his teeth, and in a grumpy tone, "I thought we were going to spend some time together, just the two of us?"

I handed him a napkin and said, injecting a good dose of sarcasm into my tone, "I'm sorry but I couldn't leave Skye behind and you were going to bring your sister along, without even telling me, weren't you?"

"But I didn't, did I?" His shirt was unbuttoned at the top, exposing his prominent Adams apple. The more annoyed he became the faster it moved.

"No, only because she was ill and you couldn't get her on the tractor."

"She's not ill, just depressed, and she pleaded with me to bring her but I thought it was best not to. I know you don't like her and she seems to be somewhat obsessed with your friend."

"Obsessed?"

"She's been drawing sketches of her and has them plastered all over her room." His chin sank. "Some of them are quite provocative."

If only you knew. "What does your mom say?"

"She was upset but she wouldn't make her take them down. Whatever Belinda wants she gets. Mom's always been like that with her. She's a little spoiled, I'm afraid."

Spoiled, manipulative, and vicious! I reached over and touched his hand. "She'll be okay. It's just going to take time."

Lots of time and a miracle.

He ran the napkin over his mouth. "I hope you're right."

Skye's colorful backpack was hanging over her shoulder, full of spell-casting paraphernalia. Her head and neck were wrapped in a red hand-knitted hat and scarf, and she was wearing a pair of Auntie's fur-lined boots, which were just the right size for her small feet. Her fake fur coat was ankle length. I bundled up, while Jonathan went outside to fetch the rope and axe. Then I went into the sitting room to say good-bye to Auntie.

I hesitated in the doorway and watched as she sat in her favorite chair with a hankie on her lap, peeling an orange. It must have been tough as she was struggling to dig her nails into its leathery skin; finally she stripped the orange, broke off segments, and bit into its flesh, sending a shower of juice all over her weathered face. Beside her sat a basket of wool and half finished hats and mitts she'd been knitting for the local children's charity. Dear Auntie Em. What would I do without her? She was more than an aunt; she was like a mother to me. She fulfilled my need for nurturing, acceptance, and unconditional love. How many years had she heard the un-earthly cries of the cottage's past inhabitants, I wondered. And how much had she been tormented by the hideous creature that haunts this place, searching for me? She'd never tell; she kept it all inside, hidden in a secluded, dark corner of her mind. But why? I couldn't let it go on any longer. I knew I had to rid this place of its haunting hellish vibes and restore its heavenly aura, before it was too late. "We're leaving now, Auntie.

We'll bring you the biggest and prettiest tree we can find."

"Come 'ere luv, I 'ave something for ya." She pulled the pendant out from under her blouse, and drew it over her head. "Put this on and keep it on and ya,' wrap up warm now, put on your wellies, and don't you go too far in them there woods. Do you hear me?"

I dropped the pendant over my head and tucked it into my sweater. "I hear you, Auntie Em. Don't worry, we'll be fine." *I hope.*

Skye had insisted that I participate in her morning ritual of yoga and meditation and my legs were a little stiff for sitting in a lotus position for so long but my mind was clear and quiet. We set off, tools in hand, into the winter wonderland, three troopers on a mission: to battle an evil entity that had plagued this area for centuries.

The air was crisp. I shaded my eyes from the bright sun as it reflected off the sparkling, virgin snow, which stretched out in front of us, untouched, except for the odd patterned tracks of rabbits and birds. It invited us to make our mark. We trudged through the meadow's heavy while blanket in relative silence. The only sound was the crunch of the snow under the soles of our boots. Jonathan reached for my hand and kissed the back of my glove. Skye sniffed and rolled her eyes, as her short legs tried to keep pace. What's wrong with her? I asked myself. She can't be jealous; she was not attracted to men and even if she was she wouldn't fancy Jonathan. She had made it clear that she didn't care for him and I suspected that the feeling was mutual, but I couldn't understand why. I had never known Skye to dislike anyone and if she did, there would have to be a very good reason. I decided that I would talk to her about it tonight. If we made it out of the dreaded woodlot alive, that is.

Jonathan suddenly bent down, scooped up a big lump of snow and began rolling it between his fingers. I knew what was coming. I let go of his hand and ducked out of the way. He hurled the snowball at me, just missing my head. I bent down, grabbed a handful and pretended to throw it at him, but instead turned and flung it at Skye. She couldn't resist; she slid the backpack off her shoulders and joined in the fun. We ran, laughed, lay on our backs, spread our arms to make angels wings, and bombarded each other with snowballs. We had no inhibitions, no hostility; we were just three young people messing around and having fun together. Until! "Emily. Emily…we're waiting for you." I froze. "Did you hear that?"

They stood motionless and listened intently. "I didn't hear anything," Skye said. Jonathan shrugged his shoulders.

I knew where it was coming from and looked towards the woodlot. It loomed in the distance like the dark palace of an evil queen, calling and daring anyone to try and penetrate its fortress walls. Calling me, daring me to enter.

Chapter 15

"It's time," I said, as I brushed the snow off my coat with my wet mitts. I could feel the woodlot's mysterious pull beckoning me. Skye picked up her backpack and flung it over her shoulder. Jonathan clapped his hands together to get rid of the excess snow that clung to his gloves, and then he stretched, inhaling the cold air deep into his lungs. I could tell he was trying to defuse the tension he felt in his gut. I was sure he remembered only too well the terrifying ordeal he encountered the last time he ventured into this dark sinister place.

We trudged, side by side, each new footprint in the pristine white carpet taking us closer to our grim destination. The celestial blue sky met with the white landscape in a beautiful contrast of color. Ice crystals floated around us like fairy dust. The air was as crisp and sweet as chilled wine, but it was laced with apprehension. When we reached the entrance of the woods, Skye stood perfectly still, drew in a deep wheezy breath, and stared fixedly at the majestic trees towering above us, her eyebrows raised and her mouth half open. "I can feel it, calling to us, pulling us in." A shiver passed through me. "It's waiting for us," she said, in a calm, unruffled voice. *But you don't know what horror lies inside its treed walls.*

I glanced at Jonathan. He was watching Skye and shaking his head. The tip of his nose and cheeks were red. "Shall we cut down the tree first?" I asked him."

"Oh, they're not going to like that," Skye said.

Jonathan sniffed and pulled the axe and rope out of his deep coat pocket. "It's you that doesn't like it." He was right about that; she had been complaining and giving us lectures about chopping down trees ever since Auntie suggested it. "Why do people feel entitled to cut down such a noble and enduring specimen expose them to an unnatural environ-ment, dress them up for a few days, then dispose of them without any consideration?" she asked. I told her that she knew I was all for saving the environment, ecology and such and so was Jonathan, but one tree from a massive grove of ev-ergreens wasn't going to make a whole lot of difference and besides, nobody put up artificial trees out here. Auntie would get her tree even if she had to chop it down herself.

Jonathan strolled around the perimeter of the woodlot; looking for a perfect tree. Like green ladies in different shades of frilly dresses, wrapped in luxurious white cloaks, they waited. Which one would be chosen for the Christmas festivi-ties? Beside and behind the evergreens, huge oak, chestnut and birch trees stretched out their bare branches, casting blue shadows on the blanket of pure white snow. "How about this one?" he asked, as he shook the snow off the boughs of a pretty Scotch pine. It was just the right size, with thick, even branches. Skye was collecting pinecones and shoving them into her backpack. "Do we have to?" she asked.

"We have to," he said, swinging the axe and driving the blade, with brute force, into the thick bark of the tree.

Skye squealed. I cringed. Jonathan rolled his eyes and tied a length of rope around its rough stem. He placed the rope and axe beside it. "We'll leave it here and collect it on the way out. We should be able to follow our tracks back here," he said, shaking the snow and pine needles off the front of his coat. *If we ever get out of here, that is.*

We entered the portal of the dreaded woodlot. The thicket was smeared with white frost; naked bushes glistened. "It's unusual for us to have so much snow this time of year. Does it remind you girls of home?" Jonathan asked, breaking the silence and attempting to make us feel more at ease.

"No, there's more of it back home, it's much dryer, and it stays for six months." My voice was hollow. I couldn't mask my fear and I wasn't up for small talk. Our boots scrunched over the frozen, snow-packed twigs and pine cones, as we trudged though the wintery forest, in search of the massive oak tree where our ritual had to take place. Flurries of snow drifted down from the upper branches of the leafless giants and landed on our heads. Jonathan led the way. "You sure you're going in the right direction?" I asked him, as I stepped into the dent of his large footprints. "This doesn't look familiar to me and I'm sure we entered the woods in a different spot before."

"It's the right way." He paused for a moment. "I'll never forget it." Skye followed close behind me, in silent determination, her little legs working hard to keep up.

What am I doing? I asked myself. I had sworn I'd never come back to this hellish place again. I was almost decapitated the last time we were here. Now I was going back to the very same place where I had to swallow the sour, sickly, gut-wrenching taste of impending death. What if Skye's spell didn't work? What if we all died? A crow swooped down from a tall tree, crying "caw, caw," fracturing my thoughts and making me cower. Someone or something was here. I could feel it.

"It's just over here," Jonathan announced. Fear mounted inside me as we entered the familiar clearing. The giant oak stood, proud and steadfast, an icon of past generations, its gnarled bare trunk baring the weight of years of torture and carnage.

Skye nudged past us and marched with haste towards the massive oak tree. Her face was lit with wonder. She took off one of her mittens and placed her hand on the rough trunk of the ancient tree, closed her eyes and sucked in a long, deep breath. "I can feel its life force, steeped in history, shrouded in secrets. It has witnessed many terrible things over the centuries. It is tired and wants the bloodshed to stop." She took another deep breath. "It wants me to know that we are not alone. Someone is watching us."

Her! The acrid feeling in the pit of my stomach intensified. I wiped the cold sweat from my brow and stretched my hands, trying hard to break away the tension. "Ask it who's watching?"

"Good grief, Emily, it's a tree. Can't we just get on with it?" Jonathan grumbled. He shuffled his feet in the snow, hands behind his back, wearing a grim expression.

Skye opened her eyes and gave Jonathan a dirty look, turned to me, and asked, "Where's the sacrificial altar?"

As if drawn by an invisible, dark, magnetic force I went directly to the slab of gray rock, now only a small portion of its original self; the sacrificial altar that I had seen in my visions. I started to brush the snow off its surface with a thick twig. Suddenly a painful, burning current ran up my arm, as if I had put my fingers on a live wire. I dropped the stick and shot back, rubbing my arm to rid myself of whatever had touched me.

"Bad vibes," Skye said, in a matter-of-fact way. She removed the spell-casting paraphernalia from her backpack and laid it in the snow beside the rock. Jonathan was pacing back and forth, his arms wrapped around his chest, pausing every once in a while to glace over his shoulder or gaze into the dense bush. "Are you okay?" he asked. I nodded my head.

Skye placed a metal dish on the altar and filled it with dried sage, lavender, rosemary and a bay leaf, and then she drizzled a little juniper oil on top. She picked up the bag of sea salt. "Come close," she commanded. "I'm going to make the protective circle now." We stood beside the slab of rock while she sprinkled the salt from the bag to make a circle around us. "You don't go out of the circle, even if something or someone tries to lure you. Is that clear?" she asked, putting a warning bite into her tone.

Jonathan frowned and then said, sarcastically, "Yes, your majesty."

"She's just making sure we know what to do," I said, in her defense. "Skye, you do remember that Jonathan and I have been here and done this before?" I was getting cold, nervous, and impatient. "We just want to get it over with."

"It can't be rushed," she said as she placed thick beeswax candles around the perimeter of the circle and two small black ones beside the dish on the altar. She handed Jonathan a box of matches. "Make yourself useful and light the candles. I will draw the energy from them." He snatched the box out of her hand. *What was with these two? I'd never known Skye to be rude and impertinent to anyone and Jonathan made it obvious that she got under his skin. They were two of the most important people in my life; they didn't have to agree with each other, but I wanted them to get along.* Skye took a piece of paper and pen from her coat pocket and wrote the name 'Merthia' in big bold letters. "This spell is supposed to be performed during a waning moon but it might work anyway."

"Might! Jenks, is this going to work or not?"

Jonathan started to shake his head. "Don't tell me we've come all this way and brought all this crap here for nothing."

Skye walked over to him, folded her arms, lifted her chin and glared at him. "Look, I'm not doing this for you." She gave me a warm glance. "I'm doing it for Emily. If you think you can do any better," she moved aside and pointed to the altar, "go ahead, give it a try."

I'd had enough. "Would you two please stop bickering with one another? You're acting like a couple of school kids."

Jonathan went to light the candles around the protective circle. Skye marched back to the altar, knelt down on the snow, set a match to ignite the black candles and dish of herbs, and then turned to me and asked, "Can I have the pentagram, Fletch, please?"

It was nestled against my chest, giving me a subtle sense of security and I didn't want to give it up. "How did you know I had it?"

"I asked your aunt to give it to you."

"You did what?"

"She knows what's going on here, Fletch. She's not as naive as you might think. When I asked her if she'd let you wear her star today, she lowered her head and said, "Bob's yer' uncle, luv. She'll be needing it.""

"She needs it just as much as I do, back at that cottage, all alone."

"She'll be fine. We know that the pentagram belonged to Merthia. It will be helpful in casting the spell." Skye stuck out her hand.

I opened the top buttons on my coat and drew the pendant out from under my sweater. "I don't feel safe here without it," I muttered.

Jonathan threw the dead match onto the snowy ground and moved towards us. "Why can't she wear it, if she doesn't feel safe without it?"

Skye ignored him and laid the pendant on the altar. "I'm ready," she said as she stood over the altar and held her hands out for us to hold. "Do not move from here, do not break the circle, and follow my instructions," she ordered.

We stretched out our arms and grasped each other's hands. The cool air was thick with candle smoke, the aroma of dried herbs and juniper oil. The woods behind and all around us echoed tribulation as the words 'you're not alone' rang in my head. We bowed our heads and closed our eyes. "Say these words after me," Skye spoke in a deep voice, with staid calmness. "We are protected by the might of the divine goddess of day and night. So mote it be. Thrice around the circle bound, evil sink into the ground. So mote it be. Blessed be the sacred tree and the goddess Helgara we call on thee, assist us now and set her soul free. So mote it be." Skye drew her hand away from mine. I grabbed it back. "It's okay," she whispered "I have to do something." She took the piece of paper with Merthia's name on it and the pendant, stretched out her arms and held them up to the heavens, as if she was about to take flight.. "Earth, water, wind and fire burn this spirit within the hour. Bond her evil to the ground, never again to be found. So mote it be. So mote it be. So mote it be." She lowered her arms and threw the piece of paper into the flames of the dish of burning herbs. The fire flared and sparks flew, as if it were angry at having to digest such a horrid morsel. Then the flame died.

There was a stillness, a silence, the kind of silence that tenses your nerves, as if a bomb was about to go off. Something moved in the woods. A branch cracked. Bushes rustled. My heart started to race. Someone was coming! Was it her? "Did you..." the words got caught in my throat, "...hear that?"

"Come out. Show yourself!" Skye hollered, into the bushes, as if she were calling to a naughty child. Out from beside a cluster of trees stepped the hard-faced Maud McArthur, the mysterious Mrs. Tilly, and between them the unpredictable Belinda. They were wrapped in heavy winter clothes and black rubber boots.

"Mum. What are you doing here?" Jonathan blurted out as he started to walk towards them.

I screamed, "Stay in the protective circle!" as I grabbed him by the coat and pulled him back.

"She's right," Skye said. "It might be a trick. They might not be who they appear to be."

Maud stepped towards the circle. "I came looking for you, son." She looked over her shoulder at Belinda. "Your sister wanted to look for a Christmas tree. We met Mrs Tilly along the way and she told us where you were." *How did she know where we were?* Maud took her gaze away from him and stared solemnly at me, her chin raised slightly, her lips drawn. "What is this? Teaching my son black magic, are you?"

"Not black magic," I latched on to her eyes, "white magic!" Then I stretched my neck and glared at Belinda. My chin quivered. "We've just cast a banishing spell."

Jonathan stepped forward. "It's okay, Mum. We were just messing around, having some fun." He looked at Skye, then at me. "But we're done now, right, ladies?"

Skye walked towards her. "Mrs. McArthur, I can explain. I belong to an amateur drama group back home and I am performing in a play as soon as I get back. It's called 'Witches in the Woods'. I asked Emily and Jonathan if they would help me practice. This is the perfect environment and I didn't think we'd be doing any harm." Belinda had her hand over her mouth, giggling behind her fingers. "I can go and get you the script if you'd like to see it?" *Good one, Skye.*

"That's all right, dear. I believe you." *What? You gullible old bat.* "You can put this stuff away now." Mrs McArthur pointed to the salt circle, with a look of disdain. "And get rid of this."

Mrs. Tilly took Belinda's arm, came towards us, and stood next to Maud. Every muscle in my body cramped. Something wasn't right.

"Why don't you step into the circle?" I asked, testing them. Belinda started to shake her head violently. Her mother slapped her on the arm. No one spoke; we just stood there and waited. "Come on," I beckoned to them, "if you are who you appear to be, it shouldn't be a problem."

Chapter 16

Mrs. Tilly smiled sweetly, and then said in a calm but scolding voice, "This is a dangerous game that you young people are playing. You have no idea what you're doing." Maud stood close to her, shoulders back and chin raised, exposing the hanging, wrinkled skin that looked like a turkeys wattle. She was surveying me with disdain. I matched her hostility with an icy glare. Belinda was on the other side of Mrs. Tilly. She lifted her hand and wiggled her fingers at Skye. Belinda looked ill. Her complexion was pasty and there were black shadows under her hooded, dull, gray-green-brown eyes. The only other person that I had known with eyes that strange color had been Uncle Reg. She lifted her eyelids and pinned her gaze on mine. Jabbed by a sudden thrust of panic I stepped back, arms to my sides, my spine rigid, every muscle in my body tensed. I felt like I had been nailed to an invisible wall.

I blinked and gave my head a quick shake, to rid myself of her hidden grip. Then I straightened my shoulders and crooked my fingers. "Come over here, inside the circle. I dare you!" Mrs. Tilly linked her arm through Maud's and grabbed Belinda's hand. "Come on, dears. Let's leave these young people to their games. I'm getting cold standing here." She smiled at Belinda and spoke to her as if she were a child. "Never mind, dear, I can help you find a tree."

"I'll see you back at the house," Jonathan called in a dull voice, as they turned to leave. His face wore a bewildered expression.

Belinda snapped her head around and turned her sharp eyes on me. Her lip twitched and rolled up at one side in a snarl, like a vicious dog. I shuddered. It was a warning, I was sure of that.

I went directly to the altar and grabbed my pendant, put it around my neck, and said a silent prayer: a prayer for help, for safety, and for peace. I prayed for a miracle. Then I helped blow out the candles and gather the paraphernalia. "Guess this was all just a waste of time," I mumbled.

Jonathan dragged his lower lip between his teeth. "And now I have my mother to answer to."

Skye flinched as she hauled her heavy backpack over her shoulder. "Now wait a minute, you two. That's not fair. I gave it my best shot, and how do you know it didn't work? The spell was complete." She stopped and drew a deep breath. "Except for one thing."

"What's that?" I asked eagerly.

She dipped her chin and slid her hands into her damp woolen mitts. "I was supposed to summon her host."

"You did," I said. I lifted my foot to step over the protective circle and hesitated. Inside, my sixth sense, that tiny voice that I had come to rely on deep with my gut, was whispering, "It's not safe out there." Jonathan scuffed the toe of his boot in the salt.

"No!" I screamed at him. "Don't do that. Keep the circle intact." I bent over and rearranged the salt with my hand to make sure there were no gaps, just incase we needed to retreat and come back to the safety of the circle. As I stood up I noticed that there were no prints in the snow where the women had stood. I stopped and scanned the area. There were no footprints, no trace that anyone had been there.

Jonathan turned. "What are you doing?" he asked.

"I'm looking for their footprints." My voice was shaky. "There are no prints in the snow." I glared at Skye, then back at Jonathan. "What do you think that means?"

Jonathan shook his head lazily, gave an impatient shrug, and then trudged ahead. But I could tell by the worried look on his face and the way his gaze searched anxiously for footprints that he was asking himself the same questions I was asking.

Skye walked up to me, hooked her arm into mine, drew me close, and whispered in my ear, "It means that that they aren't what they appear to be."

I bent my head down and put my mouth close to her ear. "Then what are they?"

She cleared her throat and said, "Deviant spirits." I gripped her arm. "I don't think your Mrs. Tilly is as sinister as you think she is, but she's definitely not of this world. I didn't sense anything horrid from her though." She lowered her voice. "But the vibes I get from Jonathan's mother were pure evil. I felt it when I shook hands with her."

I bit into my lip. "What about Belinda?"

She sighed. "I still think that deep down inside her there is a kind and gentle spirit, but you're right, evil has control over her. She looks sick and pale, as if something is sucking the life force right out of her and I've never sensed so much loathing and hate." She squeezed my arm, tenderly.

"Hate for me?"

"Yes, for you, Fletch." She raised her chin and looked into my eyes. "I'm not going to let anything happen to you."

"Perhaps, if Belinda gets sicker and weaker she won't be of any use to Merthia anymore," I said, in a hopeful tone.

"Perhaps," Skye answered, in a voice edged with regret.

Jonathan was a few yards ahead of us, following our previous tracks. His head was down and he was carrying a gnarled stick in his hand, which he used to push his way through the tangled bushes. The crunch, crunch from the thick soles of his boots, in the snow, echoed his dreary mood. I wondered if he could hear what we were whispering and if he wasn't asking himself the same questions. His head must be full of questions. I wanted to run up to him, embrace him, and tell him that everything was going to be okay. But was it?

Skye's arm was linked tightly around mine and drew me in to the left side her body, so she was snug up against me, as if she was afraid of me breaking away and escaping her grip.

She dragged her feet and struggled a little from the weight of her heavy backpack, but both Jonathan and I had asked if we could carry it for her and she had declined. The tip of her nose and high cheek bones were daubed with red.

The frosted, bare-branched giants glared down at us; their crooked leafless fingers, when disturbed, showered us with the odd sprinkling of snow. A maze of dead bushes and brambles wrapped in white cloaks lay on either side of our path. I breathed in the frosty air and the dense silence of the woods as I tramped through the snow. I couldn't wait to get out of that eerie place and get back to the cottage where at least sometimes I felt safe.

All of a sudden I felt a gust of icy air. My body tensed. I stopped. Something moved in the bushes. The air came alive with tribulation. "Did you hear that?" Skye nodded her head. Jonathan kept going. "Jonathan," I called. He stopped and turned. "Something's out there." The sound of rustling bushes and crunching snow broke through the thick silence.

Jonathan motioned us to keep going. "Let's get out of here," he said, picking up the pace. We caught up to him and followed in his tracks, with haste. He pulled back a frozen branch, causing it to lash across my face.

"Ow!" I yelped.

"I'm sorry," he mumbled. "Hey, maybe it's just my mum and sister, looking for a tree."

"And maybe it's 'her'!" I grumbled.

"Mum, is that you?" His words hung in the frosty air. No one answered.

"Shut up, Jonathan," Skye spat. "Now it knows where we are."

Did she say, 'it'? I freed my arm from Skye's hold and wove my way through the woods as fast as I could. I tripped on a fallen branch, lost my balance, but caught myself before I fell.

The sound of someone tramping though the bushes towards us was getting louder. Skye was puffing and panting, and lagging behind, burdened by her cumbersome backpack, ankle-length coat, and short legs. I waited for her to catch up. "Give that bag to Jonathan," I demanded, as I tugged on the handle. "It's too heavy and it's holding you back."

She pulled back and brushed me off. "I don't need his help."

I grabbed her arm and dragged her along. "I'm not leaving you behind."

My chest ached with tension. I could feel the clutch of the dark forest around my neck, as if the trees themselves had their spindly fingers around my throat. The sound of someone coming was catching up with us. It was behind us. I could hear its heavy breathing and smell its rancid odor. A feeling of utter terror swept over me. The words rose out of my clogged throat. "Can you smell that?"

"Yes," Skye uttered as she gasped for air.

"Run!" I screamed. "It's her!" I could feel the blood surging through my veins with every heartbeat. Jonathan was in front, moving frantically, paving our way through the bush with his stick and beating down the snow with the soles of his heavy boots. Every once in a while he'd glance back to make sure we weren't too far behind. I squeezed Skye's small wrist as tightly as I could, afraid of losing my grip, as I dragged her alongside of me.

My boot caught in a root and I stumbled. I cringed as my ankle twisted. Skye reached out and tried to steady me. But it was too late. A bush rustled behind me. I felt a presence. Skye turned and let out a blood curdling scream. Jonathan came running, wide eyed and gasping. *Oh my God!* Standing only a few feet from us was the hideous creature. Her blood-spattered dress was filthy and torn, her matted hair stuck to her ashen flesh which was split and oozing with pus. She opened her thin blue lips and hissed, "Colceathrar."

I recoiled and tried to speak—swallowed and tried again. What came out was just a high pitched squeal. Skye held up her hand to silence me, dropped her backpack on the ground and pulled back her shoulders. "Don't panic," she said. Her voice was firm but laced with dread. "This poor creature will not harm us. She is possessed by an evil entity. But what she doesn't realize is that she has control, she can fight this compulsion to kill; it is not in her true nature." Skye raised her hands to the heavens. "I command you, Odina, goddess of immortal youth. Free this innocent soul from your servant's clutches."

The creature's head tipped from side to side. Her deep-set eyes burned like two green embers on the face of a scull but there was softness in her ghastly expression. Then her eyes moved from Skye's to mine. Her soft expression changed. Her eyes became roaring fires. She stretched out her long bony fingers towards me.

I wiped the cold damp sweat from my forehead and covered my face. Jonathan pulled me back and stepped in front. "It's me you want, not her. I am Golwin, the one who slaughtered you." She rushed towards us. The smell of rotting flesh and urine overpowered me. I heaved. Her unearthly hands reached out. Grabbing Jonathan's coat, she lifted him off the ground and tossed him into the bushes. My skin started to crawl. Utter fear enveloped me.

"The pentagram!" Skye screamed.

I tugged frantically at the scarf around my neck. Her cold stinking breath touched my face. I thrust my trembling hands down the neck of my sweater and pulled out the pendant, as her disgusting fingers clawed at my throat. I pressed the metal of the five-pointed star hard against the back of her hand. The pendant burned into her skin. The air reeked of burning flesh. She shot back, shaking her hand, tossing her head, spitting and hissing like a tomcat.

"Run!" Jonathan yelled as he lifted himself from the ground.

Skye grabbed her backpack, and then she stopped to look up at the wounded creature. "Fight it," she yelled at it. "It is not the real you."

"Come on, Jenks! Hurry!" My ankle was hurting. A stabbing pain shot up my leg. All I could manage was a limping half-trot but adrenaline was surging inside me and I was desperate to reach the clearing, alive. Jonathan turned and placed his strong arm under mine to help support my weight. Skye was lagging behind, but somehow I knew that the creature would not grab her or harm her. She was safe. I was the game the creature was hunting and was so desperate to slaughter.

Pinecones and packed snow crunched under the soles of our boots. But the only other unearthly sound I could hear now was that of the towering giants and dark deadfall. They seemed to be calling my name, "Emily. She's coming for you. Run Emily. Run!" I winced and covered my ears. Finally I caught a glimpse of blue sky in the clearing between the tangled branches of the snow-coved trees. "We're almost there," I mumbled to Jonathan, as I leaned into him.

"How's your foot?" he asked.

"It hurts like hell, but at least I'm alive."

I breathed a sigh of relief but my heart was still hammering behind my ribcage as we emerged from the woodlot and into the open fields of the meadow. I collapsed on the ground beside our Christmas tree. Skye fell down beside me. Jonathan stood, staring into the foreboding forest. "On your feet, ladies, we need to get out of here, now!"

Skye heaved her tired body from the ground. "We're safe out here," she said.

"We're not safe, anywhere," he replied.

"He's right," I said, "we're not safe here or anywhere, at least I'm not. Now, would one of you help me up so we can get moving?" Jonathan took my hand and pulled me to my feet. Then he picked up the heavy rope and proceeded to tie it around the trunk of the tree. We trudged though the snow-covered meadow towing our hefty Christmas tree, sore limbs and minds full of the terrifying thoughts of what we had just experienced. I leaned into Skye and asked, "Was it Belinda?"

She nodded her head. "I think so but I'm not a hundred percent sure."

"If it was, that would mean that Maud and Mrs. Tilly were in cahoots with her," I paused, "and that the spell didn't work."

She gave me another nod. "If it was her, it probably weakened her, but now, I'm afraid, she's more desperate than ever to…"

"Kill me?" Again, Skye dipped her head.

Chapter 17

Auntie was pacing the floor. "Where 'ave ya' been? I've been worried sick, I 'ave." She looked down at my foot. "Blinking heck, what 'ave ya' been and done now? Why are ya' limping? Tripped over something 'ave ya? Like a bull in a china shop ya are or 'ave ya been somewhere ya shouldn't have?" she said in a scolding tone, and all in one breath.

I felt like I had been caught with my fingers in a forbidden candy jar, but I was sure that she knew exactly where we had been and that was why she was so worried. I played along with her game. "It's nothing, I'll be fine. Sorry we were so long but we found you a lovely tree, Auntie." I took her arm and hobbled to the kitchen window, and pulled back the flimsy net curtains. "Look at it. Isn't it a beauty? We'll set it up for you in a few minutes. Just let us know where you want it."

She leaned towards me and whispered in my ear, "Don't ya' go in them there woods again, do ya' 'ear me?" *I was right, she did know.* I gave her a reassuring smile.

Skye had tore off her boots and rushed to the bathroom as soon as we came through the back door. She had been aching to go ever since we left the woodlot and she kept stopping to cross her legs and grit her teeth. I was afraid she was going to drop her pants right there in the open field, which I'm sure she would have done if we'd been alone. Jonathan was standing in front of the blazing fire picking snow pellets off his pants, tossing them into the flames, and watching them as they sputtered and hissed. He looked despondent, and confused, and was wondering, I was sure, of the implications of what he just witnessed and how his mother and sister tied into it all.

Auntie seemed to sense his downcast mood. "Come to the kitchen and 'ave a nice cupper, Jonny," she said, as she motioned to him with her hands. "It'll warm the cockles of yer' 'eart, it will. Lugging that tree all the way from them there woods must 'ave knackered ya'. Never mind, luv, Christmas will soon be 'ere."

He turned and lifted his head. His cheeks were scarlet from the heat of the fire. "Tea sounds good, and I'm fine, Mrs. Fletcher, really." But his voice was dull and troubled. Auntie tended to my foot with an ice pack, a tensor bandage, and some smelly ointment that she called one of her mum's "home-made remedies". She instructed me to "stay off the bloody thing" and "stop buzzing around the house like a blue arsed fly" or it would "go skew-whiff again". For dinner Auntie made us a hearty pot of vegetable stew with plump dumplings; Jonathan ate with gusto, to her delight. Skye wouldn't eat the dumplings and I just picked at mine. I wasn't hungry; all that I could think of was 'her'.

Before we brought the tree inside Skye suggested that we make a snowman. "It will take our minds off of what just happened and we always made a snowman in the back yard at Christmas time," she said coyly, with a childish grin. Jonathan told her that it would likely be gone by Christmas, as the snow didn't stay very long here. "But Emily and I make the best snowmen, and Auntie would get a kick out of it, I'm sure. He could be a sentry on watch for any unearthly visitors," she teased. How could she be so playful and cheery after all we've just been through, I asked myself. My gut was still turning flips. But after I asked her if she was ever going to grow up we gave in to her antics. That was one of the things that Skye and I had in common: we refused to repress our inner child and deprive ourselves of make-believe and play. I guess we were both a little afraid of becoming monotonous adults and having to give up simple childhood pleasures. We rolled three balls for our snowman's body, gathered sticks for his arms, pebbles for his eyes, and a large pinecone for his nose. Auntie brought us one of her old scarves and a hat to make him complete. He was a fine specimen and I was glad for the distraction, but it would take more than building a snowman to take my mind off of 'her'.

We spent the rest of the afternoon decorating the tree. It stood in the corner of the sitting room, next to the hearth, adorned with Auntie's modest collection of vintage ornaments, strung popcorn, cranberries, glitter, and garland.

Jonathan weaved the fairy lights between the boughs and placed the faded angel on the top branch. Auntie stood back and "ooowed and ahhhed" when he plugged in the colored lights.

Jonathan kept trying to get me alone; he even followed me to the bathroom and pinned me against the door, but Skye wasn't far behind. She wouldn't leave us. She followed me everywhere and I didn't want to tell her to get lost or that I thought she was being childish and run the risk of offending her. She just wanted me all to herself, I concluded. After all, I was still her best friend and our time together was coming to an end. I told Jonathan that she'd be going back home in a few days and that then we'd have lots of time to spend together. I wasn't in the mood for making out anyway. I couldn't get the incident in the woodlot out of my mind and I kept wondering when and where the hideous creature was going to appear again, and how long it would take before she got her revenge.

As Jonathan was leaving, we had our usual brief touching and feeling, hot and heavy encounter at the front door. Once he had gone, Skye asked me to go up to the attic room with her. "I have something really interesting to show you," she said. Her face beamed with mischievous intrigue, like a schoolgirl who had just discovered her rival's best hidden secret.

"What is it?"

"You have to come and see."

"This better be good. You know how I hate going up there," I said and swallowed hard. "Especially after what happened today."

"It's good. I promise."

My foot trembled a little as I placed it on the bottom step and began to ascend the old wooden stairs, and I asked myself, *what the hell you are doing, Emily Fletcher? Are you crazy?*

Skye turned just before we got to the top. "Are you wearing the pentagram?"

I pulled it from under my sweater and nodded my head. "Have you got the sea salt?" I asked.

"It's sprinkled all over the room," she answered. I stood back while Skye flicked on the light switch. She scurried across the floor to the dressing table, grabbed the left side, and started to push it away from the wall. The large oval mirror wobbled. I hurried over to help her. "What are you doing?" I asked.

"You'll see." We moved the dressing table aside. "Look at this."

It was a door, a child-size door about four feet high. It had been painted over and there was no handle. Skye tapped on it to reveal the hollow sound. It looked intriguing but ominous.

All of a sudden all the horrid memories of my first encounter here came flooding back to me. I turned my head and stared at the cubbyhole that I had discovered the first time I came here to Merryweather Lodge, the gruesome cubbyhole where the cat bones had been hidden. It had been painted over too and the latch was gone.

I clenched my fingers around my pendant and shuffled

back, glancing over my shoulder, expecting the hideous creature to appear at anytime. "There's probably something really gross inside there, like someone's remains or something."

"I don't think so; I would have felt it." Skye ran her hands across the smooth surface of the painted door. "How are we going to get in there?"

"We're not. Not without Auntie's permission anyway. We can't just break down the door."

"Why not? We'll just push the dressing table back when we're finished. You can't see it behind there. You didn't know it was there, did you?" I shrugged my shoulders. "And do you think if you ask your aunt she's going to let you go in there? She took the handle off and painted over it."

"You're right. She was trying to hide it, for some reason. What a minute—how did you know it was there?"

"Winston told me."

I scrunched up my face and moved my head from side to side. "Yeah, right!"

"No kidding. He was scratching and pawing at something behind the dressing table. I thought it was a mouse. When I moved it, he just sat there glaring at the door in the wall. I'd swear he was telling me to open it. Aren't you curious?"

I was curious but I was also terrified of what we might find behind there. "Okay, let's do it."

Skye grabbed a pair of scissors from a drawer in the dressing table and ran the blade over the indented paint in the edges of the door frame. Then she dug the tip of the scissors into the crack and tried to pry the door open. It flexed but wouldn't open. Then Skye noticed a nail driven in where the latch should have been. She grabbed a knife from her backpack and dug at the nail until the head was slightly away from the wood. She then used the scissors to pry the nail free. I held my breath as she pulled the door open ever so slowly and stuck her head into the dark hole. "We're going to need some light in here; there are some matches and candles in that box beside the bed," she instructed.

I took one of the candles, lit the wick, and handed it to her. She ducked her head, held the candle in front of her, and went inside. "Come and see this, Fletch." I bent over and peeked into the dank-smelling darkness. "Come inside," she said. It was a stuffy, dismal little room, with an eerie air that made my skin crawl. On the floor of the back wall lay an old mattress with a dirty feather pillow and torn faded blanket on top. Beside it a small wooden chest held a tin cup and an old-fashioned candle holder. Skye moved the cup and candle holder and lifted the lid of the chest. She pulled out a large black book and handed it to me. I shone the candlelight on the front cover; in embossed gold letters were the words "Basic Witchcraft". It was the same book I had found in Auntie's buffet drawer the last time I was here. What was it doing in here? I shoved it under my arm. There was a box of antique toys in the corner and beside that sat a painted rocking horse. As we rummaged through the box I felt a twinge of guilt.

This place was meant to be hidden, a concealed crypt of buried artifacts, and we were excavating its forbidden contents and unleashing God knows what. Skye bent down and held the candle in front of the toy horse. It was a beautiful thing: about two feet tall with a fetching expression, carved out of wood, hand painted in bright red, green, and cobalt-blue. It had a leather harness, iron stirrups, and its mane and tail were made of, what I assumed to be, real hair. Skye stroked its mane and paused. "It looks like one of those carousel horses they used to have at carnivals and fairs. I wonder if it was Mary Eliss's?"

"Good chance," I said. I felt a cool draft. "We've got to get out of this place. It gives me the creeps and it smells of decay, as if something died in here."

"Look at these," Skye said, ignoring my comments, as she held out the candle and pointed to a stack of paintings leaning against the wall. "Let's take them out and have a look."

"What for? They're just old paintings." I was getting a little worried that Auntie might come up and discover us in here. It was obvious that it was taboo but why, I wondered. Skye was trying to lift one of the large frames while still holding onto the candle. "Here, give me that before you burn the place down." I took the candle out of her hand and hunched down under the little door. I straightened my back and drew in some air; even the attic felt somewhat comforting, after being in there.

Skye dragged the paintings across the floor. "I feel like such a snoop and what if Auntie comes up and catches us?" I asked.

"We'd hear her coming and we'd shove the pictures behind the dressing table. Stop fretting, Fletch." She blew the dust off the gold frame holding a pastoral landscape and then moved it aside. "Look at this. I bet this is your great-great-grandmother." I stared at the beautiful woman in the portrait. Her red hair was tucked under a large-brimmed feather hat. She had a pale complexion and her soft green eyes bore a sad expression. Black ruffled lace circled her robust, exposed cleavage. "Oh my God, look at the resemblance, Fletch. You look just like her."

I bent down and examined the painting. "You're right, and she was cursed with the same pea-green eyes and ginger hair, but why couldn't I have been blessed with a pair of voluptuous boobs like that?" Skye laughed, moved the portrait aside, and gazed at the one behind it. It was a painting of my great-great-grandfather sitting at a roll-top desk, with an ink-well, quill pen, and paper in front of him, a somber, starched look on his face. "Hey, does that room look familiar to you?" I asked her, barely managing the words. "It looks like it was taken in here; this must have been his office or something like that."

Skye drew close to the painting, narrowed her eyes, and then moved her gaze around the room. "You're right, Fletch, and look down there." She pointed to a cat sitting by the leg of the desk. "It's the spitting image of Winston."

We exchanged curious looks. It was identical to the cat we knew. The exact same color, the same screwed up face and strange eyes.

Suddenly I felt the presence of something behind me. I turned ever-so-slowly. "Winston! You scared me." He was glaring up at me, eyes fixated with a sort of needy expression, as if he wanted to tell me something. He glanced at the portrait then back at me. I looked at Skye, and then at Winston. "Wait a minute; you're not trying to tell me…you're not really him, are you?" "My heart started to race with emotion, excitement, dread, fear. Was it an awakening, an epiphany? I wasn't quite sure.

Skye scooped the huge black cat into her arms, took his hairy head, and moved his face gently to meet hers. "Did you come back to watch over the other kitties, to protect them from that evil creature?" The cat let out a resounding meow. Skye's eyes grew.

"That's it!" I said, "You hit it right on the head. That's why he's always wanting in here. This is where he used to spend most of his time, with his master. You said that you were picking up some strange unearthly vibes from him. Maybe he's a ghost or the reincarnation of the cat in the portrait. And perhaps he has come back to protect Winny and Winky."

Skye lowered the perplexing feline to the floor. "And maybe he has powers." She crouched down in front of him and said with a soft but firm voice, as if she were talking to a naughty little child, "Why were you trying to bury the pentagram? If you can understand me, say meow three times." The cat just sat still and poised, staring at her as if she were crazy.

The sight of Skye standing there like a little old schoolmistress, trying to get a confession out of a stupid cat, filled me with amusement. I tapped my fingers on the side of my head and burst out laughing. Skye covered her mouth and started giggling, then lost her balance, toppled forward, and landed on the ground. We were both in hysterics, until…

"You shouldn't have done that."

I froze. Skye gasped! We turned our heads slowly in the direction of the voice.

"Mary Eliss!" She was sitting on the bed, in the same position, with the same expression as the last time we saw her. But her aura was not as pleasant as before. Something wasn't right.

She turned her ethereal head in my direction. "I said you shouldn't have done that, Emily."

"Done what?" I asked.

"Opened that portal," she said, in a low voice.

"Why not? We were curious."

Skye moved towards her. Mary Eliss gave her a hostile glare. "Stay back!" she demanded angrily.

"Why was that room hidden?" Skye asked. Her tone was full of accusation. Mary Eliss's eyes grew.

I stepped in front of Skye. "Mary Eliss, we're sorry if we've upset you. We were just being nosy, wondering what was in there and what it was used for."

"It was my refuge, my hiding room. My father made me go in there when my mother was having one of her bad days. He would tell her that I had gone into the woods to play." Her pale chin dropped. "Sometimes I'd be in there for hours, but I had my toys and my Annabella."

"How awful that must have been for you."

"It was better than being beaten by my mother."

"She beat you?"

"Father said she was possessed. But I thought she was just evil." She bit down on her bottom lip. "That evil got inside me too, at times."

"Mary Eliss, your mother was possessed, taken over by the creature that haunts this place, an evil Druid priestess that's out for revenge." I swallowed. "Out to get revenge on me. She can possess the bodies of her female descendents and that means you and me, Mary Eliss."

"I know that now. But I am tired, Emily. I want it to stop. I want to rest."

"Me too, Mary Eliss, but I need your help. Is there anyway you can help us get rid of her?" She tilted her head as if she were listening for something from far away. I felt uneasiness. The air was getting cold. Her presence was becoming threatening. Her appearance was starting to change; from a pretty doll-like demeanor into something more sinister. Her lovely features were becoming drawn and gray, her eyes melting into black holes, and a subtle foul odor drifted towards me. I knew only too well what was happening. Utter fear gripped me. "Let's go! Now!" I screamed, as I dashed for the door.

Chapter 18

We flew down the stairs, through the passage, and into the parlor. I slammed the door behind us. "Wait a minute! What if she followed us? What about Auntie?" I asked, as I tried to catch my breath. "We've got to go find her." I flung open the door and raced into the passage. "Auntie Em!"

She strolled out of the kitchen with a tea towel and wet rolling pin in her hand. "What's up? What's 'append?"

I cleared my throat and gave her a reassuring half smile. "Oh it's nothing, I was just wondering where you were, that's all."

She shook her head and frowned at me suspiciously. "That funny imagination of yer's again, is it, luv?"

I sighed. "Yes, Auntie, that's it; it's just my funny imagination." As I turned to leave, I couldn't resist giving her a slight prod of sarcasm. "It's all in my imagination, according to you. But I'm sure you don't really believe that."

"Watch yer' mouth, ya' cheeky madam," she said as she walked back to the kitchen. "Ya' don't know the 'alf of it."

Her voice was croaky.

I wanted to grab her and ask her how much she knew and why she wouldn't talk about it. But I knew that would only make her mad and more defensive. "Whenever you're ready to talk about it, I'm ready to listen," I called to her. She answered with a quick grunt. I took that as an acknowledgment and I felt like I had made some progress, even though no promises were made. When I walked past the attic stairs I noticed that the door was closed but I didn't remember closing it behind me and I had been the last one out the door.

I went back to the parlor. Skye was curled up on the pullout couch, with the book of basic witchcraft tented across her chest. "What are you doing?" I asked her, angrily. "Auntie hid that for a reason. What if she was to walk in here right now and see you with it?"

"Sorry, Fletch, but there's some fascinating stuff in here."

"Put it away before she sees it." Skye lifted her upper body off the cushions of the couch, closed the book, and shoved it under the couch. "Is your aunt okay?"

"Yes, she's in the kitchen. I think we're safe, for now. Did you close the attic door?"

"No, you were the last one down the stairs."

"I didn't close it but it's closed now," I said. "We have to go back up there and put all that stuff away." I thought for a moment. "Hey, didn't you say that you sprinkled sea salt all around the room?" I could feel my pulse starting to take off, as I spoke.

"I did but now that you mention it, I don't remember

seeing it when we were up there. There is something really strange going on here."

I looked at her wide-eyed. "No shit! Have you just figured that out?"

She smiled sympathetically. "We should go back up there now and tidy up the room."

"Now? What if she's still there?"

"I don't think she will be but even if she is, I don't think she can harm us. She possessed the ghost of a little girl who, as far as we know, had a kind spirit. The legend says that only those with an evil heart can kill for her."

"Do we know that for sure?" Skye shrugged her shoulders.

"Well," I continued, "better be safe than sorry, as Auntie would say."

"I'll go and do it; it was my idea to snoop, after all," Skye said as she headed for the door.

"Wait, I'll come. I can't let you go by yourself and you're going to need help moving that dresser back. Do you have any more sea salt?"

"It's up there, in my backpack, unless it's been taken."

"There's some in the kitchen, in an old coffee tin but we'll have to get Auntie out of there first."

The Kitchen smelled of almond, butter, and freshly-baked cookies. Auntie was standing by the little gas stove, her head cocked towards the kettle waiting for the first hiss. She was wearing her brown hair net, but there were no curlers underneath. Her apron held smears of butter, jam, and flour.

There were three china cups on the table with a plate full of shortbread biscuits and one rice cake, for her picky guest, I assumed. "Ahaaa, 'ello luvs. I was waiting for ya." *She was?* "Sit yer' selves down, we'll 'ave a nice cupper, we will." I shot Skye a 'what do we do now?' look. She shrugged. My head and guts were still in turmoil, reeling from the thing I had just witnessed. I needed wine, not tea.

Auntie stood patiently, her head to one side, with a warm glow of contentment on her face. The kettle gurgled then burst into a full whistling shrill. Auntie grinned as she turned off the stove and extinguished the blue flame. She lifted the kettle from the stove with her apron-covered hand and poured a little bit of boiling water into the teapot, swirled it around, emptied it out, added the tea leaves, and inhaled the whirling steam. Then she smiled and put the teapot on the table to steep. How does she do it? I asked myself. She looked so calm, so content wallowing in the simple pleasures of her ordinary life, wrapped in the arms of this fairytale cottage. But most of the time it was more a house of horrors than a fairytale cottage and she must have known that; she had hinted that she knew, but what kept her from talking about it, what made her so immune to its menacing vibes and ghostly apparitions?

She poured the tea into our delicate cups, handed one to me, one to Skye, took a sip from the third one, and placed a biscuit in her saucer. Auntie strolled into the sitting room, motioning us to follow and farting like a trumpet as she walked. Skye waved her hand in front of her face; what has she been eating? I wondered. "Come on, luvs. I've got something to tell ya."

The tiny colored lights twinkled on the proud looking Christmas tree by the hearth, and the flames from the fire crackled and danced. The air was alive with the scent of mulberry, pine, and everything Christmas.

She placed her cup on the end table, being careful not to spill, took the shortbread biscuit from the saucer, eased her plump bottom into her favorite comfy chair, and propped her slippered feet on the tapestry stool. Auntie knew how to live in the moment and to savor the simple things in her life. I vowed to live like that one day, when all this ghostly stuff was put to rest, if it ever 'was' put to rest.

She brushed the biscuit crumbs from her apron with her hanky and said, "Listen 'ere, luvs, I 'ave something to tell ya." *This was it, she was going to admit to her cover- up, tell us all her secrets and help us get rid of HER!* We listened intently. "Martha's coming to spend the day with us on Friday and tomorrow I'm going shoppin' and to the pictures with 'er." Her old eyes sparkled. "I'll get the bus into Salisbury and Martha said she'll bring me back 'ere in 'er brother's car." She leaned against the back of her chair and took another sip of tea. I waited. Was that it? Was that all? "Don't you have something else to tell us, Auntie Em?" I asked, with a pleading smile.

She rubbed the side of her head and drew her untrimmed eye brows together. "Don't think so, luv." Then eagerness flashed from her eyes. "Oh yes, don't go drinkin' anymore of that there wassail. I 'ad some last night and it made mu tummy go all queer, give mu self a good dose of salts this morning I did." *Yes we know, we were downwind of it. Is that all?* I sighed.

"That's nice, Auntie, it will get you out of the house for awhile and we're looking forward to seeing Martha again." I gave Skye a critical nod. "Aren't we, Skye?"

She was staring at Winston, who was sitting by the hearth staring at her. "Yes, of course. I can't wait to see her again."

"You don't have to get the bus, though, Auntie. I'll drive you."

"Can't bring mu self to go in the old car, not yet." She sniffed, lowering her head while she dug into her apron pocket for her hanky.

I went to comfort her, but she turned her head and pushed the button on the T.V. remote control, indicating that she didn't need my consoling and that she didn't want to talk about it. *Her grief, just like everything else was getting swept under the rug.* "Enjoy your show, Auntie; we'll be back in a minute." She just grunted.

I crooked my finger as a signal to Skye. She rose and followed me to the kitchen. "It's on the top shelf of this cupboard," I said as I stretched my arm and reached for the toffee tin containing the sea salt. It was full to the brim. "It's been topped up. Auntie must be using it too. *But where was she getting it from?*

"I told you; she knows a lot more than she lets on."

"I know that, but I don't know why she won't talk about it. I'm not going to confront her though; I've done that before and she gets really upset. Pour us some wine, will you? We're going to need it, if we're going back up there."

Skye set two glasses on the table and popped the cork off a bottle of Auntie's raspberry wine. "Why didn't you tell her that we wouldn't be here when Martha comes?"

"Why won't we? Where are we going?" I asked.

"You don't remember? Fletch, what's wrong with you? Friday's the twenty first, the day before I go home and we are supposed to be going to celebrate Winter Solstice at Stonehenge. Now do you remember?"

"Oh right." I raised my chin and glared at her. "I'm just forgetful, not stupid, and can you blame me with all this horrible stuff going on? It's a wonder I don't lose my mind altogether."

She handed me the glass of wine and smiled at me compassionately. "I know, Fletch, but it will all work out in the end. I swear."

I took a swig of the comforting elixir and stuck out my little finger. "Pinky swear?" She gazed at my finger, then turned away and said in a croaky whisper, "Sorry, Fletch."

"I thought as much." I took another hefty swig of my wine, set the glass on the table, and ordered her to "grab the salt and say a prayer."

I sniffed the air and listened intently as we climbed the old wooden stairs. My feet were heavy and my body was stiff. Skye was in front of me, her hand clutching our bag of salt. She drew a deep breath and gripped the knob on the door. I gritted my teeth; every cell in my body was rigid. *Please let it be safe. Please don't let her be in there.* Skye opened the door, fumbled on the inside wall for the light switch, flicked it, and then went inside. I stood by the opened door.

"It's all clear," she whispered. I stepped from behind the door and walked slowly, tentatively into the room. Skye moved with haste, scattering the sea salt, like seeds onto a ploughed field. Her gaze flitted here and there, and I could almost hear the thumping of her heartbeat as she dashed around the room. I just stood there, still and quiet, trying to swallow the lump that was lodged in my throat, watching, waiting for her to finish, and praying that the creature would not return.

Things were not the same as we had left them. The paintings were gone, the rocking horse and toy box were on the floor beside the bed, and some of the toys had been removed. Mary Eliss's china doll Annabella was lying on top of the bed. "Hurry up, Jenks, let's put this stuff back and get out of here." She shoved the bag of salt into her backpack and started to gather the toys. I pulled back the door as far as it would go, grabbed Skye's bag, and propped it against the hinge of the door, just in case we needed to make a quick getaway. "Why would someone or something put the portraits back and leave all this stuff out?" I moaned, as I went to put Annabella back on her seat.

I ran my fingers down the tiny fasteners on the back of the doll's dress where I had first discovered the note that Mary Eliss had written. Where did it go? Was it all a dream; is this whole thing just a nightmare? There was something about this doll, a sort of comforting feeling. Her painted blue eyes seemed to beckon me and whisper my name. I brought her up to my face, captivated by her soothing aura, and snuggled into the soft warmth of her red velvet dress; the faint smell of lavender emanated from her porcelain form. Something touched my face. Her tiny fingers were alive, and caressing my cheek! I threw her on the floor. There was a presence behind me. "Meow!"

"Winston!" I screamed.

Skye came rushing out of the secret room. "What is it?" she asked breathlessly.

"The doll's hand moved." I was still trembling.

"Is that all? I thought the creature came back. Help me get this stuff put away, so we can get out of here."

I stared at her, wide eyed. "Is that all? Skye, the doll was animated; its hand caressed my face! It was so…unreal."

"Think about it, Fletch; does any of this stuff seem real? We are in touch with another dimension and anything and everything is possible."

She was right. Nothing should surprise me. "It feels like I'm in some sort of twilight zone," I said, as I picked the doll up from the floor.

Skye sighed. "Like I said, you got a shitload of karma to sort out. The rest of us are just secondary actors on your movie."

"It's a pretty scary horror movie, Jenks. Too frickin' scary!"

We tried to place everything exactly as we'd found it,

but we couldn't fix the door and it would be obvious that someone had broken in. Before we left the room, I tucked Annabella into the bed and drew the blankets around her neck. "What did you do that for?" Skye asked.

"I wanted her to be warm and comfortable," I replied, as I watched Winston climb onto the bed and curl up in a ball beside her. "Do you think they're two lost souls looking for their masters?"

Skye smiled. "Or two souls out on a journey to seek revenge for their masters."

"I hope so; I will take all the help I can get."

Back downstairs, we took our wine from the kitchen into the sitting room. All my senses were alert, on guard for any sudden noises, strange smells, or paranormal activity. My body felt weak and tired from all the tension and stress. Auntie had already gone to bed. I snuggled into the corner of the chintz sofa by the fireplace and sipped my wine. Skye sat in Auntie's chair and put her feet on the tapestry stool.

The ambience of the little room felt as comforting and safe as it always had: an idyllic scene of all things country-cottage and Christmas-y. An array of sentimental treasures, along with boughs of holly, mistletoe, and pine sat on the mantel and the buffet. The fire blazed, the candles burned, and the Christmas tree lights flickered. The only sound was that of the crackling logs on the fire and the tick-tock of the old grandfather clock in the hallway. We sat for a few moments, in quiet contemplation, sipping and thinking, trying to steady our nerves. There was so much I wanted to ask her, so much I needed to say. She was the one who broke the silence. "You do want to celebrate the Winter Solstice at Stonehenge, don't you, Fletch?"

"Of course I do." But my inner voice was warning me not to go and the thought of participating in a ritual, at Stonehenge, on a pagan Sabbath filled me with dread.

Chapter 19

I guzzled the rest of my wine and refilled my glass. "I'll break the news to Auntie, but she's not going to be happy with us and I'd really wanted to be here when Martha came. I still haven't been able to get her on the phone, which is really odd, because I've been calling her at all times of the day. I want to know what she wanted to talk to me about." I thought for a moment. "But Auntie did say Martha was coming for the day and we wouldn't have to be at Stonehenge until late afternoon, right?" Skye gave me a nod. I sat up, repositioned myself on the sofa, and lowered my voice. "There's something else we need to talk about, Skye."

Her smile disappeared "Okay."

"Why are you so hostile to Jonathan? Why don't you like him?"

She fluffed her hair with her fingers. "What makes you think I don't like him?"

"Oh come on, Jenks. I'm not stupid. It's obvious."

She sniffed and said, defensively, "He doesn't care for me either."

"I know, but I don't understand why and I haven't had time to ask him, so I'm asking you."

She poured herself another glass of wine, walked over and flopped onto the sofa next to me. Her soft black curls fell over her shoulder blades and I could smell her vanilla and peaches body lotion. I was uncomfortable. I moved back to the corner of the sofa to put more room between us. The pheromone she was emitting was enough to turn a nun. "Okay, Fletch, this isn't going to be easy for me but it has to be said. I've been meaning to tell you for a long time but I just kept putting it off, hoping that one day you might feel the same." *I don't like where this is going.* She took a deep breath. "Ever since we were teenagers I've had feelings for you...and not the sort of feelings you have for a friend." Her chin dropped. "You know what I mean. I would have told you I was gay and I would have stopped seeing you if I hadn't had a sense that somewhere, deep down inside, you'd had those sorts of thoughts about me." *God, she's so intuitive.* She reached for my hand. I pulled back. I could feel patches of pink growing on my cheeks. There were tears pooling in Skye's big brown eyes. *I couldn't bring myself to tell her that her senses hadn't failed her, I had had those sort of thoughts about her, but they were only fantasies, dark shadows, unacceptable tendencies that I allowed myself to act out in the safety of a secret place in my mind. But I'd had the same thoughts and fantasies about guys.* She looked away. "I guess my intuition must have been wrong."

She was waiting for me to say something, hoping against all hope. A lone tear trickled down the soft skin of her perfect cheekbone. I handed her a tissue. I wanted to hug her but I was too afraid.

We sat side-by-side in silent ponder, afraid to touch, afraid to speak, afraid of what the other might say, think, or do. I felt like a cannonball had dropped in my stomach. I had to say something. "I'm not gay, Skye. I'm deeply in love with Jonathan."

She looked up at me and smiled but she still had tears in her eyes. "It's not that black and white, Fletch. You can't help who you fall in love with. It's not unusual for someone who considers themselves straight to be attracted to someone of the same sex. But don't worry, I won't come on to you again, but I had to give it a try. I knew you were falling in love with Jonathan; I just didn't know how much. And I knew that this was my last chance to tell you how I felt. If I'd left without telling you I'd never have forgiven myself." She lowered her head and stared at the wine in her glass. "He's a good guy, Fletch, and has an old spirit, like you. The reason why he's been cold to me is either he senses my feelings for you, or he's just plain jealous of our relationship. I've noticed him looking at me looking at you, so I suspect the first is true. As for me, its pure envy, I'm afraid." She turned to face me and pleaded, "But I'll be nice to him from now on, I promise." She took my hand. I wanted to pull away but I didn't. "I'm so sorry, Fletch. Can we still be friends, please? Can we put all this behind us and be like we used to be? You are my best friend, my forever friend." Her chin quivered. My eyes filled with tears. I turned and threw my arms around her. "You are my forever friend too, Jenks."

We hugged and consoled each other, just like we always used to. She pulled away from my embrace, looked into my eyes, and said, "Can we forget about this now?"

"I'll try." I sniffed, as I wiped the tears from my eyes. "Besides, there are more important things on my mind right now. I'm so scared Jenks—terrified of what's going to happen next. Merthia won't stop until she gets her own back. Haven't you come up with anything other than what we did in the woodlot?" I asked her, injecting a good dose of disappointment into my voice.

"I've been casting spells, chanting, visualizing her tied to a tree and being burned alive," she said. I cringed. "But there is one other thing we could try."

"I'll try anything," I said.

"Hypnotism," she whispered.

I sat up and reached for my drink. "You want to hypnotize me?"

"I'm thinking, if I can take you back to when you were Merthia's cousin, you might be able to tell me more specifically what happened to Merthia, and where she's buried. If we know where her remains are, we could dig them up and burn them."

"Is that what we have to do? Will that expel her and send her back, forever?"

"I don't know, but it worked on the Vampire Chronicles."

I shook my head, mockingly. "You watch too much of that shit. She's not a vampire."

"It's worth a try. You might reveal some pertinent information which could lead us to banishing her."

"How do you know you can take me back to that area? My soul might have had hundreds of incarnations. And what if you take me back to a life when I was struggling with some horrid disease or one when I was a bum on the streets starving and destitute or worse, a prostitute?"

Skye laughed. "A bum I could see, but a prostitute? Not! You could have been a beautiful princess riding bareback on a handsome stallion to meet your gorgeous prince charming, or better still, maybe you were the voluptuous Marilyn Monroe. You've always wanted blond hair and big boobs." We stared at each other and then tossed our heads back and burst out laughing.

The wine was starting to take effect. Skye stopped, wiped a dribble of wine from her chin with the back of her hand, and said, "Seriously, Fletch, let's do it."

I sniffed and regained my composure. "Why not, what do I have to lose?"

It was getting cold. I walked over to the hearth and threw a couple of logs and some paper on the dying ashes in the grate. The fire flared to life. Winky was curled up in her favorite spot, on the sheepskin fireside rug. The fluffy black and white feline lifted her head and stared up at me with a cantankerous expression. She didn't like to be disturbed. Winny, I assumed, was waiting for me on my pullout bed in the parlor. She had grown accustomed to sleeping with me and had become a close companion. Winston was sitting like a stone statue in the corner of the room. I suddenly realized that he shouldn't be here. "Winston? Didn't we shut you in the attic?"

Skye walked towards him cautiously, then bent down and stroked the back of his head. She was a little unstable. "Yep, it's him all right."

I scanned the strange cat, perplexed. "But how did he get back down here?"

"Isn't it obvious, Fletch? He's the ghost of your great-great-grandfather's cat."

I bent down and studied him closely. He started to purr. "He doesn't look like a ghost." I straightened up. "But then again, nothing would surprise me here."

"Lay down on the sofa, Fletch." Skye commanded.

"Why?" I asked anxiously.

"I'm going to rip your clothes off and ravish you."

"What!"

She shook her head. "Just kidding, stupid. I'm going to hypnotize you."

"You do know what you're doing, don't you?" I asked her.

"Well, sort of," she said with a dismissive crooked smile.

"Jenks! Have you or have you not hypnotized someone before?"

"I've tried but it never worked very well. But I've done more research, and now I have it perfected," she added with haste. "I think," she mumbled as she poured herself another glass of wine.

I threw myself on the sofa. "Do it!" I ordered her. My voice was shaky and there was a knot starting to form in the pit of my gut. "But make sure you bring me back from wherever the hell you take me." Her eyes gleamed down at me, and there was an eager look on her face. "Get a pen and paper. Make sure you write everything down."

She dug in her backpack and pulled out her writing pad and small nib fountain pen. Then she took another mouthful of wine and raised her glass to me. "To you and me, Fletch, forever friends, forever…" She grabbed her throat, choking and coughing, as she tried to speak. "It went down the wrong way," she sputtered, thumping her chest.

"You're drunk, Jenks." *I was going to get hypnotized by someone who was intoxicated?* Skye didn't usually drink that much but when she did it made her silly and giddy, like a schoolgirl. I, on the other hand, could drink a couple of bottles and still keep my composure.

"Lay back and close your eyes, and let your body relax. Imagine being in a happy place, a calm, secure and peaceful place." She spoke in a low, slow, soothing voice. *There's no way that this was going to work.* "Feel your feet, legs, stomach, chest, arms, neck, and head relax. You are in a peaceful place." *Nothing was happening.* "You are feeling sleepy, every cell in your body is at rest. Feel yourself sinking down,

down…" My eyes were getting heavy. "You are in a dark tunnel. There are many doors on either side of you." I could see the doors. "Do not enter." My body was drifting, down, down, as if there was no gravity. It was dark but I was not afraid. I felt like a butterfly, free from the confines of its co-coon. "You are a Celtic maiden. Your uncle Loki is a high druid priest. Your name is Colrea." It was getting cold. I saw a light at the end of the tunnel but was far, far away.

I was spinning round and round in the dark abyss. My mind was in turmoil. Words, like rubber balls bounced around in my head; not gay—ghost cat—bury it—secret room—malevolent spirit—sacred ground—mom. Words all jumbled together like misfit pieces of a puzzle. "Find the por-tal to your home, Colrea." Skye's voice was distant and un-clear. I was almost there. The light was bright and warm. "You are almost there, Colrea, and when I clap my hands you will wake up." Her voice faded into a trailing vapor, and then disappeared into the dark ether. Something was propelling me forward. I came out of the tunnel and into the light.

There was a garden, a large magnificent garden with fountains and manicured trees, shrubs with pink and white blossoms, and numerous flowers of vivid colors. The grass was a brilliant emerald green. I was wearing a long pink, frilly dress, white gloves up to my elbows and high laced boots. There were ribbons in my hair. The air was alive with floral perfume. I was captivated by its splendor. There was a laby-rinthine ahead with perfect clipped hedges. I am moved to-wards it, drawn by an uncontrollable magnetic force. I didn't want to go in there, but I was being pulled in, into a wall of impenetrable hedges.

There were tourists jostling and giggling along the narrow green tunnels. They didn't see me. I kept walking. A couple in formal old-fashioned clothes hesitated as they passed me by; the lady's arm was linked with the arm of her gentlemen escort. She was carrying a fancy parasol. She looked right at me. It was my mother's face! "Mom, wait!" She was gone. The walls were closing in on me. I felt claustrophobic. A tiny, hideous looking creature flitted in front of my face. It was glowing like a firefly. It cocked its head from side to side. Its devilish red eyes were staring at me. Its pointy little teeth gnashed. It flew into my face. I felt its sharp teeth on my nose. There was blood and excruciating pain. In an instant it was gone. There was no blood, no pain. It was still and quiet. The tourists were gone. I was alone, lost and deathly afraid; moving with great haste through the bends, sharp turns, and long stretches of dense hedges, searching desperately for a way out of this unrelenting maze. My long dress was tangled around my legs; my laced boots were hurting my feet and pinching my toes. There was a twig sticking out from one of the hedges; I pushed it aside as I hurried past. It became a snake, slithering between my fingers. I shivered and screamed, and shook my hand forcefully to rid myself of the horrid creature.

Someone was behind me. I lifted up my dress and started to run. It was bitterly cold. I could see the icy vapor from my breath. Something smelled. My legs felt as though they were going to collapse. I fell to the ground. The smell was over-powering. I heard a faint echo from far, faraway, "Be strong, Emily. Connect to the magic within you." Slowly I turned my head.

Chapter 20

It was the hideous creature. She was covered in carnage. Bits of human flesh were stuck to her tattered gown. A blood-stained axe was in her hand. Vile yellow discharge trickled down her pasty chin. I cringed and shuffled back into the hedge.

I could hardly breathe. There was a rustling in the bush beside me. I grasped my throat. A cat jumped out. It was a black cat with a wrinkled face and bulging yellow eyes. It was Winston. He stood between me and the creature. His back was hunched, his fur stood erect. The creature's mouth opened. Millions of maggots poured out. I turned my head and vomited into the bush. I was trembling in fear for my life, and Winston's. The creature hissed and snarled as it glared down at the brave cat. The cat hissed back, then flexed its claws and leapt at the creature. Winston was dead. The creature was on top of me. I heaved from the smell of her cold sticky flesh.

A voice called from somewhere in the distance, "Come

back. Come back…" I could feel something dark emerging from the deepest recesses of my soul: anger, hate, bloodlust. "Use the pentagram, Emily. The pentagram…" *Skye*! Suddenly I was seized by the fact that none of this was real. I shoved my hands down the front of my frilly dress and clasped my fingers around my five star pendant and closed my eyes.

I could feel the familiar soft fabric of the cushioned sofa underneath me. Skye was standing over me. Her eyes were like saucers; her face showed utter panic. She was screaming in my ear, "Wake up!"

I rubbed my eyes and tried to focus. The sour taste of vomit still lingered in the back of my throat. The creature's revolting essence and her stench were still with me. My fingers were tightly wrapped around the cold metal of my pendant. I held my hand to my head as I tried to sit up.

Skye put her arm around my back to assist me; she was shaking. I was dazed, my throat was dry, and my head was throbbing. Skye put the rim of my wine glass to my lips. I shook my head. "Water" I mumbled. She exchanged the wine glass for bottled water. I sipped as I tried to regain my shaken equilibrium. I suddenly remembered the dead cat. "Winston! Where's Winston?"

Skye pointed to the hearth. He was curled up beside Winky and Winny, snuggled into the fluffy fibers of the fireside rug. "He left the room for a few moments, and when he came back he had Winny with him," Skye said. "He walked with her, to the rug, and waited until she had fallen asleep before he curled up beside them." Her voice was a hoarse whisper. She looked into my eyes with an expression of utter disbelief. "Where did you go, Fletch? You were tossing and turning, then your whole body started to vibrate." She sucked in a deep breath; her dark eyes were puddles of water. "Then you started to change." She sobbed. "You were morphing into some sort of ugly creature. I kept clapping my hands and calling you. Didn't you hear me?" She flopped on the sofa beside me and put her hands over her face. "I screwed up. I should have told you to wake up when I clapped my hands but I forgot and then I tried to tell you when you were already under."

I pulled her hands away from her face and looked into her watery eyes. "Hey, I'm back now and look on the positive side: you were finally able to hypnotize someone. You put me under and took me back to another life."

She blew her nose into a tissue. "Where were you, Fletch?"

I thought for a moment "God knows. Somewhere in the eighteen hundreds, I'd say."

"Eighteen hundreds? You didn't go back to the Druid era?"

"It was like one of those hodge-podge dreams—bits and pieces of your life and emotions flitting in and out of scenes, of people and things that have happened, or perhaps, are yet to happen. I was in a labyrinth, running around searching for the opening." I felt the muscles in my head tighten as I flinched. "Then she came." I sniffed. "Oh my God, Jenks, it was so horrible. It felt like I had tendrils of poisonous vines growing and spreading inside me." Skye grimaced. My eyes started to sting with the threat of tears, and my throat was parched. "I don't know how much more of this shit I can take. I feel like running away from this place and never coming back."

Skye took my hand. Her skin was smooth and warm, her touch comforting. "Be strong, Fletch. If not for yourself, do it for your aunt. She needs you here. Merryweather Lodge needs you. Jonathan needs you. You have to get rid of this curse. There is a way and you will find it." She sighed and lowered her head. "I've tried everything I know but nothing has worked." She lifted her finger and pointed to my heart. "Somewhere inside there is the key to unlocking this mystery and only you can solve it; I'm sure of that now."

"What about my regression? What do you think it all meant?" I asked her, through sniffles and sobs.

"I don't know where you were, but it sounds more like a dream than a past life regression, or maybe it was a bit of both. A labyrinth would represent a maze of unresolved emotions, choices, regrets, losses, questions, and fears, and your life for the past few years has been a tangled web of emotions." She gazed into my eyes and squeezed my hands gently. Her eyes were red and droopy. "You have to be the spider that catches the fly, Fletch."

I turned my face away from hers. "Thanks for the metaphor."

Skye yawned. "I'm sorry I haven't been more help to you."

"Go to bed, Jenks. You've done everything you can and

that's all I could ask for."

She got up off the sofa. "Can I sleep in the parlor with you…on the floor, I mean? I don't want to sleep in the attic room tonight."

"I'm never going up there again and I don't want you to either," I ordered.

"Okay, Fletch, goodnight." Skye ambled to the door. Winston rose from his spot on the fireside rug and followed behind her, as if he'd been commanded to do so.

"Good night, Jenks. I'll be there in a minute."

I dragged myself off the sofa, stoked the fire, and gathered empty wine bottles. Auntie liked a "tidy house" when she got up in the morning and if I left anything out of place she would nag at me and quote one of her favorite sayings, "Cleanliness is next to Godliness." As I was rinsing the wine glasses in the sink and gazing out of the little kitchen window I noticed some odd shadows in the yard. I dried my hands on the tea towel, moved a little closer to the window, and pulled back the net curtains.

The yard was bathed in soft moonlight. Oh my God! Our snowman had been squashed; his head, body, and accessories were sprawled all over the snow-covered lawn. And beside his remains with a sick in her hand…I blinked to make sure my eyes were not deceiving me…was Belinda.

She was standing completely still, like a carved life-size figurine of a young girl; her shoulders were slumped and her head hung. She was wearing only a simple dress and her pigtails were tied with red bows. I stared at her for a moment, wondering what she was doing and how long she'd been standing out there in the cold. Then she moved, lifted her head, dropped the stick, and put her hands to her stomach and starting rubbing her belly in a circular fashion, as if she was trying to tell me that she was ill. Her eyes were on me, as I stared at her through the window. *What was with her? She must have walked all this way, by herself. She'll freeze to death out there.* The thought of leaving her there to freeze entered my mind but my conscience quickly brushed it off. She looked so forlorn, like a little girl lost and alone.

I went to the back door, shoved my feet into my boots, and wrapped Auntie's heavy cardigan around my shoulders. The air outside was icy cold. I could see my breath. The snow crunched ominously under my heavy winter boots. Belinda was gone! I couldn't find any fresh footprints; there was no indication that she had ever been there. I went around to the side of the house. The dismembered parts of the snowman were there, scattered about, but where was Belinda? I walked around to the other side of the cottage. "Belinda," I called, loud enough for her to hear, but soft enough not to disturb those inside. *Where could she have gone?* I drew the cardigan around my arms as goose bumps ran up and down my skin. All of a sudden a sensation of foreboding swept over me. I searched the darkness. A disembodied voice rang in the ether. "Emily, Emily, two by four. I saw you at the cellar door, I pushed you on the dirty floor and cut you with a chainsaw." *Where was that voice coming from?* My pulse started to race, my hands formed tight fists. "No!" I screamed. "You won't win. Bitch! I'm going to send you back to the dark dimension from where you came."

I ran back inside, my adrenaline pumping, my heart thumping behind my ribcage. I was more determined than ever to get rid of this curse—to get rid of her! Was that just an illusion, was that really Belinda out there or was it another trick to make me think I was going crazy? What if that really was just Belinda? What if she was wandering about out there, in that dreadful cold, with nothing on but a thin dress? I knew I wouldn't be able to sleep, thinking about her out there possibly freezing to death. Should I phone the McArthurs? I decided to call Jonathan on his cell phone. I needed to talk to him anyway. I needed to hear his voice.

"Hello." His voice was groggy.

"Jonathan, it's Emily."

"Emily. What's up? Are you all right?"

"I'm okay." I glanced at the clock by the curio table. It was eleven o'clock. "Sorry to call you so late; were you sleeping?"

"No, just laying here. My sister's got some sort of weird music on in her bedroom. I was just about to get up and tell her to shut it off."

"You're at your parents' place? Belinda's there?"

"Yes, my mum called me to come over. Apparently Belinda's been having some problems and I'm the only one she'll talk to. Why did you call?"

She's manipulating you, stupid. "I just wanted to hear your voice. It seems like forever since we were together, just the two of us."

"That's hardly my fault." There was harshness to his tone.

I was immediately on the defensive. "Well, it's not my fault either."

"I'll come over tomorrow after work."

"Okay, whatever." I slammed down the receiver and marched into my makeshift bedroom. Skye was fast asleep on her bed of cushions. I was reeling from the unearthly taunting and Jonathan's cold tone and lack of interest. I grabbed my journal, dropped onto the pull-out-couch, and scratched the side of my head with the nib of the pen.

Dec. 19th

Dear friend, I need someone to talk to and you're my only confidante, right now. I'm scared. No, I'm terrified. Of what's happening here. I don't want to lose Jonathan but I'm afraid that he might be losing interest in me and I'm deathly afraid of what might be going on with Belinda. Is she trying to win him over, to get her disgusting hands on him? And who is she…really? I love him so much and I can't bear the thought of losing him. I haven't even made love with him yet. I want, so badly, to wrap my legs around him and feel him inside me. Why hasn't he been more persistent in trying to sleep with me? Perhaps, like me, in the back of his mind are the terrifying thoughts of what she might do. Merthia and that past life are ripping at every part of my being. I am exhausted. I have always felt the mysterious pull of another dimension and I have glimpsed it so many times, in my recurring dream, visions, distant echoes, emerging from the deep recesses of my soul. Like a plant stretching towards the sun, this other life is drawing me farther and farther away from my physical existence and into its realm. I am sick of all this shit! I just want to be normal. If it wasn't for Auntie, Skye, my dad, and Jonathan, I'd let her take me.

I tossed my pen and journal on the floor and proceeded to pull out the couch and make my bed. Thoughts were chasing around in my head like caged rats. I wanted to go to sleep and never wake up. As I was taking off my sweater I suddenly remembered that I'd left my pendant in the sitting room. I'd taken it off and placed it on the sofa beside me when I woke up from being hypnotized. I had to take it off every now and then as it weighed so heavily around my neck but I needed to know where it was at all times—around my neck, around Auntie's or somewhere close at hand. Skye had told me that a true spirit would not be able to remove it from around my neck, it would scorch their hand.

I slipped into my warm flannel pajamas and headed back to the sitting room. The passage was cool and held its usual foreboding air. The pendant was not on the sofa where I'd left it. I looked around the room. Nothing. "Perhaps Skye brought it into the parlor or maybe I took it into the kitchen when I was cleaning up," I mumbled to myself. As I walked into the kitchen I noticed that the cellar door was open.

I moved towards the door, cautiously. There was something on the stairs. I turned my head, not wanting to look into the creepy black hole and felt for the light switch on the inside wall. I turned and peered down the stairs. "Winston!" The strange black cat was sitting on the bottom step with the silver chain of my pendant hanging out of his mouth. "What are you doing with that? Bring it here you naughty cat." He dropped the chain, scurried up the stairs, and flew past me, almost knocking me off my feet. I looked down at the silver pendant lying on the stair. *You can't leave it there; you have to go and get it.* I pulled the heavy wooden tool box from beside the back entrance and shoved it against the cellar door. The door stayed open the last time I did this, I reassured myself. I narrowed my eyes and peered into the dim, dark hole.

Chapter 21

I took a long, deep breath and said a silent prayer. Then I shot down the stairs, grabbed the pendant, and scurried back up. My blood was pumping through my veins so fast I thought I was going to faint. I clicked off the light switch, moved the tool box, and closed the door. Leaning against the hard surface of the door, I tried to catch my breath and regain my equilibrium. *He was taking the pendant back down there to try to bury it again, that I was sure of. But why?* All of a sudden the wooden door became icy cold, like an iceberg against my back. I bolted away and into the passage. *There's something about that cellar. It has a presence that's even more ominous than the attic room.* I rubbed my arms to rid myself of the cold, the goose bumps, and the eerie sensation.

As I passed Auntie's bedroom door I felt compelled to go in and check on her. I placed my hand on the brass knob, turned it, and opened the door ever so slowly, so as not to disturb her. She was making quick, repetitive snorting sounds under her thick patchwork quilt. There was a faint smell of wild rose talcum powder and lily of the valley lingering in the air. Her majestic old-fashioned wardrobe loomed against the wall. Silhouettes of precious cat ornaments, photo frames, and trinkets adorned her mahogany dressing table, small chest of drawers, and bedside tables. Her false teeth were submerged in a murky liquid inside a Toby mug on the little table closest to her bed. I remembered what happened the last time I was here, when I put the mug to my lips and almost swallowed the disgusting liquid inside. I flinched at the thought of it.

This was Auntie's private retreat, full of her dear old things, but she looked so vulnerable here, all alone with no protection. I went to the foot of the bed and hung her pendant over the brass bedpost, and then I went to Auntie's side, looked down at her sweet wrinkled face and put my lips to her soft cheek. *Sleep tight, Auntie Em. Don't let the bed bugs bite.*

The next day, when I told Skye about Winston and the pendant she suggested that we let him bury it and see what happened, but I wasn't comfortable with that. The pendant had protected me and saved my life on a couple of occasions. The creature was terrified of it. Merthia had called it the old symbol of the goddesses of light. To have it buried in the cellar floor was unthinkable, at least for now.

Jonathan phoned and told Auntie to tell me that he couldn't make it, that he had an important project to finish, and that he'd pick us up to take us to the airport at ten on Saturday morning. Skye's plane was leaving at three in the afternoon. Auntie said he was still at his mom's and driving back and forth to work from there. I was tempted to go over there and find out what was going on and ask him why he hadn't asked to speak to me or why he hadn't driven over to see me. But then I thought it best to leave it alone. I'd confront him after Skye left. I was sure, well almost sure, that he was just leaving us alone to spend time together and didn't want to be a third wheel. But I had no idea why he was spending so much time at his parents' house. It scared me think of what was happening over there.

Tomorrow Skye was leaving to go back to Canada. Today Martha was coming to spend the day with Auntie and Skye and I were going to the Winter Solstice at Stonehenge. I had asked Jonathan to join us but he declined.

I could hear Auntie's off key, high-pitched voice ringing throughout the cottage. "Good king Wenceslas last looked out on the feast of Stephen…" She'd been in the kitchen since early morning, peeling fruit, rolling pastry, and kneading dough. The cottage smelled heavenly and looked so charming, all dressed up in its Christmassy attire. Why couldn't it always be like this? I asked myself.

Martha was due to arrive at two. We were going to stay and visit with her for a couple of hours before we headed off to Stonehenge. Auntie was not happy when I told her that we wouldn't be here for tea and where we were going. "It's bonkers, if ya' ask me; flittin' about them there big stone thinga-mabobs with the devil's children, getting up to all kinds of mischief, and all night long, in the freezing cold," she said.

"By gum our Emily, sometimes I think ya' 'ave a few tiles missing on yer' roof." Then she gave me a toothless grin and patted my hand. "But I luv ya' anyway." When I explained to Auntie how much Skye wanted to go and how it was a once-in-a-life time opportunity for her, she was a bit more understanding. I also emphasized the fact that Martha was coming to visit her, not us, and that they needed time together to reminisce and to get reacquainted. I was planning to try to get Martha alone before we left and ask her what she had wanted to talk to me about, as I had not be able to contact her by phone.

By one forty-five Auntie had taken out her curlers, put in her teeth, hung her apron in its proper place on the hook behind the pantry door, and set a fancy table with her best china and Nottingham lace table cloth. She had planned to have an early afternoon cream tea, which consisted of scones, strawberry jam, real butter, thick cream, and an assortment of teas. Then, later she planned to make them an evening supper instead of the traditional English tea. Auntie was stepping out of her usual rigid routine and going all out for her friend.

It was two ten and Martha had still not arrived. Auntie kept glancing at the clock in the middle of the mantel, while she sat in her favorite chair, knitting. The more she looked at the clock, the faster the needles moved in her hand. Two thirty arrived and she was starting to get edgy. "I'm sure she'll be here soon, Auntie Em," I reassured her. "She must be caught up in traffic."

"Auntie stuck her knitting needle into her curly gray hair

and scratched her head with its nib. "Always been on time 'as Martha. Never known 'er to be late."

"Why don't you give her brother a call to see what time she left?" I suggested.

She rose from her chair, went to the window, and peered out through the heavy lace curtains. "I suppose it wouldn't 'urt to give 'im a call." She retuned a couple of minutes later, shaking her head. "No one's 'ome."

"Well, something must have delayed her. She'll be here soon, I'm sure."

It was four o'clock and still no Martha. Auntie had already finished two hats, and had started on a pair of mittens. She was watching her afternoon soaps, sipping tea, and nibbling on a plate full of ginger biscuits. It was time for Skye and me to leave, but I kept asking myself, how could you go and leave her like this? We had called Martha's brother's house three times but there was still no answer. I was not sure what to do.

Auntie must have read my mind or noticed Skye's gestures towards the clock. "You girls go and do what yer' gonna do. I'll be all right. She might turn up yet."

I crouched by the side of her chair. "But I don't like to leave you alone and worried about your friend."

She placed her knitting on her lap and started rewinding a ball of wool between her fingers with great speed. "Some mate she's turned out to be. She couldn't even be bothered to phone to tell me she can't make it. Don't you worry about me; I'm a bit cheesed off but apart from that I'm as right as rain, I am. Now get going and don't fret."

Before we left I crept into her bedroom, took the pendant from the bedpost, and put it around her neck. I told her not to take it off while we were gone and I reminded her that it was her mom's lucky star. She just mumbled, "It were that, mu luv, it were that."

"What do you think happened to Martha?" Skye asked as we stepped out the door.

"I don't know, but my gut's telling me something's wrong."

"Mine too," she said.

Rows of vehicles were parked on either side of the verge, and the parking lot was full. I managed to maneuver my way between a white van and a red Peugeot. We followed the stream of people carrying flashlights, lanterns, and extra winter clothing, working their way towards the ancient stones along the fence on the side of the road. It was dusk; the sun had already set. I could see lights flashing and heard the sound of drums, bells, and chanting as we got closer to Stonehenge. Skye was dressed in her colorful hippy attire, with flowers in her hair and a couple of warm blankets over her arm. I had my old tartan bag tossed over my shoulder with snacks, flashlights, bottles of water, and a small bottle of Auntie's homemade brew, but I had no idea if I'd be able to take it in with us or not. We hadn't bothered to find out what the restrictions were or how much security was going to be there. All we knew was that it was free and the gates closed at ten the next morning. Sunrise was going to be at five past eight and we had to leave right after that to be back at the cottage for when Jonathan came to take us to the airport.

We were at the entrance. There were floodlights illuminating the area around the great monoliths. Police were at the gates, and they were patrolling the perimeter, but no one searched our bags and there were no signs telling us that alcohol was prohibited. My wine was safe. We started to work our way through the crowds of people. There were all manner of pagans, hippies, Druids, sun worshippers, witches, warlocks, wizards, and plain-clothed tourists, curious to experience this pagan, spiritual event; the shortest day of the year and the birth of the new sun.

We entered the stone circle and watched a reveler beating his drum. We stood with the group of people that encircled him; some were draped in black hooded robes, others were dressed in colorful gowns with wreaths of ivy in their hair. Their eyes were closed, their heads were raised, and they seemed to be in some sort of trance as they swayed and hummed to the beat of the drum. "Hmmm…" We moved on to another circle of people. It was a hand fasting ceremony— a pagan wedding, an old Celtic ritual. A young couple with shaved heads stood in the center of the circle; their wrists were tied together with rope. A priestess was standing in front of them with a long staff in her hand. She called on the ancestors and four elements to protect them. They exchanged some simple vows and rings. After the priestess blessed them she untied the rope from their wrists, then she instructed them to jump over a broomstick to finalize their reunion. The couple kissed, and the crowd cheered, rang bells, and honked horns.

A man wearing a fur hat with antlers on it was handing out little cakes. I took two greedily from the tray and handed one to Skye. It was dry and had no taste. I grimaced and looked at Skye. "Vegan?" I asked. She nodded her head. There was a man with beady eyes and a long white beard blessing a pile of crystals on a small rock. A group of people chanted and danced, dressed like hippies with sprigs of mistletoe in their hair and tambourines in their hands. White witches recited incantations. Cameras flashed and candles flickered against the dark night canvas. The place was alive with magical merriment. I was captivated by the high-spirited energy of everyone around me. But there was a stirring deep down inside me, a warning of something yet to come.

I took Skye's arm and led her away from the lights. "Let's sit down for awhile; my feet are getting sore," I said, as I took one of the blankets off her arm and spread it on the ground behind a giant slab of blue stone. Skye gathered her ankle-length, orange skirt around her short legs and sat down beside me. I gazed up at the sliver-plated moon that peeked from behind dark clouds; they looked like the shadows of giant bats sailing across the sky. I hoped that it would not rain. I took off my gloves, opened my bag, took out the bottle of wine, and unscrewed the top. "So, is it everything you'd thought it would be?" I asked, after I shoved my hands back into my gloves, took a swig from the bottle, and then passed it to Skye.

"The best is yet to come, Fletch. I can't wait to see the sun rise between the stones and see the Archdruid conducting the welcoming ceremony. It's all so—" she took a deep breath, "—intoxicating!" She draped her blanket over our legs. "You're not feeling it, Fletch?"

I removed the wine bottle from my mouth. "I'm just worried about my aunt and all the other shit that's going on." I could feel the tears swelling up inside me as I looked into her face. "I'm going to miss you, Jenks, my dykey best friend."

She giggled and laid her head on my shoulder. "I'm going to miss you too, my witchy best friend."

I handed her the bottle. "Do you really think I have a psychic gift?"

"I think you do, Fletch."

"But how do I use it?"

"If I knew I'd tell you. Maybe you have to go back to that other life to find it."

"We tried that, remember?"

She sat up and gave me the bottle. "I have an idea! This place is where your ancestors conducted their ceremonies thousands of years ago and you said you dreamt about running around theses stones with Merthia, and the stones are said to have magical powers."

"So?"

She turned around to face the huge slab of rock. "Take off your gloves and put your hands on it," she said.

I placed my bare hands on the icy cold stone and cringed.

"Can we get this over with? This thing is freezing."

"Now close your eyes, breathe deeply, and concentrate. Think of how it might have been back then, when you were Colrea. Call on your ancestors to take you back to that time." *I wasn't sure that I wanted to go.*

The stone was getting warmer. "Look into your soul, dig deep, and excavate that life." My head was getting fuzzy. I started to spin, round and around. I tried to free my hands but they were cemented to the rock. I felt dizzy and sick to my stomach. The spinning stopped. I opened my eyes. It was still nightfall. My hands fell from the rock. I looked for Skye; she wasn't there. The atmosphere was different now.

Chapter 22

I heard voices, lots of voices, some in a language I didn't understand. "Find her, you imbeciles. She has come back and she cannot escape. There is nowhere for her to go." I recognized that voice but—could it be...

Shadows of screaming vultures circled overhead. The air was crisp and biting. I moved back from the stone and gazed around the area. The ancient monoliths were smooth and uniform, in a perfect circle. Fires inside the circle lit the sky and the air reeked of wood smoke, sweet herbs, and death. I rose from the ground and peeked around the blue stone. There were clusters of people, some in long white robes, others wore dark hooded cloaks. One of the groups closest to me was performing some sort of slaughtering ceremony. They were jabbing sharp spears into the backs of cows. The poor blood-stained creatures were failing and tossing their heads. A man was wrapped in the hide of a newly-slain cow. He was drenched in blood and guts from the meat. Two younger men sat beside him, their mouths covered in gore from eating raw flesh. I winced and swallowed the nausea that was working its way up from my gut.

"Over here. She's over here." A group of men with long beards were running towards me, spears held high in their hands. My heart started thumping madly. My first impulse was to run but I knew it would be useless to try to escape them.

I tuned to the stone, pressed my hand on its frigid surface, and prayed. *Take me back! Oh please, God. Take me back.* Someone grabbed my arm. Petrified with fear, I froze. Then I turned to face my captor. He was wearing a sheepskin over his shoulders and a dirty white tunic gathered at the waist with a rough piece of rope. His gray beard was matted and a necklace of tiny bones hung around his dirty neck. The other men gathered around me, looking me up and down, wide-eyed and babbling to each other in a strange language, fascinated, I was sure, with the oddly dressed spectacle of a woman in front of them. One of the men poked me with his finger. I grimaced.

They dragged me between the stones and into the circle, through the crowed of primitive people. Everyone stopped and stared at me. The air was thick and fetid with the stench of feces and sweat. I felt like a lamb being led to the sacrificial altar, and perhaps that was exactly what I was. The blood was gushing through my veins like a raging river. They stopped and threw me, face first, on the ground. There was a moment of foreboding silence. Someone was marching towards me. It must have been someone of great importance as the people moved back and bowed their heads.

A woman stepped in front of me. I raised my head. My gut clinched. It was her, my dreaded rival. "Merthia." My voice was a croaky whisper.

"Get up!" she commanded. I scrambled to my feet. She was rapped in a luxurious wide-hooded cape of purple silk; her long red hair flowed loose over her shoulders. Her green eyes held long lashes that cast spidery shadows down her high cheek bones. She smiled mischievously; her teeth were like pearls between her scarlet lips. She was stunning. But I knew all too well that buried inside that beautiful, bewitching facade there was an evil, hideous creature. "You are an imbecile, Colrea. You thought you could come back here without me knowing. I know everything." She tossed her head. "And now, finally, I am going to get my revenge."

I wiped the mud from my face, stood tall, straightened my back, and tried to look brave, but inside my guts were churning over and over. "If you could have killed me you would have done it by now. You told me the last time we met that the time and place had to be just right." I peered around. "But I don't think that this is the right place or time."

Her face was wild with rage; her green eyes latched on to mine and glared furiously at me. "We'll see about that." She turned. "Bring my axe!" she called to the men behind her.

I wasn't going to die without knowing more and I wasn't going down without a fight. "Before you slaughter me, would you have the decency to answer some questions?" Her eyebrows creased. A satanic grin spread across her lips, as if she were amused. My throat was tight and I was struggling to give voice to the words. "Are you still using Belinda to conduct your evil deeds? Will you free her if you kill me and will you leave my aunt alone?" I cleared my clogged throat. "You told me that Mrs. Tilly was your real mother, Hagmanis. Is that true? Were you lying? And were you lying about Belinda being my aunt's biological daughter?"

She whipped her head back and cackled like an old witch. "Cousin, you are absurd. I care nothing about decency, and I am under no obligation to tell you anything." She moved closer to me and stared me in the face. "But I won't deny you the truth." She stroked my face with one of her graceful fingers. Then she dug her sharp fingernail into my skin and trailed it down the side of my cheek, drawing a line of blood. I flinched. My hand shot to my face. "After all, Colrea, we are cousins," she said. "Tell me, did you really believe that that eccentric old witch was my mother? Stupid! She is merely a pawn in my game, a mischievous old faerie that I brought back to assist me. As for your feeble old aunt—" Her eyes grew wider. "I am going to cut off her head and slice her into little pieces."

I gasped, and my hands formed a fist. "My aunt is not feeble, I can assure you. What will you do with Belinda?"

Her mouth became a sour grin. "I haven't decided yet." She turned and shouted, "What is keeping you, imbecile? Bring me my axe!"

I swallowed hard but the lump stayed in my throat. I was desperate to know the truth before I died. "Is Belinda Maud's real daughter?"

The man with the axe was hurrying through the crowd. "Of course not; are you so stupid that you could not sense that? Have you lost all of your powers?" She chuckled and reached for the crude, bloodstained axe. "Like your friend Helgara and all the goddesses of light, you are powerless."

"Why did you say that Merryweather Lodge was built on sacred ground?"

"Enough questions! Kneel down and bow your head, cousin." *Surely she couldn't really kill me? This was another world, another dimension. None of this was real. Was it?* Two men came forward, grabbed my arms, and pushed me to the ground. She lifted the axe. I bowed my head and prayed.

A soft voice, like that of an angel, spoke. *Was I dreaming? Was I dead?* "I am not powerless, Merthia." I lifted my head ever so slowly. It was the goddess I had seen in my vision, my radiant friend Helgara. She had hold of Merthia's axe-swinging arm. "There has been enough bloodshed, Merthia. It's time to stop the carnage." Merthia's face was seething with rage. Helgara looked down at me and smiled sweetly. "Rise, Colrea." I lifted my trembling body from the ground. Helgara turned her eyes to Merthia and said to me, "The reason she called the ground under the cottage sacred is because she and her evil mother are buried there."

An elderly lady dressed like a gypsy was pushing her way through the mob of people. There were gasps and moans, and fear on their faces as they moved back to let her through. "Who are you calling evil? Let my daughter go, at once!" There was something about her that reminded me of someone

I knew and I recognized that voice. "Does she have the amulet?" the strange woman asked.

Helgara smiled and lowered Merthia's arm. "Hagmanis, you have come to join us," she said. Suddenly I felt something tugging at me. I felt disjointed, disembodied. My head was spinning around and around. Then, darkness.

"Wake up, Fletch. You're going to miss it."

My eyes popped open.

Skye was staring into my face. My heart leaped with utter relief. "I'm back! How long have I been gone?"

"A few hours. You fell asleep. I thought it was the wine and I didn't want to wake you."

I lifted my head. "You've been sitting here beside me all night."

"Yes, but I wasn't alone." Her eyes lit up. "This really cute girl came and sat down beside me. I gave her some of our wine." She hesitated. "Well, one thing led to another."

I sat up. "You've been making out with some strange girl, while I was about to get slaughtered?"

"Slaughtered?" Her eyes grew and she touched the side of my face. "Where did you get that scratch?"

I put my hand to my cheek. "Ow." *How could that still be there? Wasn't it all just a vision, a dream? Or did I really travel back in time?*

I pulled a pen and note pad out of my bag. "I'll tell you all about it." I handed her the pen and pad. "Write this down while it's still fresh in my memory." I tried to remember every little detail but it was slowly becoming a foggy blur, drifting from my memory like a dark cloud across a stormy sky. But there were a few details that I could not forget, like the voice and demeanor of Merthia's mother, the wicked sorceress Hagmanis. It was getting light. The sun would soon rise.

All the tourists and pagans were gathered in a large circle, as the sun drifted, like a giant yellow saucer, up between two of the huge ancient stones. Everyone cheered. The herald lifted a long bronze trumpet known as a carnyx, held it vertically in his hands, and blew. Arthur Pendragon, the Druid leader, stood in the center of the circle. He was wearing a long while robe with a red dragon on the front. He made an offering and blessed the newborn sun. The grove members spoke in unison, saying, "Grow strong, O' newborn sun." The senior Druidess came forward. She was also dressed in a white robe with a red dragon on the front. Bits of foliage and mistletoe ran through her braided hair. She turned to the north and raised her arms. "Hail to the fertile darkness of the north. Life and light is reborn." She turned to the east. "Hail to the gentle breeze of the east. Life and light is reborn." She turned to the south. "Hail the rekindled spark of the south. Life and light is reborn." And finally she turned to the west. "Hail the trickling drop of the west. Life and light are reborn." We said a prayer to the Great Spirit for world peace and for protection of mother earth. I sent a personal prayer, for protection for me and for peace at Merryweather Lodge.

On the way back to the car I tuned to Skye and asked, "What was she like?"

"Who?" she asked.

"The cute girl you met."

She grinned. "She was here on holiday from the States and she gave me her phone number. She was my princess charming, Fletch."

I smiled and nodded my head.

When we got back to the cottage we learned that Martha had not been to visit Auntie and there was still no one home at her brother's house. I could tell that Auntie was upset. She kept sniffing and fiddling with her hanky and it looked like she had been baking since early morning. There was a full English breakfast waiting for us when we got back, with bacon, eggs, sausages, and piles of pastries. She had forgotten that I didn't eat meat and about her guest's so-called allergies.

Skye was in the parlor, gathering the last of her things before Jonathan was to arrive to take us to the airport. I went to see her and to say goodbye. I sniffed back the tears as I entered the room. "Hey, Jenks, thanks for coming. I'm going to miss you."

She reached up and threw her arms around my neck. "I'm going to miss you, too, Fletch." Then she took my hand and led me to the couch. "Sit for a minute," she said. "I have been thinking. If Merthia and her mother are buried," she looked down at the floor, "under here, maybe burying the pentagram in the cellar is the key. Think about it; it's an ancient symbol of protection and healing. People used to inscribe it on graves and chests to keep the contents safe. Maybe if the pentagram is buried on top of Merthia's and Hagmanis's remains, and the ground is consecrated, they will be sealed in, forever."

A twinge of hope built inside me. "And that's why Winston has been trying to bury it." But then I shook my head and said, "No, it's too easy."

"Maybe, but you have to give it a try." Skye handed me a pad of paper. "Here, I've written some things down, with the instructions on how to consecrate the ground after you've buried the pentagram. But don't do it alone; it's much too dangerous."

"What about Belinda? I have to do something to help her, now that I know for sure that she's my cousin."

"But you still don't know that for sure, Fletch. All that Merthia said was that she wasn't Maud's daughter, right? And Merthia has lied to you before."

"Yes, but I just assumed..."

"Don't assume anything, Fletch."

There was a tap on the door. It was Jonathan. "Well, la-dies, are you ready?" He looked tired and downcast and there were dark shadows on his chin and under his nose. He hadn't shaved.

We drove Skye to the airport and said our goodbyes. I made her promise that she would email me once a week and call me as soon as she got home. I also told her to make sure she contacted her princess charming and to let me know how that went. Even though I was sad to see her go, in some ways it was a relief. I would finally get to spend time with Jona-than. I also hadn't had any time to be alone or to work on the book I was writing or try to pick up some freelance work. But I knew before I did any of that, there was something much more important that I had to take care of.

Jonathan was as quiet on the way home from the airport as he had been on the way there. He seemed to be in another world, gazing out the window as if searching for some lost soul. "What's wrong, Jonathan? I thought you'd be somewhat relieved when Skye left. You weren't exactly...welcoming to her."

He took his eyes off the road and gave me a quick glance. "I'm sorry, Emily. You're right. I should have been friendlier to her but I had a feeling that she didn't approve of our relationship and—"

I cut him off. "And what?"

"Oh, nothing, I just had the feeling that she wanted you all to herself."

I wasn't going to get into this. "Aren't you the least bit curious to know what's been going on?" My voice was getting louder. "I mean the paranormal stuff." He never answered. "And you haven't even asked me how the Winter Solstice was."

"I heard all about the solstice from the two of you in the back seat on the way to the airport. And I thought things had quieted down, in the paranormal realm."

"No, Jonathan, it's only gotten louder." I told him everything that had happened, my dreams, my visions, and the occurrence in the cellar. I even told him about my experience at Stonehenge, but I left out the bit about Belinda not being his mother's biological daughter.

He just sat there in quiet contemplation, not saying a word. When I finished, I told him, in an angry tone, that I wasn't making any of it up, I wasn't crazy, and he was to stop trying to push it all under the rug like Auntie did and that he had to help me get rid of Merthia. He looked across at me and said, "I know, I know, we need to put a stop to this once and for all. The thought of my mum and sister being involved in all of this stuff…" He hesitated. "Well, I just can't get my head around it."

As we were driving down the narrow dirt road that led to the cottage, we passed a police car. What were the police doing here? I felt a sudden wave of apprehension.

Chapter 23

I dashed into the cottage. Auntie was sitting in her comfy chair, holding her handkerchief to her face. Her eyes were red and puffy. I squatted by the side of her chair and reached for her hand. "Auntie, what's wrong? What's happened?"

"It's Martha," she sniffed. "She's gone." She put her hanky to her nose and gave a loud blow.

"Gone where? Back to Australia?"

She dabbed her eyes. "Gone for good, luv. They found 'er in a ditch, on 'er way 'ere she was." She gnawed on her bottom lip and sniffed. "Dead as a doornail, all chopped up into pieces, she were, just like Lizzy and some of the others." I shuddered. Her puffy red eyes peered down at me. "The bobbies wanted to know why I didn't call Fred, 'er brother, when she didn't show up. I told im' we called umpteen times but no one was 'ome. They said 'er brother and 'is wife were 'ome all evening." She gave me a puzzled look. "What do ya make of that?"

Jonathan came over and put his hand an Auntie's shoulder. "I'm so sorry, Mrs. Fletcher. Can I make you a cup of tea?"

"She needs something stronger than tea," I said to him. "Bring her some brandy and pour me a glass while you're there." Jonathan came back from the kitchen with two glasses of Auntie's homemade blackberry brandy and a glass of whiskey for himself. I had never known him to drink whiskey before.

He stood in front of the fire, his head bowed, staring into the glass of amber liquid.

Auntie took a sip of her brandy. "It ain't proper to be drinking at this time of day, it ain't."

"You need something to calm your nerves. You've just had a terrible shock." I pulled the tapestry-covered stool up beside the arm of her chair and sat down. "I think you have an idea of who might have done this." I looked into her face. "Don't you, Auntie Em?" She turned her head. "Look at me, Auntie. This stuff has gone on far too long. You can't pretend it's not happening any more. It's time to put an end to this curse that has plagued Merryweather Lodge for God knows how long. I don't know what you've experienced here or how much you know but I'm going through hell."

She took hold of my hand, gave it a gentle squeeze, and said, "Best not to talk about it, luv, its bad luck. Once you start talking about it, yer doomed, and I ain't leaving this 'ere cottage, our Emily, not unless they take me out in a wooden box, that is." Her bottom lip quivered. "They're all 'ere, ya see luv, m' mum, m' Reg and all the others. I won't leave them. I won't, not for all the tea in China. And I ain't selling Merryweather Lodge, our Emily, so don't try and talk me into it. It's supposed to be yours when I kick the bucket. Your Uncle Reg loved the bones of this place, he did." She burst into tears.

I suddenly realized why she wouldn't talk about the paranormal activity here. She thought that if she admitted that the place was haunted, I would try and talk her into selling it, and she was also under the impression that if she was to start talking about it things would get much worse. I knew it was a common superstition among the folks around here but I hadn't realized that Auntie believed in it with such conviction.

I leaned over and put my arms around her. "Drink your brandy, Auntie; we'll talk about this later." I didn't want to upset her anymore than she already was. As I pulled away from her, I noticed that she wasn't wearing the pendant. "Where's your mom's pendant?" I asked her hastily.

She touched her neck, and then fished inside the neck of her blouse. "Don't ya ave it, luv?"

"No, I put it around your neck before we left last night and made you promise that you wouldn't take it off, remember?"

She had a bewildered look on her face. "No, luv. I don't remember."

"It's probably in your room. I'll go get it for you."

She grabbed hold of my wrist and whispered, "I gave it to you. I want you to wear it."

I smiled and took her glass. "Let me fill this up for you."

As I walked towards the kitchen I caught Jonathan's attention by tossing my head to one side and motioning him to follow me. He had been staring into the fire while rearranging the logs with the iron poker.

"We have to find the pendant," I said as soon as I got him alone.

He grabbed my waist, drew me close to him, kissed me tenderly, and asked, "Are you okay?"

I nodded my head while running my fingers over the stubble on his chin. "I'm just worried about my aunt right now. And you?"

He dipped his head and sighed.

"Jonathan, what is it? Please tell me."

"I don't want to burden you with my problems. I'm just worried about my family. Belinda is behaving bizarrely and she's sick all the time, but they can't find anything wrong with her, physically, that is. She throws temper tantrums when I leave the house, and last night she ran away." He paused for a moment. "My mum found her a couple of hours later, wandering in the woods. We have an appointment to see her doctor on Monday; hopefully he'll change her prescription or suggest some more tests. My mum's miserable and fretting all the time; my dad's drinking too much and working long hours laboring on other farms to subsidize his income. He's hardly ever home and I can't say I blame him. And now someone else has been butchered. How is your poor aunt ever going to get over this?" His chin dropped.

I put my arms around his broad chest and buried my face in his neck; it was moist and there was a slight sweaty odor. He hadn't been showering. "You know how tough she is. She will get over this eventually. It's going to be all right, Jonathan. Once we get rid of Merthia and this curse, everything will be fine, including my aunt and Belinda. Your sister is still being controlled by that unearthly creature; you do realize that, right?"

He drew back. "She's sick."

"Get your head out of your butt, Jonathan." His eyebrows arched but I had to speak my mind. I couldn't let him continue pretending and covering for her. "She's not sick, she's possessed. And where do you think your sister was last night? Isn't it a coincidence that she wandered off at the same time Martha was slaughtered—and on a pagan Sabbath?"

He lifted his chin and met my indignant gaze. "Wait a minute. You can't possibly think that Belinda did that? She would have been covered in blood for one thing."

"And when your mother brought Belinda back was she wearing the same clothes that she left in?"

"I don't know." He was starting to pace.

"It's not her fault, Jonathan. Merthia has had control over your sister ever since she was born." I wanted to tell him that Belinda wasn't his mother's biological daughter but I didn't know that for sure. Merthia could have been lying to me again. "She has been using Belinda to get back at me and to perform her evil deeds." I took his hand. "But we are going to expel that hideous creature once and for all. I have the key

257

now; so all we need is Auntie's pendant." I gave his hand a gentle squeeze. "Will you help me?"

He leaned forward and pressed his lips to mine, and then he put his mouth to my ear. "We'll give it another try but if it doesn't work, you have to leave this place. It's not safe for you here."

No shit! "I'd go if you and my aunt came with me." He didn't answer. I took the brandy bottle off the counter, filled the glasses, and then I handed one to Jonathan. "Take this to my aunt while I go look for her pendant." He left the room glum-faced, his steps slow and sluggish.

The first place I went to look was in her room. I searched everywhere: under her bed, in the wardrobe, through her drawers. I even rummaged through her dirty clothes in her laundry basket and the cedar chest at the foot of her bed. I felt so guilty going through her personal stuff but I knew she wouldn't do it herself, and I knew now that the pendant was the key to getting rid of the hideous creature, Merthia, and freeing Merryweather Lodge. I looked in the bathroom, the kitchen, the parlor, the sitting room. I also checked the curio table in the hall. There were only two places left to look, two dreaded places. But why would it be in the attic or the cellar? Auntie wouldn't have taken it off in either of those places. She very seldom went into those rooms anyway, but I knew someone who did, and he was sitting on the kitchen floor staring up at me. I bent down and peered into his strange yellow eyes. "Winston, have you taken Auntie's pendant? Go find the pendant." I was startled by the sudden sound of someone clearing their throat.

"He ain''t gonna answer ya, luv, but if 'e does, let me know; 'e'd be worth a bob or two." She shook her head. "I know ya got a few tiles missin', our Emily, but pretty soon the 'ole roof's gonna be gone." She forced a smile. "But I luv ya anyway." Even at this difficult time of shock and grief Auntie could conjure up a good dose of sarcasm and humor. "How are you feeling?" I asked her.

"Like I've been pulled through a bush backwards. I'm gonna make m' self a cupper and take something for m' 'ead. It's splitting."

"You shouldn't be taking pain killers with brandy."

She sniffed. "It's only aspirin. Maybe it'll put me out of m' misery."

"Don't talk like that, Auntie Em." I put my arms around her chubby form. "I don't know what I'd do without you."

Her watery eyes gazed up at me, and tears trickled down her dear old face. "Yer' all I've got now, luv."

I could feel the tears welling up inside me as I held her close. "I won't leave you. I'm going to put an end to this curse once and for all." *I hope.* "Are you ready to tell me about what's been going on here? Do you remember what happened on the night that Uncle Reg died? And what about the incident in the woodlot with that horrid creature and Belinda? You must remember that." I waited for an answer. "If you're worried about that silly superstition, don't be. It's not going to get any worse just because you talk about it. It can't get any worse."

She pulled away from me and reached for her pills on the cupboard shelf. Then she filled a glass with water, threw the pills to the back of her throat, took a mouthful of water, and swallowed hard. "Ya know enough, our Emily." She shuffled towards the kitchen door. "Best if ya leave this place and never come back."

I could feel the fury of utter frustration building up inside me. I stepped in front of the door and stared her right in the face. "Is that want you want me to do—leave you here and never come back? Leave you all by yourself to suffer the same demise as Uncle Reg or worse to end up in a ditch some-where, butchered like poor Martha?"

She gasped and fumbled inside her apron pocket for her hanky. *How could I have been so insensitive, after all she's been through, after the shock she's just had? What is wrong with me?* I opened the door and stepped aside. "I'm so sorry. I didn't mean to be so cruel. I know you'll talk to me about it when you're ready."

She shoved her soiled hanky back into her deep apron pocket. "When I'm ready and not before." Then she asked, "Can ya drive me to Martha's brother's 'ouse tomorrow? I've gotta see 'im and tell 'im 'ow sorry I am." Her eyes were heavy.

"Of course I will. Perhaps you should go and lay down for a while." She ambled through the doorway, dragging her slippered feet. "Do you have any idea where your mother's pendant could be?" I called after her. Her head moved from side to side, indicating that she did not know.

I chucked back the rest of my brandy and went to talk to Jonathan. He was sitting in Uncle Reg's worn wingback chair, drink in hand, gazing at the flickering Christmas tree lights. "It's a bit early to have the tree lights on."

He jumped, jolted from his reverie. "They were on when I got back from the toilet. I thought one of you had come in and switched them on."

"I didn't and you know what my aunt's like for saving electricity."

"It must have been one of your unearthly friends then."

Or her. "Friends? Have you any idea what it been like for me here?" I flopped on the sofa and buried my face into my hands. Jonathan came over and sat beside me. "There isn't a moment goes by in this cottage when I don't fear for my life and for my aunt's life. I have thoughts of the creature jumping out at me from behind every door, coming down the basement stairs with her bloody axe. Every shadow is a ghost, every sound a warning cry." I sniffed and sobbed, trying hard to restrain the pent up emotions that were bubbling inside me. Jonathan put his arms around me and drew me in. I snuggled my face into his woolen sweater; it was warm and calming.

"Like I said, if we're not successful in getting rid of her this time you've got to promise me you'll leave this place."

I sat up. "Leave you and my aunt?"

"It's the only way. As long as you stay in this area, she's going to haunt you until she gets what she wants. I have a friend who owns a flat in Kent. I might be able to get him to rent it to you and your aunt. I could drive down there on weekends to visit you."

"My aunt wouldn't move from this cottage; you heard what she said. And even if I was able to convince her to move, how do we know that Merthia wouldn't come after me there? We don't know how far she'd travel to get her revenge."

"Aren't spirits supposed to be bound to a specific area?" he asked.

"I think so but she's not your normal run of the mill ghost, is she? What we have to concentrate on now is finding that pendant and burying it. I've checked everywhere except the attic and the cellar." I rested my head on his shoulder. "And I'm not going in either of those rooms, a least not by myself."

His lips brushed my forehead. "Let's go take a look then." My skin started to crawl at the thought of going back there again.

Chapter 24

I knocked back the rest of my brandy, put the glass on the side table, and followed Jonathan through the passage and up the attic stairs. I was feeling a little light-headed from the alcohol and my legs were wobbly. The closer we got to the portal at the top of the stairs the weaker my legs became.

Jonathan opened the heavy wooden door. The cold ominous air of the room wafted towards me, like a ghostly fog. I stood on the top step, peeking inside. "Are you coming?" Jonathan asked, as he entered the room.

"I'll just stand here and wait, if you don't mind." I held the door with both hands, just incase, and told him where to look. Things had been shifted again. The doll was back on the covered ottoman, not in the bed where I'd left her, and the rocking horse and box of toys were sitting beside the dressing table. Skye had put them in the secret room. Who keeps moving them, I wondered? I was soon to find out.

The pendant was nowhere to be found. "What about the

cat?" Jonathan asked as I went to close the door. "We can't shut him in here."

I hadn't noticed Winston sitting behind the door. "He can stay in here; this is his home. This is where he used to spend time with his master. We can just leave him here; he walks through the closed doors." Jonathan's brows rose as I closed the door; he gave me a sour grin but didn't question my seemingly bizarre comments. I realized I had neglected to tell him who I thought Winston really was, so was this entire paranormal stuff becoming commonplace to him? Was he growing accustomed to it? Or did he think I was going loopy? "There's only one more place to check," I told him, as he came down the stairs. "The pendant has to be down in the cellar. Winston's probably stolen it again and taken it down there."

"I suppose he wanted to keep it for himself, to wear on special occasions," Jonathan said, jokingly.

"No, Mr. Snide, he keeps trying to bury it."

"What?"

"Never mind, I'll tell you about it later; just go down there and look for it," I ordered as I yanked on the handle of the dwarf-sized cellar door. He had to crouch down and lower his head to get through. "There's a light switch on the right, just behind the door," I told him as I held on to the handle securely and hid behind the wooden frame, not daring to look down into the deep dark hole. "Look for lumps or scratch marks on the floor; it could be buried in the dirt." I knew that even if Winston had buried it, without the blessing and without the ground being consecrated it would have no effect. At least that's what Skye had written in her notes. It seemed to be taking Jonathan a long time and I was starting to worry for his safety. "Hurry up, Jonathan, you're too vulnerable down there," I called to him.

"It's not here," he called back to me.

"Are you sure? Keep lookin; it's got to be there."

I could hear his footsteps on the stairs. "I told you it's not there."

I closed the door behind him. "We have to find it, Jonathan. It's our last hope."

He thought for a moment. "We'll ask your aunt again when she wakes up from her nap. If she was wearing it when you left, then it's got to be in the cottage somewhere. I'm sure she'll remember what she did with it in time." *In time? How much time did we have?*

"Where are you going?" I asked as he walked past the sitting room towards the front door.

"I'm going to give my mum a call and tell her what's happened."

"Where's your cell phone?"

"Belinda took it and she won't tell me what she's done with it. I'll get a new one on Monday."

Before he picked up the receiver he asked, "Is it okay if I stay overnight? I can't leave you and your aunt alone, not after what's just happened."

Something stirred inside me. "Of course you can."

I heard him arguing with his mother on the phone and

telling her that he was staying here and that was the end of it! I was happy to hear him sticking up for himself, finally. Maud seemed to have some unnatural power and control over her son. I knew now that there was something sinister about her, but I couldn't figure out what it was and what role she played in this mystery. But I knew all too well what role his sister was playing.

Auntie was still sleeping and snoring like an old fish wife. The brandy and aspirin had knocked her out. I took some of my precious sea salt, sprinkled it in a full circle around her bed, and said a silent payer to protect her, and then I went into the kitchen to make us something to eat. Auntie didn't believe in using microwaves or any other "new-fangled" appliances, so there were no quick pre-cooked meals to be heated in her kitchen. I sliced some thick white homemade bread, smothered it in butter, and started chopping some fresh vegetables for a salad. "Can I help?" Jonathan asked as he stepped into the kitchen.

I stuck my paring knife into a plump tomato. "You can put the kettle on."

He came up behind me, nuzzled his face into my neck, and nibbled on my skin. It gave me goose bumps all over. "I've had enough tea; my mum drowns me in it. Does your aunt have any beer?"

"There should be some in the pantry but it won't be cold."

"I'm British, remember; we don't drink cold beer." Jonathan walked towards the pantry, leaving my neck damp and wanting more. His tall muscular form moved with such a commanding power, such an alluring grace. I couldn't take my eyes off his wide shoulders and firm, perfectly sculptured butt. I had forgotten how tantalizing and gorgeous this man was; right from his silky black hair to his compelling dark brown eyes, to his sexy cleft chin, all the way down his long, sturdy legs, and all the luscious stuff in between. His body begged to be touched, to be stroked, and to be licked in all its succulent places.

He sat at the table, pulled back the tab on the large beer can in front of him, and put it to his mouth. He must have felt my eyes glued to him as he lifted his head and rose from the table. "I'm sorry, what was I thinking, you wanted tea, right?" he asked.

"Yes, please; no, maybe I'll have red wine; there's some in the corner cupboard." The buzz that I had got from the brandy had worn off and gloom was setting in. I needed a little something to brighten my low spirits. "What am I going to do if we don't find the pendant?" I asked him, as I placed a bowl of salad and big chunk of bread in front of him.

"He stuck his fork into the bowl of leafy greens. "Like I said, it's got to be here somewhere. It couldn't have just disappeared."

"Don't be naïve, Jonathan. As you well know, anything is possible around here." I suddenly thought of Auntie and how long she'd been sleeping. "I'm just going to check on my aunt and see if she's awake yet. I'll be right back." There was a sense of dread in my gut as I walked through the passage to her room. The door was ajar. She always closed her door. The salt ring was still there but Auntie was tossing, turning, and moaning as if she were in pain. I went over to her bedside. She must have sensed my presence as her eyes opened almost immediately. "How are you feeling, Auntie?"

She raised her torso, while I lifted and fluffed the pillows behind her.

Her old eyes wrinkled at the corners as she adjusted them to the light. "What time is it, luv?"

I glanced at my watch. "Five o'clock."

She threw back the blankets. "Flippin 'eck. It's tea time; gotta get up and make us something to eat."

I pushed her legs back under the blankets and tucked her in. "You'll do no such thing. I've made us some tea and I'm going to bring you yours."

"Hey, I'm not ready for the nackers yard yet, I ain't." That was Auntie's way of telling me that she was still healthy and shouldn't be put out to pasture yet.

"You've had a terrible shock and you need your rest. Stay here and I'll bring you some tea," I insisted, a little surprised that she didn't argue about it as she usually would have done.

"Bring me another one of m' pills. I'm still feelin' a little poorly," she said as I walked out the door.

"I'll be back in a few minutes," I reassured her before I closed the door. I heated some of her of her favorite chicken soup in a pot on the little gas stove, sliced a piece of pound cake and a small portion of bread, and set them on a tray with a cup of tea, a glass of water, and her pill bottle. But when I got to her room she had fallen back to sleep. I laid the tray on her bedside table and left the room. Jonathan was busy clearing the table.

"She's gone back to sleep," I told him. "She'll probably be in her bed all evening." He tuned to face me, lifted his eyebrows, and gave me a warm, seductive smile. I knew what he was thinking, and a subtle sexual energy was already starting to build inside me.

After we washed and dried the dishes, Jonathan grabbed the bottle of wine and two glasses and tipped his head, motioning me to follow him. He led me into the sitting room, set the glasses down on the wooden chest that served as a coffee table, poured the wine, handed me a glass, and raised his. "Alone at last."

I shook my head "We will never be alone, not as long as that hideous creature is around. She's probably watching us right now, just waiting for us to get really close."

He took the glass out of my hand, placed it on the chest, then grabbed my waist and pulled me hard against him. "We are going to get very close and nothing is going to stop us."

My body was ready and aroused, but my mind could not let go of what had just happened. "This doesn't seem right, Jonathan, not after Auntie's best friend has just been murdered." His mouth was already caressing the nape of my slender neck and his long fingers were working their way from my waist to my breasts. My crotch was starting to throb. "Did you hear what I said, Jonathan?"

He withdrew, stepped back, and said in a chilly tone,

"When will it be the right time, Emily?" He walked towards the hearth, threw a log on the dying embers, and started jabbing at it with the iron poker. My eyes followed him, peeking at a forbidden place that I had fondled many times in the privacy of my own mind, a place that was now bulging with arousal. I couldn't stand it any longer. I took hold of his sweater and whipped him around, grabbed his hand, and forced him onto the fireside rug. His mouth was on mine, wet and sensuous, his tongue probing the inside of my mouth. His fingers fumbled with the buttons on my shirt. "Wait," I said, putting my finger on his lips. "What if Auntie comes in and finds us like this? I would die of embarrassment. Let's go into the parlor. She won't come in there without knocking when the door is closed."

I stopped in and checked on Auntie as I passed her bedroom. She was snoring contently under her thick patchwork blanket, as the elaborate brass headboard gleamed like a massive crown behind her head. She must have been awake at some point as all the food on her tray was gone. On my way to the parlor I kept wondering if Merthia was watching us and if she was going to suddenly appear, seething with jealousy and wielding her axe. We closed the parlor door.

I got Jonathan to help me to pull out the couch and make my bed. I could almost smell the raunchy pheromones that he was emitting as he tucked in the sheets. My whole body was pulsating with a lusty eagerness, like a lioness in heat. He started to disrobe, pulling his bulky woolen sweater over his head. His chest was muscular with a dark dusting of hair.

Then he undid the buckle of his belt, undid his fly, and dropped his jeans. I gasped with delight, under my breath, at the sight of the huge swelling in his underwear. It was hard not to stare but I forced my gaze away from him and started to undress. I got down to my bra and panties and stopped. He moved towards me, completely naked, his private parts hard and erect. I stared up at him coyly. He unfastened the hook at the back of my bra and tossed it on the bed, and then he bent down and drew my panties down my legs and under my feet. As he came back up he touched my thigh gently with his moist lips. I trembled. He curved his big hands over my naked bottom and held me still while he kissed me. I could feel his stiff manly parts pushing up against me. Both of our hearts were pounding, but it was hard to distinguish between the two. "I love you," I whispered, against his mouth.

My crotch throbbed with an intense need that I had never felt before. He took my arm and guided me onto the bed. I turned to him and ran my fingers through the hairs on his brawny chest. Slowly I slid my tongue down, down to the dark line of hair that ran from his bellybutton to his genitals. Then I stopped. Needy moans escaped from his lips. His damp skin tasted salty and sweaty; its tantalizing, natural, manly scent filled me with an erotic sensation. His mouth found my breasts. My nipples bellowed as his tongue explored their peaks. He slid all the way down my body. My legs parted; he caressed the inside of my thighs with his tongue, teasing me with anticipation. *Breathe, Emily, breathe,* I told myself. His head was between my legs. I arched my back and moaned until the wave of arousal came to a climax. Never have I felt so much erotic pleasure. He pulled himself up and slid on top of me. I dug my fingernails into the blanket as he pushed himself inside me and thrust, over and over until he too, climaxed in a shuddering finish. We lay there, still, relaxed, wrapped in each other's arms, not saying a word, basking in our own satisfaction. Until…crash!

Chapter 25

"Auntie!" I threw on my housecoat, dashed out of the door, and into her room. The bedroom door was open. Auntie was sitting on the side of her bed, rubbing her eyes. Her stubby little legs were dangling over the edge of the mattress. Broken pieces of china and pottery were scattered all over the floor, beside the dressing table. They were her precious cat ornaments. *Oh shit! It must have been her! We've made the creature mad and now she's taking it out on Auntie. Thank God I put the protective circle around her or she would have...* "Auntie Em, are you okay?"

She struggled to her feet. "Thought I 'eard a noise." She slipped her feet into her fuzzy bedroom slippers and shuffled towards me. Her hand shot to her mouth when she looked down at the floor. "Bloody hell! Who did that?"

I bent down and started to pick up the shattered ornaments. "It was the ghost, Auntie. Who else could it have been? You know, the one that torments you, the one that haunts this place and murders and butchers people." I could feel my body tensing at the accusation in my voice "The one that you refuse to acknowledge."

"What happened here?" Jonathan asked as he walked through the doorway.

Auntie placed the waste paper bin beside me and said, in a slurred but snappy voice, "It were the cats. I've caught them up there on m' dresser before, I 'ave. I'll give m' what for if I see them up there again."

I had never seen any of the cats climbing up on the furniture before and why was it only the cat ornaments that were smashed while everything else on the dressing table was intact? "It was Merthia!" Cries of utter frustration were starting to build up inside me as I shifted my gaze back and forth between the two of them. "I'm sure that both of you have a good idea of who it was, and if we don't find that pendant soon and put a stop to her, it's going to get worse."

Auntie walked over to the bedside table, fished into her Toby mug, pulled out her false teeth, and maneuvered them into her mouth with her hanky. "No good crying over spilt milk," she said, shoving her hanky up the sleeve of her full-length flannel nightgown. "It will all come out in the wash," she mumbled, as she left the room.

I threw my hands up and looked at Jonathan. "Auntie loved those ornaments. Why wasn't she upset to lose them? It was a warning, you can be sure of that. Merthia will be back and she's madder than hell now," I dipped my chin, "after what just happened between us."

Jonathan stayed that night and we made love, again and

again. Auntie had made a bed up for him on the sofa but after she'd gone back to her room for the night, he crept into the parlor and climbed in bed with me.

The next morning he left early to go to his parents' house. Auntie and I spent the day wrapping Christmas gifts and baking. She was somber, quiet, and wore a sad expression for most of the day. I missed her singing and listening to the Christmas carols on her stereo. She had called Martha's brother and asked if she could call in and see them, but he was on his way to the police station and he asked her if she could come over on Boxing Day. She said she would.

That evening before I went to bed I heard a rustling outside. I dismissed it at first as the wind and then I remembered that Auntie sometimes forgot to let Sam in before she went to bed. He wasn't in his usual spot on his woven rug in the corner of the kitchen. When I opened the back door I saw the shadow of someone walking away from the cottage. It was the shadow of a short, plump woman in a long dress. "Hello," I called. "Can I help you? Were you looking for someone?" She disappeared into the darkness. Sam came strolling up to me from his dog house; as I bent down to pet him I noticed a large wicker basket on the bottom step. I took it inside and peeled back the purple tea towel that lay on top. There was a brown bag marked sea salt, a small bottle of lavender oil, some dill, fennel, sage, cinnamon sticks, acorns, and four colored candles. I took it into the parlor and shoved it under the pull-out couch. The sea salt would come in handy but Auntie hated lavender and dill. I assumed it was some old gypsy lady

or one of the superstitious locals bringing a token of condolences and protection to my aunt.

At six o'clock on Christmas morning I found myself wide
awake, staring at the low ceiling. I had been trying to quiet
the nagging voices in my head for over an hour but I couldn't
seem to put them to rest. Yesterday the local vicar had come
to see Auntie. He offered her his condolences at the loss of
her best friend, handed her a card, and wished her a Happy
Christmas from him and his dear wife. He just stood at the
door wearing a fake smile and glancing here and there, as if he
were afraid that someone was watching him, and when
Auntie invited him in for a cup of tea he stiffened, shook his
head, and then turned and fled. Some of the neighbors came
over in the evening for a cup of Wassail and munchies. Auntie
had put on a huge spread and she looked more cheerful than
she had the day before. Jonathan had popped in for a few
minutes; he had been on his way to his uncle's in Chillsbury
for a Christmas Eve family supper.

Christmas Day used to be my favorite day of the year. I
would wake up early on Christmas morning wide-eyed and
full of anticipation, anxious to see what Santa had brought
me. Sometimes my mom's sister and her family came to
spend the holiday with us and I'd have to share my room with
my cousin Kim who was three years younger than I was. I
adored her. She loved to dress up in my clothes and play with
my old dolls. I'd make a snowman with her on Christmas Day
and take her tobogganing on the hill behind our house; we'd
make sugar cookies and cupcakes and then decorate them. I

would pretend that she was my little sister. I had always wanted a sister. I wondered what Kim was doing right now? I wondered how my dog Merlyn was and if he'd remember me when I got back. Our neighbors were looking after him while we were gone. I thought about my dad, and how this would be his first Christmas without Mom. How was he holding up? He had promised to call me today. I missed my mom so much; like me, Christmas was her favorite time of year. Auntie had invited the McArthurs for Christmas dinner and the thought of seeing Maud and the unpredictable Belinda again made me nervous, although I was happy that Jonathan was going to be here, and I was looking forward to seeing his dad again.

I pushed my arms into my soft terry housecoat and shoved my feet into the warm slippers that Auntie had bought me. Then I strolled into the kitchen and poured myself a hot cup of coffee from the automatic coffee maker I'd bought in a department store in Sainsbury. I'd had a feeling that I'd be up very early this morning so I had set the timer for six. I needed my coffee in the morning as much as I needed my wine in the evening. I knew that I would have to curb both of these un-healthy habits eventually, but now was not the time. Sam nuzzled his cold nose into my hand. I bent down and patted him on the head. "Merry Christmas, Sammy; I wonder what Santa has in your stocking." His tired brown eyes peered up at me lovingly, and then he turned and strolled to the back door. The icy winter air struck me with a jolting blow when I opened the door to let him out. It was still pitch dark. Out in the country when there was no moonlight, the night is as black as a raven's wing.

"Good morning, luv. Happy Christmas."

I gave her a gentle squeeze. "Merry Christmas, Auntie Em. You're up early."

"Gotta get that there bird ready for the oven and fix us a nice big breakfast," she said, as she carried her kettle to the stove and ignited the gas burner. "But first we've gotta go see what Father Christmas 'as brought us." Her tone was low and sweet, as if she were talking to a little child. But I was glad that she was cheery; having her agreeable would make the day a little more tolerable.

I poured myself another cup of coffee. "Come on then, Auntie Em, let's go open some gifts."

"Hold your horses, can't be doing anything without my first cupper," she said, in a teasing tone, as she scooped the loose tea leaves into her tea pot.

We carried our cups into the sitting room. I switched on the Christmas tree lights and lit a couple of candles while Auntie put a match to the fire. There were a few neatly-wrapped gifts under the tree and four bulging, hand-knitted stockings hanging over the mantel, each with a name embroidered in gold silk on the front. Auntie had started to knit them in November, as soon as she found out that I was going to be spending Christmas with her. They were for my benefit I was sure, not hers. She still liked to think of me as a child. I handed her the red one marked Emy and I took the green one marked Emily Anne. There was also one for the cats and one for Sam. "I wonder what Santa has in our stockings? You first, Auntie," I said with a girlish giggle.

She sat down in her comfy chair, took a piece of the crystallized fruit from the glass bowl on the side table, popped it in her mouth, and then shoved her hand into the woolen stocking. I had stuffed it with her favorite chocolates, toffees, bath salts, talcum power, and some miniature cat ornaments that I hoped would replace the ones on her dressing table. She beamed as she pulled out her trinkets and sweets.

She looked at me with an eager expression, like that of a little girl waiting for her mother to open her hand made gift. "It's your turn now, luv. Let's see what Father Christmas brought you."

I dug into my knitted bag of little treasures. There were scented soaps in fancy boxes, bubble bath, a small carton of Jammy Dodgers—my favorite English biscuits—some mittens (hand knitted of course), a pen with my name on it, an address book and, at the very bottom, a little blue velvet box with a note wrapped around it, secured with an elastic band. I looked up at Auntie with a curious 'What have you bought me?' expression. She had a wide grin on her face.

My fingers peeled off the elastic band impatiently and unfolded the note. Elation started to well up inside me as I read the words.

"My dear Emily, please forgive me for not delivering this to you in person but I knew that our time alone today would be limited and I wanted you

to have this for Christmas. I know that this is your favorite day of year and how much you like sur- prises. I have loved you since the first time I met you as a young girl, in your uncle's pasture. Some- thing resonated inside me a feeling, of recognition, longing and affection too deep and too profound for words. I cannot imagine my life without you. Our love has endured many incarnations. Our souls were born to be together for eternity. I love you with all of my being and I want to share my life with you. Emily Anne Fletcher, will you marry me? Love, your soul mate, Jonathan."

I sniffed as a signal joyful tear trickled down my cheek. I glanced up at Auntie as I fumbled to open the little blue box. She was still beaming. I gasped with delight. It was much more than I'd ever imagined my engagement ring to be. A large, raised, emerald-cut diamond flanked by four tiny round diamonds set in a band of white gold.

"Put it on," Auntie instructed eagerly. "Gave it to me yesterday 'e did, told me to put it in yer stocking, and 'e asked me what I thought, bless 'im. I told 'im 'e were as fit as a butcher's dog and if my niece knew which side 'er bread was buttered she'd say yes."

The ring was a perfect fit. "I have to call him."

Auntie looked at the clock on the mantel. "It's too early, luv, best wait for awhile; ya don't want to wake up the whole 'ouse."

"I'll call him on his cell phone," I mumbled to her as I rushed out of the door and headed for the telephone in the hallway.

A groggy voice muttered through the other end of the receiver. "Hello, Happy Christmas."

"I will...I will...I will!" I cried down the phone, and then, with a crafty grin, I placed the receiver back on its stand.

We un-wrapped the rest of our gifts. Skye had bought me a necklace with a forever friends charm on it, and Auntie a book about cats and their so-called, magical powers. She sniffed and put it aside. My dad had sent me money, enough to tide me over for the rest of my stay, and Auntie a gift card to buy herself some flowers at the local florist.

We spent the rest of the morning preparing for our festive Christmas dinner and getting ready for our guests. I kept holding up my hand and admiring the gem that adorned my finger. The delicious aromas of roast turkey, gravy simmering on the stove, plum pudding bubbling in the pot, spiced apple cider, cloves, and cinnamon wafted through the cottage. Christmas carols blared from Auntie's old radio on the corner shelf and for the first time in a long while the cottage felt homey, warm and unthreatening, as if it had rid itself of its pesky dark shadows. On the surface, part of me felt light, joyful and unburdened, but deep down inside me stirred a fearful apprehension at the thought of the pending arrival of our dubious guests. What would they think of Jonathan's proposal?

Butterflies stared to flutter in my gut when I heard the

McArthurs car pull up on the gravel driveway.

Auntie took off her soiled apron, laid it over the back of the kitchen chair, smoothed down the front of her dress, and went to answer the door. Maud was the first one who stepped inside the door; she was carrying a plastic bag full of baking, and looked glum-faced as usual, complaining about the weather and the bumpy roads. John followed behind her, with a cheerful smile on his drawn, pale face. He'd aged considerably since the last time I saw him and his partially bald head now held just a thin halo of white. Belinda, I assumed, from the provocative way she was dressed, piercings and all, was back to her old self, and she didn't look ill at all; on the contrary, she looked positively thriving and cute in a slutty sort of way. Jonathan gave me a quick peck on the cheek as he walked through the door carrying an armful of parcels. "What would everyone like to drink?" I asked, as I ushered them into the sitting room, took their bags, and placed their parcels under the tree.

"Whiskey for me, love, if that's not too much trouble," John asked in an eager but feeble voice.

Maud shot him a dirty look and said to me, firmly, "Tea for me."

"Me too, luv," Auntie said, as she opened a box of chocolates. "Don't want to get tipsy before supper, I don't."

"I'll have white wine and make it a double," Belinda demanded, as she looked me up and down with contempt, as if I were a piece of trash.

"I'll help you," Jonathan said as he followed me into the

kitchen. As soon as we were alone, he swept me up in his arms and kissed me passionately. My heart leaped in response. Then he took hold of my hand, brought it up to his face, and gazed at his ring on my finger. "Are you ready to make our announcement?" he asked enthusiastically. A sense of anxiety washed over me as I carried my tray of drinks into the sitting room.

Chapter 26

I distributed the drinks. John McArthur took his greedily from the tray before I could hand it to him. Maud cleared her throat and gave her husband another reprimanding glance.

I sat on the floor and snuggled up beside Jonathan. He draped his arm over my shoulder and held me close. I nestled my head into the crook of his arm, fully aware of the resentful cold eyes upon me. "Are you ready?" he whispered. I put the rim of my wine glass to my mouth and took a big swig. *As ready as I'll ever be.*

He pulled himself up from the floor and reached for my hand. I stood tall and proud, my chin slightly raised, hand in hand with my handsome price charming, ready to defend our intention at any cost, but on the inside I was shaking like a quivering coward.

"Emily and I have an announcement to make." His voice was clear and final, his countenance steadfast and proud. He lifted my ring finger for everyone to see. "We are engaged." Auntie clapped and giggled. Belinda gasped. John's red face beamed. Maud rose from her seat, wide-eyed, her thin lips drawn tight. It looked like her ample breast was going to explode. "No! You're too young!" she shouted. I swallowed hard, as I suddenly remembered where I'd seen that demeanor and heard that voice before. Could this really be her? Mary Eliss's words rang in my head: "Watch out for the malevolent spirit. She is the master of disguise and deceit." Maud's face was seething with hate and anger, but then she appeared to re-think her reaction, and after a few seconds of silence she softened her stance and spoke again in a lowered voice, "You're too young to be married."

Auntie cleared her throat and leaned forward in her chair. "Now, now, let's not go makin' mountains out of mole hills. They are a bit young, I'll give ya that, but as we well know," she glared at Maud, "in our days younguns were married when they were much younger than these two, they were. Besides I'm sure they're not getting married yet for awhile." Again she looked over at Maud and said, "So don't go getting your knickers in a twist." Maud plunked herself down in her chair, but not before she threw me an icy scowl.

John McArthur struggled to his feet and raised his glass. "A toast to the happy couple." Auntie put her hanky to her mouth to stifle a loud burp, and then lifted her cushy bottom out of her chair, held up her glass, and said, "To my lovely Emily Anne, and little Jonny." Maud lifted her cup from its saucer, reluctantly. Belinda just rolled her eyes and kept her hands firmly planted on her lap. She was visibly fuming.

I helped Auntie set the dinner table and prepare the vege-

tables while Jonathan carved the turkey. We squeezed ourselves into the chairs around the old kitchen table. It groaned
under the weight of Auntie's huge, traditional Christmas
feast. Jonathan sat on one side of me, his miserable sister on
the other. I could feel the dislike and hostility emanating from
her as she shuffled her chair closer to her mother and further
away from me. The atmosphere was laced with tension and
gloom although some of us were trying hard to be cheerful
and festive. First we pulled the traditional Christmas crackers.
They contained party hats, tiny trinkets, and little pieces of
paper with jokes written on them. We went around the table
and read our riddles and jokes. When it came to my turn,
Belinda slipped me her piece of paper and took mine. I
shrugged and held it in front of me. Then I froze, as I read the
words she had written: *Gotcha bitch! I'm pregnant!* I didn't
know what to say. I just sat there, staring dumbfounded at the
piece of paper. Why was she telling me this? Did anyone else
know? I hadn't thought that she was seeing anyone but it was
probably a one-night stand knowing her. Why was she being
so smug, as if she had one over on me? Then something
clicked in my mind. No! It couldn't be. The creature was invisible when she raped Jonathan. That was just too unthinkable, too disgusting.

"Blinkin' heck our Emily, it's like waiting for paint to
dry." I looked up. Everyone was staring at me. Should I read
it? That would wipe the smug look off her face.

"Oh, it's a duplicate, the same one you had, Auntie," I
lied, and gave Belinda a hostile look out of the corner of my

eye. "Pass the turkey. I'm famished," Jonathan said, fracturing the awkward silence.

We ate heartily, drank four bottles of wine, and exchanged polite, idle chit-chat. Every once in a while Maud would flash me a chilly glance or Belinda would prod me purposely with her elbow. But I ignored their petty threats and teased by holding up my hand and admiring the gorgeous gem on my finger. Everyone wore their party hats except Belinda. John's was pink and shaped like a crown. Through its top his dappled, bald head protruded, looking like a shiny bowling ball wrapped in fancy paper. He looked hilarious and I couldn't help but snicker.

Before the McArthurs left I managed to corner Belinda as she came back from the washroom, something I had been trying to do all evening. "Was that a joke?" I asked her. "You're not really pregnant, are you?"

Her cold, wild eyes latched on to mine. I moved back as I felt the sting of their fury burning into my soul. "Jealous? Bitch!" she said as she pushed me against the wall. Then she hacked up a wad of phlegm and spit in my face. I wiped the disgusting gob from my cheek. My hands squeezed into fists. I gritted my teeth. I wanted so much to lash out at her, to scratch her face and rip her hair out, but I had to think of Auntie and Jonathan. "I'm going to kill you!" I snapped.

She grinned mischievously. "He was delicious," she said as she gave me the finger and walked away.

I asked Jonathan if he could stay the night but he said that he'd promised his mother that he'd spend Christmas night at their house with them.

Auntie was fast asleep in her comfy chair, her head laid back on the cushion, chin raised, mouth half open, making her usual grunting sounds. I sat beside the hearth and stared at the tiny twinkling lights on the tree; they shone like jewels against the old stone fireplace. This was supposed to be one of the best days of my life. I was engaged to the gorgeous Jonathan McArthur, my prince charming, the man of my dreams, my literal soul mate. But all that I could feel were *her* prickles, all that I could hear were Belinda's words. He was delicious and all I could think about was how I was going to kill *her*. It didn't matter to me anymore, if we killed Belinda as well as Merthia. Besides I was beginning to think that they were one and the same, that Belinda was not being possessed or used by Merthia, but that she was Merthia. I needed to find the pendant. *Please God, help me to find the pendant.* I covered my face as the tears of utter desperation ran down my cheeks.

"Don't cry, Emily." I gasped, and slowly removed my hands from my face. Standing in the doorway, like an angel, surrounded by a white aura, was the radiant, angelic form of Mary Eliss. She smelled of lavender and wild flowers.

I was so happy to see her. "Oh, Mary Eliss, can you help me, please? I need to find my aunt's pendant and bury it. It's the only way to get rid of the monster that haunts this place and bring peace to me and Merryweather Lodge."

She smiled sweetly. "Look in the basket that the faerie left you. But I must warn you, it's not as easy as that. I have to go, Emily. I'll help you whenever I can." She was starting to fade. "Please thank your aunt for taking my playthings out of the hiding room. Goodbye, Emily."

"No! Please don't go. There are so many things I need to ask you." But she was gone.

I lifted myself up from the floor, dashed into the parlor and pulled the basket from under the couch. "Look in the basket the faerie left you," Mary Eliss had said. The faerie… Mrs. Tilly? I removed the bag of sea salt and rummaged though the herbs in the basket. Nothing. I took a deep breath as I opened the brown bag and shoved my hand into the coarse salt. My fingers touched a piece of metal, and I breathed a long, slow sigh of relief. I went immediately to the telephone to call Jonathan, and he said he would be over right after breakfast the next day. Auntie was going to visit Martha's brother then, and Jonathan and I were going to banish this evil creature Merthia from Merryweather Lodge, forever!

Before I went to bed I wrote in my journal.

December 25th

Dear friend, This Christmas day has been a paradox of emotion. Like Merryweather Lodge its contents have contained both good and evil. All that I want to do is rid this place of its negative energy and free myself of this vengeful spirit. I want to live here in the arms of Mother Nature, in this simple enchanted little cottage, where life is unrushed, uncluttered and unworldly. A place where my spirit can find peace and my mind has time to ponder. I

*want to get married here, have children and live
happily ever after with the people I love. But first I
must expel Merthia and her evil from Merryweather
Lodge, and from me. I have managed, with the help
of my friend, to put most of the pieces of the puzzle
together. I pray that the ones that are left are not
the important pieces. It isn't going to be easy and I
fear for my life. God help me.*

That night I couldn't sleep. I kept tossing and turning,
doing everything I could think of to turn off the nagging, running commentary that was going on and on in my mind. At
one time I thought I heard footsteps and voices coming from
the attic room, but as soon as my feet touched the floor the
sounds stopped. Then there was that pesky song that I had
heard from Belinda's unmoving lips, playing over and over:
"Emily, Emily two by four. I saw you at the cellar door. I
pushed you on the dirty floor and cut you with a chain saw." I
put my hands to my ears and wished it away but it kept coming back.

When I did finally fall asleep, the demanding shrill of
Auntie's kettle woke me up again. Where was she? Why
hadn't she taken it off the stove yet and why the hell was she
up so early? I grabbed my housecoat and headed for the
kitchen. I felt tired, bedraggled, and my dry mouth tasted like
rotten eggs. I took the tea towel from the draining board and
placed it over the handle of the kettle before removing it from
the stove. Its piercing shrill was hurting my ears. "Auntie

Em," I called as I wandered into the passage. Then I heard the loud flush of the toilet. Auntie came out of the washroom red-faced and rubbing her tummy. "Cor blimmy, I'm never gonna eat that much again. It were all them there sweets, put a spanner in m' works, they 'ave, and opened the flood gates." I wasn't sure I wanted to hear that. She let out a thunderous fart as she passed by me. "Better out than in," she mumbled. I hoped that her upset stomach did not put a spanner in my works. She had to leave if I was going to cast my spell and bury the pendant.

Jonathan arrived at ten o'clock. Auntie insisted that he sit for a cup of tea and some of her homemade scones. She drank a cup of tea and took another dose of Epsom salts. She was starting to feel a little better and was ready for her visit with Martha's brother. We had decided that Jonathan would drive Auntie to Salisbury while I prepared for the ritual. I was a little reluctant to stay in the cottage by myself but there was a lot of preparation and I desperately wanted to get it over with.

Before Auntie stepped out the door she walked up to me and placed her hand on the five- pointed star around my neck and said, "You keep that 'ere and don't go takin' it off. Do ya 'ear me?" I nodded my head and wondered if she had some idea of what I was up to. It wouldn't have surprised me in the least if she did.

Jonathan held me close and whispered in my ear before they left. He told me to phone him right away if I sensed any paranormal activity in the cottage. I just smiled and thought to myself, is he kidding? I felt it almost all the time. How could I not sense it? The cottage positively pulsated with paranormal activity.

I walked outside to see them off. It was overcast, breezy, and threatening rain. After they pulled out of the driveway, I turned to face the cottage and feasted my eyes on its story-book façade; its stone walls, thatched roof, tiny spider web windows, and black wooden shutters. Suddenly there was lightness in the air. I was consumed with a warm, loving feeling, as if the arms of the cottage were reaching out to me, like a mother reaching for its child. Or perhaps it was the souls of my ancestors embracing me, pleading with me to set them free from the clutches of the hideous creature. "Help me," I whispered. Then I heard a sound, like footsteps, on the gravel driveway. I looked around but I couldn't see anyone. "Sam, is that you? Sammy!" I called. He came strolling around from the side of the house, seemingly unenthused at being called and having to get out of his dog house. I hurried back to the cottage as I had a strong feeling that I was being watched.

Inside, the rooms had taken on a foreboding air, more ominous than I had ever felt before. I took my basket of herbs and notes into the kitchen and started to prepare the potion for our ritual. Everything I needed was in the basket that the faerie or Mrs. Tilly, whoever it was, had dropped off. How did she know what ingredients to bring me? She must have found out what I was about to do. But how? It had occurred to me that it might be a trick—that the ingredients had been tampered with and would make

Merthia stronger rather than banishing her, just like it did the last time Mrs. Tilly gave me the recipe for a banishing potion. But Skye had given me this recipe and I had no way of getting these herbs from anywhere else. I had to take a chance; what choice did I have? I read from Skye's notes. At the bottom of them she reminded me that this was a purification ritual and that I needed to bathe and put on clean clothes before I performed it. I had forgotten all about that.

I dashed into the parlor to gather some clean clothes and headed for the bathroom. Then it suddenly dawned on me that I had forgotten to lock the doors. Auntie never locked the doors during the day. She would say that there was more funny goings on inside a house than outside of it and she was right about that, especially here, but I was all alone and I had heard something, or someone, moving outside. The wind was starting to pick up and I could hear it pushing its way through the cracks of the doors and windows. As I was turning the lock on the front door I thought I heard a woman's voice coming from outside. I opened the door ever so slowly and peered outside. I was immediately assaulted by a gust of wind. "Hello! Is anyone out there?" *What was I doing? Was I crazy?* It could be any unscrupulous character. It could be *her*! I stared up at the ominous clouds racing across the sky; indigo-blue, gray, black, coiling and uncoiling, chasing each other like demons across the vast infinity. Thunder rolled in the distance. *Oh shit! That's all I need, a thunderstorm.* I had always been afraid of thunder and lightning. It carried with it a sinister and threatening air and reminded me of some of the scary movies I had watched as a child. Now I was forced to act in my own scary movie with the climax of my performance yet to come.

Chapter 27

I pushed my wind-wept hair away from my face, went inside, and turned the lock on the door. A feeling of dread, vulnerability, and fear consumed me. Someone was out there, that I was sure of, but who and why? Pull yourself together Emily! I told myself. There is a job to be done and you're the only one who can do it. "There's nothing to fear but fear itself," I muttered as I hurried through the narrow passage way, past the attic stairs, and into the bathroom.

With haste I turned on the brass taps and drizzled some scented bath oil into the claw-footed tub. I wanted to have everything ready and waiting for when Jonathan returned. He was going to stop at a tobacconist's shop to pick up some matches, after dropping Auntie off at Martha's brother's house. We were almost out of matches and I needed them for lighting the ritual candles. Jonathan had said he'd be back in about an hour and a half. I tried to block any negative thoughts from my mind as I submerged my weary form into the silky, soapy water. It was hard to think only positive thoughts, because every time I bathed in this tub I was reminded of the time that the ghost of my great-grandmother came in here, morphed into the creature, and then possessed me. But she did leave me the pendant, and now I knew why.

I squeezed my eyes tight and tried to block out the thoughts of it all. How was I ever going to erase all of those dreadful memories? Was I ever going to be able to live in this cottage without the fear of something or someone jumping out at me from every shadowy nook and cranny? I washed my hair, soaped myself, rinsed off and resisted the temptation, to lay back, submerge my head in the luxurious floral scent of the hot soapy water, and never come up, but that would be a coward's way out. I dried myself off, wrapped the soft white bath sheet around my lean form, and went to the mirror. As I wiped the steam off the glass with a facecloth and stared at my blurred image, I noticed someone behind me in the reflection; it was a beautiful woman in a purple hooded cloak. I gulped and turned my head quickly. No one was there and when I looked back, the image in the mirror had gone. I could not smell *her*, I could not feel *her*, but somehow I knew she was there. "Leave me alone!" I screamed, as I shivered and climbed into my clean clothes.

There was a chill in the air, not a bundle-up-warm, nippy kind of chill, but a flesh-crawling, heebie-jeebies, menacing kind of chill that made my blood run cold. I placed my hand over the pendant around my neck and crept into the kitchen where I began preparing my consecrating elixir. I followed Skye's instructions, blessed the water, and added the lavender oil for eternal sleep. Then I snipped the herbs into a small wicker basket; fennel for purification, cinnamon for healing, sage for clearing away negative energy, dill for protection, and the acorn seeds of the sacred oak for new beginnings and peace. I flinched as lightning flashed through the window above the sink. Thunder roared and rolled overhead, as I chopped and prayed that the lights would not go out. I inhaled the aromatic fragrance of the fresh herbs as I looked out of the little kitchen window and watched the wind and rain lashing against the sturdy old cherry tree in the back yard. Its branches flailed erratically like seething serpents.

There was a knock on the door. The knife fell from my hand and into the sink as my stomach clenched. I went to the window in the sitting room to see if anyone had pulled up in the driveway but there was no vehicle there. Whoever it was must have walked here. The knocking was getting louder. I hesitated in the hallway. My mother always told me never to answer the door when I was home alone, especially not to strangers. But how was I to know if this was a stranger? It could be one of Auntie's neighbors needing help or in distress. Or it could be some deranged rapist or even *her*! *Oh stop it, Emily. Ghosts do not need to knock on the door.* "Hello, who is it?" I called through the thick wooden door.

"Let us in! We're getting soaked," a muffled voice called from the other side of the door.

It sounded like Maud McArthur.

"My Aunt's not home," I called back.

"It's cold out here; can we please come in?" Us? We? Did

she have her crazy so-called daughter with her? "I have some-thing to tell you about your aunt." Auntie? What could have happened? My inner voice was shouting a resounding "No!" as I pushed on the lock and opened the door.

Maud came barging in like a stampeding bull, shoving the door back and thrusting me against the wall. Belinda fol-lowed, head bowed, now in her sickly little girl disguise. They were bone dry. Something was very, very wrong.

"What about my aunt? Has something happened to her?" My hands were starting to shake. Maud gave me a blank look. "You said you had something to tell me about my aunt."

She tossed her head back and laughed. "I lied. Your aunt's an imbecile!" Where had I heard that term before?

I stood right in front of her, face to face, my arms folded and my back straight, trying my best to add an air of intimida-tion but my insides were trembling so bad. "Look, you can't just barge in here spewing insults. My aunt was kind enough to invite you all for Christmas dinner. Have some respect." Her eyes were growing, her thin lips drawing tighter and tighter. "What do you want? Why have you come here?"

She stiffened and faced the challenge. "I came to talk to you about my son." Her breath smelled like a dead rodent. Belinda was standing behind her, twirling her loose hair around her fingers, and humming softly. Maud turned and slapped Belinda on the back of her head. Belinda cringed, and then she growled at her mother like a wild dog. "Shut up!" Maud snapped. "Can we come in and sit down?" she asked in a much calmer tone.

Disregarding my better judgment and my gut, I stood aside and ushered them into the sitting room. Maud lifted her chin and sniffed the air as we walked past the kitchen. "What's that smell?" she asked, abruptly.

"Dinner," I replied.

"Really?" She sniffed, and then went directly to Auntie's chair and parked her large bottom between the arms. Belinda sat in the corner of the sofa, gnawing on her finger-nails like a frightened little child. Then she started picking her nose and putting it in her mouth. My stomach heaved.

I looked at her mother, and without thinking, I asked, "What is with her? One minute she's a teenage diva, ready to rip my head off, and the next minute it's like butter wouldn't melt in her my mouth, Miss Goody Two Shoes. Now she's an adult-sized, little kid, a sickly little kid. She needs help."

The muscles at the corners of Maud's mouth twitched. "I think you already know what's wrong with her. Don't you?"

No, Emily, don't acknowledge that you know anything, I said to myself. This is not your adversary Merthia and her evil mother Hagmanis; this is Jonathan's nasty Mom, Maud McArthur, and his sick sister, Belinda. If I pretend not to be suspicious of them maybe she'll just say her bit and leave. Maybe; my palms were sweaty. "Jonathan said she has schizo-phrenia but I didn't realize that these were the symptoms." I leaned forward in my chair and asked calmly, nervously, "You wanted to talk to me about Jonathan?"

She ignored my question, squinted, and stared at my neck. "Where is your aunt's amulet?"

I had tucked it inside my polo-necked sweater. "My aunt's wearing it."

She frowned and said, in a threatening voice, "Liar! Give my son his ring back and tell him you can't marry him." Her teeth clenched. "I forbid you to marry him!"

I stood up but restrained my anger, for fear of what she might do. "Please leave, now."

Her jaw clamped shut; her eyes squeezed into slits. Her features were starting to change. My heart was taking off on a tangent. She flew off the chair and charged towards me like an angry beast. I turned and ran, heading for kitchen and my protective bag of sea salt. She raced behind me, as if she had speed running through her veins. I reached for the doorknob. Then I felt a pair of powerful hands and claw-like fingernails sinking into my shoulders. They grabbed my arm and twisted it forcefully around my back, causing me to cringe. I squirmed and thrashed and tried to pull away but she had gained the strength of ten men. "Get the potion!" she hollered at Belinda. Her voice was deep and hollow, as if possessed by a demon. *Where was Jonathan? He should have been back by now.*

The deranged teenaged child ambled in front of us with a vacant expression, as if she were in some sort of trance. She lifted her pale, limp hand to the doorknob. "Now!" her mother demanded. Belinda shot back and gasped when she opened the door. Winston was sitting, poised, right in front of the doorway. He seemed different—larger, bulkier, and his posture seemed it indicate that he was on guard. "Never mind him. Get in there and bring me the potion." Belinda moved one foot in front of the other. The enigmatic black cat hissed and raised his back. Belinda moved back, made a pitiful moaning sound, and then she started rocking on her heels and sucking her thumb. Maud shoved me towards the door, my hands behind my back, held in her vise-like grip. "Move out of the way," she commanded Belinda. "What is wrong with you? You used to eat those things alive." I shivered. "Scat!" Maud screamed at the cat. As soon as she put one foot over the doorway, Winston leaped at her, latching his claws and sinking his teeth into the pale, loose flesh of her leg. Her scream ripped the air apart. A stream of blood ran down to her ankle, over her sturdy brown shoes, and on to the floor. Her eyes grew huge. I could feel her body tensing with fury but Winston stood his ground, guarding the kitchen, his ears pinned back, his back arched, his fur erect, as if he were a sentry protecting a fortress from an evil villain.

Maud turned and threw me on the ground with such force that it rendered me numb. The fear that was congealing deep inside my soul had tuned into utter panic. I stared up at her. Her face was haggard and wrinkled; scraggly, steely gray hair hung over her pointed, ugly features, and her clothes were faded and threadbare. She shared only a mere resemblance of the Maud McArthur I knew. Now she was more like the old crone I'd seen in my vision at Stonehenge, more like the evil sorceress Hagmanis. "Have you possessed Maud McArthur?" My chin quivered as the words came out of my mouth.

Her lips curved into a sardonic grin. "Of course not, imbecile!" She glanced at Belinda. "Only my daughter has such a gift. I killed that stupid, feeble woman a long time ago. I do believe you have visited her grave."

"You killed Maud McArthur? What grave?"

"Of course I did, but not before I stole her identity and image. She is buried in the faerie's garden along with her useless seed." She chuckled like an old witch. "Colrea, are you so naive? I had to take her place and raise these children so as to fill their soul's destiny and bring them together."

I tried to lift myself up but she raised her long bony finger and pointed it at me, warning me not to move. Fear, rage, and hatred burned inside my soul like a blazing fire. "So you are the evil sorceress Hagmanis." I moved my gaze to Belinda. "But that is not your daughter. She is a mere pawn, a slave, a poor child possessed by an evil spirit. Jonathan could never love her; he thinks only of her as his sick sister."

Her eyes became large and red, like the windows of an inferno. "Golwin will love her. He has already planted his seed inside her."

I was fuming! I couldn't stand it any longer. Yanking myself off the ground, I charged towards her, arms stretched, reaching for her neck. Belinda hissed as she came behind me and sank her teeth into my back, like a ravished vampire, right through my thick sweater and into my flesh. I arched my back and clamped my fingers around Hagmanis's neck as a jabbing pain shot up my spine. She pried back my fingers as if they were made of dough, lifted me off the ground with the front of my sweater, and said, "Where is the amulet?" Her eyes were on fire, her breath putrid.

"Put me down and I'll show you." My whole body was trembling.

She threw me against the wall. "Get it now!" she commanded.

I shoved my trembling hand down the front of my sweater, pulled out the pendant, and held it in front of my face. Skye had told me that the pendant would burn them if they tried to remove it from around my neck. I hoped and prayed that it was true. "The key to the mystery, I assume."

Her untamed eyebrows shot up as she stepped back. Out of the corner of my eye I could see Belinda approaching. She had a tall brass candlestick in her hand. I turned to face her and held out the pendant. "Stay back," I warned her. She charged towards me, candlestick raised above her head. The blunt instrument struck me on the side of my head. I felt a sharp jab of pain and dizziness. And then—darkness.

"Come, Emily. Come." I forced my eyes open. Leaning over me, staring me right in the face, were the emerald, unblinking eyes of Mary Eliss. There was a strong smell of gas in the air and a sulfurous taste at the back of my throat that was making me gag. My eyes burned. My head was pounding. "Come, Emily." She was motioning me to the back door.

I managed to lift myself to my hands and knees and crept towards the door. I reached up for the knob, grabbed it, and pulled myself up. Then I turned it and pushed, praying with all of my soul that it would open. The door opened, and I stumbled out onto the stone steps, into the brisk fresh air, breathing in great gasps of it, deep into my lungs as I coughed, heaved, and wiped a trickle of blood from the side of my face with my sleeve. I stumbled back through the doorway, covered my mouth and nose with my hand, and dashed into the kitchen and turned off the gas. Then I opened the windows. "Mary Eliss," I called. She was gone. I looked for Winston but he was nowhere in sight.

The potion was still on the draining board and the pendant was still around my neck. *They tried to gas me and if it wasn't for Mary Eliss waking me up, I'd be dead. I had to perform the ritual before they came back. Where was Jonathan? Why wasn't he back yet? Maybe I should call him? No, there was no time. I had to move fast!* I gathered the paraphernalia and notes from the kitchen as quickly as I could and headed for the cellar.

I paused for a moment at the top of the stairs, said a silent prayer, and then hurried down into the damp, dingy hole. I laid the basket and notes by the shelves and placed the candles in their appropriate corners; east yellow, south red, west blue, and north green. Then I got on my hands and knees and started digging with my bare hands in the dirt. I had forgotten the trowel and I wasn't going back upstairs for it.

As I was digging, out of the corner of my eye I noticed a flicker of movement in the dark shadows. Suddenly a swarm of ghostly little lights flew towards me; they were in front my face, in my hair, nipping at my nose and my ears with their tiny sharp teeth. They were the same pesky imps that I had seen on Beckon Hill, the ones Skye had called will o' the wisps or corpse candles. I batted and swatted the horrid little creatures with my hand. "Go away. Shoo!" Something spooked them. They flew up the stairs and in an instant they were gone.

The air was turning icy cold. I stuck my hands back into the hole and dug frantically, then took the pendant, shoved it into the ground, and covered it with dirt. Ignoring the foul smell and cold eerie feeling that now enveloped me, I lit the four colored candles. There were only two matches, so I lit one of the candles and used its wick to light the others. I'd save the last match, just in case. I was just about to sprinkle the herbs when I heard the sound of soft footsteps coming down the stairs.

I held my breath and turned. The candles started to dance erratically. Moving methodically, as if in a daze, Belinda descended the stairs. She was filthy. Her clothes were dirty rags, her damp matted hair stuck to her forehead and cheeks, a line of dry snot ran from her nose to her chapped lips, and she smelled of feces. In her hand she lugged a rusty old chainsaw. Then it suddenly dawned on me that I had forgotten the bag of sea salt. A wave of sheer panic swept over me. *Oh my God! How could I have forgotten that?* "Stay away," I warned her. "This is going to free you as well as me." She kept coming towards me, her head bowed, her crude weapon by her side. Every muscle in my body tensed and my heart was hammering behind my ribcage. I took a step back and swallowed hard. She stood in front of me, lifted her sad eyes slowly to meet mine, and then she hoisted up the chain-saw with both of her hands. *There's no way she's going to be able to pull that starter cord. She's too weak, too fragile.* I took a tentative step towards her. She lifted her weapon higher, as if it were made of cardboard. I jumped back. Her back went ramrod stiff. Her eyes rolled to the back of her head. A small feeble whimper came from her chapped lips, "Help me." She started to shake, violently, as if she were having a seizure. Then she began to mutate; her clothes became a blood-stained white gown, her hair yellowed, the smell she was emitting was more like cat pee than feces. I knew all too well what was happening. It was *her*, my rival, my cousin the druid priestess Merthia, in her hideous form. I moved back, way back, until my spine was against the cold, dirt wall and then I froze, too terrified to speak, too terrified to move. She lifted the chainsaw and put her hand to the cord. A fear, worse than any fear I had ever felt, reached inside my soul and gripped me. *She was going to kill me but I wasn't going down without a fight. What did I have to lose?* I took a deep breath and prayed.

A surge of adrenaline gushed through my veins. I lunged at her, gritting my teeth and roaring with as much threat, as much force, as I could muster. She put her hand out and pushed me to the ground. Her mouth opened, pale yellow mucus oozed from between her jagged teeth. "Colcesthrar," she spat. Then she pulled the cord on the chainsaw and fired it up. I sank to my knees and cried out, in utter desperation. "Mamma, Grandma, Uncle Reg, Mary Eliss, Martha, all of you that have been tortured by this creature….help me! Please help me!" All of a sudden the walls began to shake, as if we were having an earthquake. Then they began to pulsate like the rhythm of a giant heart. Harrowing cries and moans came oozing out of the walls, and up from the ground. The creature froze. Her eyes glared down at her feet. I shuffled back. Hands of all sizes, severed hands, bloody hands, were pushing their way through the dirt floor. The creature moved her feet. Two of the gory hands reached up and grabbed her ankles. She yelped and struggled to free herself. But the hands were steadfast and pulled her deeper and deeper into the earth. Like a snake shedding its skin, the evil creature's dark spirit was sucked into the abyss.

Belinda's tortured form collapsed on the ground, and then crawled to the corner and curled up like a poor abused animal. I grabbed my bottle of blessed water and sprinkled it over the ground, along with the herbs and a handful of fresh dirt. "With the elements of earth and water I cleanse this space." Then I took a candle and walked around the perimeter of the room. "With the elements of air and fire I cleanse this space." Then I lifted my arms. "With the elements of spirit and by the power of the Divine, I cleanse and consecrate this place. So mote it be, so mote it be, so mote it be."

"It is done," I whispered to the poor dejected, adult-sized, little girl as I took her arm and helped her up from the ground, and up the stairs. The kitchen felt warm, welcoming and peaceful. I wrapped Auntie's hand-knitted sweater around Belinda's shoulders and led her to the table. "Sit there while I make us a nice cup of tea." Her hand was cradling her stomach.

The front door opened. A man's voice called, "Emily!" It was Jonathan. "I'm sorry I'm late. The car broke down on the way there. I tried to call but the line was dead," he called out, all in one breath. He gasped when he saw us. "What happened?"

Auntie followed behind him. "We're okay," I assured them. I looked at Auntie and then at Jonathan. "Welcome home. It's over. She's gone," I said with a smile. But the tiny mysterious voice inside me whispered, *Are you sure?*

I set my pen and reading glasses down on the antique desk in front of me and closed my writing pad.

ABOUT THE AUTHOR

I grew up in southeast England; in a mining village lovingly nick-named, "The place that time forgot". I came to Canada when I was 21 years old, in search of adventure and a new life. I now live in Alberta with my hockey crazy husband, lazy ginger cat, and adorable Shetland Sheep dog. We have two grown children. They are the gems in my treasure chest.

As far back as I can remember the pen and paper have been my faithful companions and story telling my forte. As a child I would sneak away from the mundane adult world, find a private retreat (usually behind the garden shed) and imagine. There in my own little sanctuary I'd conjure up all kinds of intriguing tales and colorful characters. In my teen years my journal became my confident, revealing all my hidden secrets, private fantasies, and wild notions within its pages. Later I started to write poems, articles, and short stories, and pondered the thought of becoming a writer.

When I immigrated to Canada I buried my dreams under layers of real life clutter. I chose a safe and practical career in child care, married, and raised a family. But my creative spirit kept trying to dig its way out. I was asked to write articles and editorials for our local church. I taught a story time class at the school, which lead me to writing a children's book. I wrote an article about my husband's prestigious grandfather and sent it to our local newspaper. They printed it. I kept sending them articles, they kept printing them. I was surprised at the compliments I received from the editor and readers. It was evident to me then that I had excavated my creative spirit.

I decided to take a comprehensive writing course to improve my technique. With help from a proficient and supportive tutor, who told me I had a gift, I began to cultivate my skill. My articles started to sell and I received an assignment from a major Canadian magazine. I have spent the past twenty-five years writing books, short stories, articles, and editorials. Come visit me at www.paulineholyoak.com

For your reading pleasure, we invite you to visit our web bookstore

WHISKEY CREEK PRESS

www.whiskeycreekpress.com